Never With Me

NEW YORK TIMES BESTSELLING AUTHOR
KAYLEE RYAN

Copyright © 2022 Kaylee Ryan

All Rights Reserved.

This book may not be reproduced in any manner whatsoever without the written permission of Kaylee Ryan, except for the use of brief quotations in articles and or reviews.

This book is a work of fiction. Names, characters, events, locations, businesses and plot are products of the author's imagination and meant to be used in a fictitious manner. Any resemblance to actual persons, living or dead, or actual events throughout the story are purely coincidental. The author acknowledges trademark owners and trademarked status of various products referenced in this work of fiction, which have been used without permission. The publication and use of these trademarks are not authorized, sponsored or associated by or with the trademark owners.

The following story contains sexual situations and strong language. It is intended for adult readers.

Cover Design: Perfect Pear Creative Covers
Photographer: Wander Aguiar
Editing: Hot Tree Editing
Proofreading: Deaton Author Services, Editing 4 Indies
Paperback Formatting: Champagne Book Design

Never With Me

Prologue

RAMSEY

I BLINK HARD.
   Once.
   Twice.
Three times.

I refuse to let the tears fall. Not this time.

I stare at the bruises that surround my wrist. It's easy to make out the fingerprints. I'd show them to my father, but I know it won't matter. He's created the same type of bruise multiple times. Besides, he's just told me that I'm to marry the man responsible for my new markings.

My father doesn't care that the man hurts me or that he has a different woman warm his bed every night. All he cares about is binding our families together. He doesn't care about what I want. He never has. I've spent my life living under his thumb.

I can't take it anymore.

For the first time in my life, I'm going to defy him. I'm scared of the repercussion of doing so, but I'm even more scared to spend my life married to a monster.

"No." My voice is flat and void of any emotion. I learned a long time ago that showing him anything other than obediance isn't tolerated. I don't let him see that his demand has cut me to the quick and that my heart will be forever broken from the man who was supposed to love me unconditionally. Protect me.

"What did you just say?" Anger ramps up in his voice.

Slowly, I lift my head and stare my father in the eye. "I said no."

His nostrils flare, and if it were possible, he'd have smoke coming out of his ears. In all of my twenty years of my life, I've never uttered the word *no* to the man until just now. The look on his face and the way he's clenching and unclenching his fists tells me he's not the least bit impressed. Not that I expected him to be.

My entire life, he's dictated my every move. What I wear, who I'm friends with, and who I date. Currently, it's Robert Barrington, the third, my current boyfriend, and son of my father's business partner. We've been dating since high school, if you want to call it that. Robert does what he wants and keeps me around for when he needs to put on a show. I'm well aware that he's cheated on me multiple times. In fact, it's a daily occurrence. It doesn't bother me. In fact, it's a relief that he's finding it somewhere else.

"You will do as I say," my father spits.

"No." I'm calm on the outside, but my insides are shaking. Rage appears in his eyes, his voice, and he scares me. They both do. I glance out of the corner of my eye and see my mother sitting on the wingback chair sipping her wine. I didn't have to see her take them to know that she's also taken anti-anxiety medication that I'm sure she washed down with said wine.

My mother is weak. She bows down to my father like the good little trophy wife she is, and it makes me sick. I've begged her more times than I can count to leave him. We can run away together and live a happy life, but she refuses. She claims she loves him and she's nothing without him. He's brainwashed her, and it breaks my heart, but at this

"I don't date," I remind her.

"I know, and you know that I have been begging you to get back out there. Don't let the hands of one man, or in your case, two men, keep you from the loving touch of another." Her voice is gentle. "Besides, I have a good feeling about this."

I ignore her "good feeling" comment. "They're all the same." I know that she means well. I also know this is a big marketing campaign for her and her new photography business, but I'm nervous as hell to walk out there and have to face a man I don't know and spend time with him. The only reason I agreed is because Palmer will be there the entire time taking pictures.

"Not true, and you know it." She points her index finger at me.

"Fine. I know, but I just… I'm better off on my own. I've worked hard to get where I am the last two years. I'm good with where I am in life."

"Are you not lonely?" she asks.

"I have you and the boys," I say, referring to my cousins. My aunt Carol is a mom to nine rowdy boys. *Nine!* Crazy, right? They opened their arms for me just as Aunt Carol and Uncle Raymond did. They're more like my nine brothers instead of my nine cousins. They're all protective of me, even the three who are younger. Hell, they might be younger, but they're all taller than I am, and they're all built. I'm not sure what Aunt Carol fed them growing up, but damn. Yes, they're my family, but I can admit that they're all gorgeous.

"Come on, Ramsey. You know what I mean."

"I don't let myself get lonely. I work too many jobs. If I allow loneliness to creep in, that gives me time to think, and I just don't want to go back there, Palmer. I'm my own person and living on my terms. Coming from my background, there's nothing more freeing."

"I love you, Ramsey." She leans in and gives me a hug. "You are so strong. I promise today is going to be fun—just a photo shoot. I'll be there with you the entire time, and I swear to you he's a good guy. I would never ask you to do this otherwise."

"I trust you." I do trust Palmer. She and I became fast friends working abused and pushed around, and your every move is dictated, getting away from that is freedom. Freedom, I had to walk away from my parents to obtain. I have no regrets, and I'm going to make damn sure that I never will. I don't need them, and I want to know that no matter what life throws at me, I don't need their money or their connections to succeed."

She reaches over and lays her hand over mine that's resting on my lap. "I'm sorry. I just want to see you happy."

"I am happy. Happier than I have ever been." I'm telling her the truth. Since moving to Willow River, life has never been better.

"I still think you need that special someone to take that happiness up a notch." She wags her eyebrows, and I laugh.

"There are battery-operated devices that serve that purpose just fine." I know they exist, but I don't have one. Most days, I'm too damn exhausted to even shower before bed, let alone give myself any kind of self-love.

"Nothing like the real thing, my friend." She laughs as she pulls into the parking lot. "Sit tight. I'm going to set up and make sure your date is here and ready."

"Oh, maybe he's going to be a no-show." I make a production of crossing my index and middle finger on both hands, and she rolls her eyes.

"Stay put." She points a finger at me before climbing out of the car. I remain seated while she reaches into the back seat to grab her camera bag. "I'll be right back. Get your blindfold ready." With that, she closes the door. I watch her as she walks behind a row of trees.

I've been to Willow Park many times over the last two years. It's full of beautiful landscapes and park benches. There's a brick wall that's great for photo ops, and a ton of beautiful landscaping. There's even a small pond with a bridge that crosses over it. It's almost something out of a fairy tale. I know that's why Palmer chose this location.

I just wish she hadn't chosen me.

A knock on the window pulls me out of my thoughts. "Ready?" Palmer asks. Her beaming smile reminds me of why I agreed to this blind-date photo shoot. Palmer is my best friend. She's mine, not an acquaintance of my parents or because I have money or status. She's my bestie for me, and I would do anything for her, even if it means subjecting myself to the awkwardness of a blind date.

It's not just the blind-date part. I don't do well around men I don't know and trust touching me. That's why I work behind the bar at the Willow Tavern. I've been offered to work the floor, but I like the barrier that the counter provides me. Never again will I let a man touch me if it's not my choice. This brings me to today. I googled blind-date photo shoots, and they're pretty intimate. They look fun, but that's for someone who's... normal. Not a girl who was touched by the rough hands of her father and her ex-boyfriend. They don't have the fear that lives inside me.

I groan as I push open the car door. "Palmer, this is going to be a disaster." I wipe my sweaty palms against my thighs.

"No, it's not. Trust me, Rams. This guy, he's one of the good ones. He'd never hurt you or me. I promise you with all that I am that I know him. I wouldn't put you in this position with a man I didn't trust."

I pull in a deep breath. "Okay."

"Okay." She smiles. "Hand over the blindfold, woman." She wiggles her shoulders with excitement. "I'm so excited for this. Thank you so much."

"You're welcome. Can we get this over with?"

"So impatient," she teases as she helps me slide the blindfold over my eyes. She links her arm with mine. "There is nothing in our path. We're going to take slow, steady steps. It's not far," she says, guiding me to the meeting spot.

"What if he hates me?" My insecurities run deep. Sure, I know guys like what they see, but I can hear my father and Robert in my head telling me I'm nothing without them.

"What if he falls in love with you?" she asks, her voice full of wonder.

"Come on, Palmer, we both know that's not going to happen. I'm the ice queen, remember?" I repeat the words Robert said to me so many times I lost count.

"Fuck him," Palmer snaps, her voice heated. "You're beautiful, and trust me, this guy, he'd be lucky to have you."

He laughs, and the sound washes over me like a cool breeze on a hot summer's day.

"You love me, and you know it," Palmer fires back. She's not the least bit bothered by her brother's comments.

"You know I do, little sister," he replies. He glances over at Palmer, and I can see the love he has for her. My shoulders relax further, and suddenly, this entire arrangement doesn't seem so bad.

Chapter Two

DEACON

HER NAME IS RAMSEY, AND SHE'S A FUCKING KNOCKOUT. I've heard the name many times over the past couple of years, but I've never had the chance to meet her. Hell, she's been to my house to swim with Palmer, but it's never been while I was there. Now, here she stands before me. Her long dark hair and her big blue eyes are staring at me with so many different emotions. I wish I knew her well enough to read exactly what she's feeling, what she's thinking.

When Palmer called me last week begging me to do this photo shoot, I made up every excuse in the book to get out of it. However, my baby sister knows how to get me to cave, and here I stand. I had no idea what I was in for, but I never in my wildest imagination thought I'd be standing in front of the most beautiful woman I've ever seen.

My sister's best friend.

Way too young for me.

Sexy as hell.

"It's nice to put a face to the name," I say, dropping her hand when I realize I'm still holding it. I miss the feel of her soft skin instantly.

"You too." She smiles shyly, and my cock twitches.

"So, have you ever done this before?" I ask her. I already know the answer. Palmer assured me the woman I'd be photographed with was beautiful and just as nervous as I was.

It's not that I'm nervous. I just have work to do. I'm thirty-two years old and working my way toward partner at the law firm where I've been since passing the bar. I don't have time for blind dates, especially those that are being photographed by my baby sister.

"No. Never. I actually tried like hell to get out of it." She shrugs.

I feel my mouth lifting at the corners. "That makes two of us. She's relentless."

"That she is." Ramsey laughs lightly, and the sound washes over me. "So, how do we do this?" I ask her.

"Well," my little sister breaks into our conversation, "think of it like an engagement shoot."

I turn my eyes back to Ramsey. "You ever been engaged?" She's young, like Palmer, so I highly doubt her answer is going to be yes.

"No. You?"

"Never." We turn to look at Palmer. I point at Ramsey and then myself. "Never been engaged."

"Come on. It's not hard. Work with me, people." Palmer laughs. "Just hug, and be playful, and think about how you'd pose if you were engaged."

"Yeah, not helping," I tell her.

"Ugh. Fine. Hold on." With one hand still holding her camera, she pulls her cell phone out of her pocket and taps the screen. "This." She shoves the screen in my face, and I take it.

I hold the phone so that Ramsey can see the screen as well. I flip through the pictures that look fun and also intimate. Ramsey steps closer, and her floral scent wraps around me like an embrace.

As I flip through the images, I feel her body stiffen next to mine. "Are you okay with this?" I ask her softly. Surely Palmer didn't force her best friend into this.

"Yeah, I promised Palmer."

I glance up and see my sister standing a few feet away, messing with her camera. "You can back out if you want. Don't do this if you're uncomfortable." I turn my attention back to Ramsey as she exhales and stands a little taller, her shoulders straightening.

"I can do this."

It sounds like she's trying to convince herself more than she is me. Something about her words, the square of her shoulders, and the tone of her voice has me wanting to encourage her and tell her to leave at the same time. I know Palmer can be a lot. She could also sell snow to an Eskimo. My little sister is convincing as hell when she wants to be.

"Hey." I wait for her to look at me. "If you're uncomfortable, we can stop this now. She'll understand."

Ramsey gives me a slight smile that hits me right in the center of my chest. "I'm good, Deacon. Thank you." Her words are softly spoken, and the look in her eyes tells me that she's on board. She might be nervous, but she's not going back on the promise she made my sister.

I nod and hold my hand out for her. "Let's explore." I give her what my momma calls my charming smile and wait for her to place her hand in mine. When she finally does, I give her hand a soft squeeze, hoping that it will offer her comfort.

"Yay. Okay, this is good," Palmer says from behind us. "Just do you. I'll take pictures," she instructs.

I look over at Ramsey and playfully roll my eyes, which makes her laugh. Her blue eyes sparkle in the sunlight, and my lips once again tip into a smile. "So, what do you do?"

"What don't I do." She laughs. "I have three jobs. Well, not three full-time jobs, but three jobs all the same," she rambles. It's obvious that she's nervous, and for some unknown reason, that has me feeling protective over her.

"Wow. Three. That's a lot. How do you manage to juggle all three?" Our hands are linked, and we're walking down the paved path of the park. It's lined with trees, casting shadows in front of us and offering some shade from the hot Georgia summer sun. I can hear the shutter of Palmer's camera behind us, but I ignore it, giving Ramsey all my attention.

"I work at the Willow Tavern five days a week. My shifts vary whenever they need me, but I usually have my schedule several weeks in advance. I also work two days a week for At Your Service Catering. That was my first job when moving to Willow River, and then I just filled in at the Maid for You Cleaning Service. I worked there part time before I started at the Willow Tavern."

"Damn," I mutter. "Do you ever have time for yourself?" My sister snorts, and I turn to glare at her over my shoulder.

"Come on, Deacon." Palmer laughs. "Pot"—she points at me—"meet Kettle." She indicates Ramsey. "You're both workaholics. I'm still surprised I got you both out here with me today."

"I do have to work later." Ramsey sticks out her tongue at my sister. I have to remind myself that she's too young for me so my mind doesn't wander to that tongue, and images of what she can do with it invade my mind.

"The Tavern?" I guess.

"Yeah. I work most Friday and Saturday nights. I don't mind it. The tips are better on weekend nights."

"Oh, over by the brick wall," Palmer instructs.

With Ramsey's hand still laced with mine, I lead us to the brick wall. Pressing my back against the wall, I pull her to stand in front of me, my hands landing on her hips. Her breath hitches and my cock takes notice.

"Is this okay?" I ask her. My voice is soft. It's not that I care that my sister hears us, but something about the moment and the position we're in, my hands gripping her hips, and her leaning into me, makes it more intimate, more just for us.

"I'm okay." Her body visibly relaxes as she says the words.

"Come on, you two. You know what this is supposed to look like," Palmer encourages.

"Ramsey?" She's looking at my chest. Slowly, so not to scare her, I place my index finger under her chin, and her eyes meet mine. "I'm going to have to touch you for this. Maybe even kiss you," I say, pulling her a little closer. She flinches a little at that, and I try not to let it affect me.

"I looked up a few of these type of shoots on YouTube," she confesses. "They were holding each other and kissing, and… yeah, she's going to want that." She motions her head toward my sister.

"What do you want?"

Her blue eyes hold mine. "I made her a promise."

"Tell me what's off-limits." I can see it in her eyes, she's uncomfortable, and I want to know why. Not just because it will make this easier and less awkward, but something primal in me sees a woman in her shell, and I want to help her come out of it. That's not something I've ever desired before, but my gut tells me that Ramsey needs to know she's in control here.

"My wrists," she whispers. Her voice is so low I wouldn't have heard her had I not been giving her my absolute attention.

"Don't touch your wrists?"

She nods. "And maybe if you could tell me what we're doing before we do it?"

She doesn't want me to touch her wrists, and wants to know my actions. I scan for scars or bruising and see nothing. Someone has done something to make her feel this way. That has to be it. I swallow back the rage that someone hurt her, and give her all my attention. "I'm going to place my hand against your cheek." The corner of her mouth tips in a barely-there smile, but I catch it. "Is that okay?"

"That's okay."

Slowly, I raise my hand and do as I told her, resting my hand against her cheek. Everything in the background fades away. I don't hear the other patrons at the park or the cars driving by. I don't hear the click of my sister's camera. All I see is this beautiful woman who has so obviously been hurt in the past. "I don't know who hurt you," I say, keeping my voice soft. She tenses up a little as she closes her eyes. "Hey." I wait for her baby blues to land on me once again. "Never with me. When you're with me, you never have to worry about me hurting you. I know you don't know me, but you do know her." I nod to where I'm sure my sister is standing, clicking away at our intimate position. "She would never put you in a situation with someone who would hurt you. I'm not that man."

"I know she wouldn't."

"Good. Now, my guess is that we have maybe thirty seconds before she starts begging us to move out of this pose." I playfully roll my eyes, and she giggles. The sound weaves its way around me, and I want to hear it again and again.

Too young for you, Setty. I just need to keep reminding myself of that.

"You take the lead, Ramsey."

"W-What?"

Her surprise tells me control was not something men, or a man from her past, let her have. "You're in control. Do what feels right, and I'll follow your lead."

"I-I don't know what to do."

"Just do what feels right." I hold my hands out to my sides and give her a cocky grin. "I'm all yours." Her face flushes a light shade of pink, and I'm certain it's not from the Georgia heat.

Letting my arms fall to my sides, I stand stock-still, patiently waiting for her to decide. Slowly, she lifts her hands and rests them against my chest. "Is this okay?"

"It's all okay, Ramsey. Anything you want."

She thinks I'm talking about the photo shoot, and I am. However, there is a deeper part of me, the part that's captivated by this beauty, that knows I would follow through with any request that she makes of me. It's a damn good thing this is just a project for my sister. Ramsey is way too young for me, and being around her stirs something inside me. Something new and primal. I can't act on it, of course. She's my baby sister's best friend. I can, however, make this easier on her, and that's what I intend to do.

There's a cautious smile on her face as she lifts a shaking hand to my cheek. She's staring up at me in awe. As if she can't understand how I would give her free rein to touch me. There's a slight tremor as her palm rests against my cheek. "I'm going to cover your hand with mine," I tell her softly, keeping the instruction just between us.

"Okay."

My large hand covers her small one, causing her to pull in a shuddering breath, but to my surprise, the tremble disappears. "I'm going to lean in close, Ramsey." She gives me a subtle nod of permission, and I close the distance, resting my forehead against hers.

"This is gold!" Palmer calls out.

Her statement pulls me back to the fact that it's not just me and Ramsey in our own little bubble. "Sounds like we're doing it right." I chuckle.

"Yeah," Ramsey agrees. Her voice is soft and breathy, and my cock notices. *I* notice. I make a mental note to keep the lower half of my body from touching hers.

"Let's try something different. Deacon, why don't you lift her to sit on the wall, right over there." Palmer points to a half brick wall that matches the one we're leaning against. "And just let nature take its course," my sister instructs.

"She's enjoying this," I say as I angle away and stand to my full height. "You okay with this next step?" I ask softly.

"I am." Her smile is a little wider than when this first started, and I'll take that as a win. She drops her gaze to our hands. I turn my hand over, offering it to her, and she slides her fingers between mine.

Together we make our way to the half brick wall. "I'm going to lift you up." I wait for her nod before I step in front of her, gripping her hips, and easily lifting her to the wall.

"You did that effortlessly."

I flex my muscles, making her laugh.

"Oh, god, put them away," Palmer teases. "This isn't one of those cheesy 'look how strong I am' kind of shoots, Deac." She laughs.

"The lady asked to see the goods," I fire back.

"Hey." Ramsey slaps at my chest, and I capture her hand, holding it there. With that move, I step between her legs.

"You're supposed to be on my team," I tell her. She surprises me when she wraps her legs around my waist, holding me closer. The act is done before I can stop it. My hard cock is lined up against her pussy, and when she sucks in a breath, I know there's no denying it. "I'm coming in close," I warn her.

I brace my hands against the wall she's sitting on, and I'm shocked when she wraps her arms around my neck. The pose is intimate with her wrapped around me, and I can only imagine the smile on my sister's face, but I can't think about that right now.

"I know I should apologize." My eyes flash to where my cock is nestled against her pussy. "But I can't. You're gorgeous, Ramsey. You can't hide that, and I can't hide what being close to you does to me."

I clamp my mouth shut, giving her time to process my confession. I should take a step back and break the connection, but her legs are still locked tight around my waist, and I told her she had the control.

She pulls me closer until we're hugging. "Thank you, Deacon," she whispers.

I want to ask her why she's thanking me. However, the feel of her body pressed tightly against mine takes over, and I'm lifting my arms, wrapping them around her, returning her embrace. Her floral scent engulfs me, and I inhale deeply.

I faintly hear my sister squeal with excitement, but I don't dare break this connection. I'm a smart man. When there's a beautiful woman in my arms, she gets all my attention. Even a workaholic like me can figure that out.

Still holding her close, I stroke her back gently, and I feel her relax into my touch. It's funny, up until about twenty minutes ago, I was cursing myself for giving in to Palmer after her insistent begging. Now I'm glad that I did. I never imagined this is how today would have gone, but I'm enjoying myself. I'm enjoying my time with Ramsey. But regardless of this connection I feel with her, nothing can ever happen between us. I'm too old for her, but damn if I'm not going to enjoy every minute of the rest of this day with her.

Chapter Three

RAMSEY

This isn't me. I don't let men get close. It has to be the golden eyes. Maybe it's his strong arms as they wrap around me. Or could it be the feel of his large hand engulfing mine? It's all of that and more. Could it be his brutal honesty and the openness I see in those honey-colored eyes? It has to be the way his hand feels as it trails slowly up and down my back. It's his woodsy scent and the way he just met me, but it already feels as if he knows me.

Not at all what I expected.

Realizing I'm wrapped around him like a spider monkey, I ease my hold, pulling back. I've never had a man be so patient and kind with me. My hand rests against his cheek, and the texture of his beard is foreign under my palm. My ex was clean-shaven, as was my father. I can't explain my desire to just feel the rough of it against my skin.

"Ramsey." Deacon's voice is gruff, pulling me out of my thoughts. His eyes are darker, full of something I can't name. "Can I touch you too? Your face, I mean?"

I nod, because speaking is out of the question. There's a lump in my throat the size of the entire state of Georgia. Slowly, he raises his hand. I don't know if it's to not spook me or to give me time to change my mind, but as soon as his warm palm is pressed against my cheek, I close my eyes, letting the soothing touch of his skin seep into me.

"Ramsey." His voice is clipped but has me opening my eyes all the same. "Can I kiss you?" His eyes widen just a fraction as if he can't believe he asked the question. I wait for a few heartbeats for him to take back his request, but he remains silent, waiting patiently for me to answer him.

Slowly, I nod.

His thumb caresses my cheek. "I'm going to need your words this time, sweetheart."

"Yes," I say without an ounce of hesitation. It's sad that this man will be the first that I kiss by my own choosing. To me, this is my first kiss. That's the only explanation for the way my heart is racing.

"You sure?" He leans in close.

"Y-Yes."

"Palmer?" he calls out for his sister.

I stiffen. Is he toying with me? One strong hand grips my thigh, which is still locked tight around him, while the other softly caresses my cheek.

"What's up?" I faintly hear her ask.

I'm still as I wait to see what's going to happen. I'm not even sure that I'm breathing. When he opens his mouth to speak, and his words register, I pull breath into my lungs.

"You're going to want to make sure you get this." That's his final warning to either of us before his lips descend on mine.

I freeze, my body goes rigid in his arms, which causes him to pull back. "Ramsey?"

"I'm sorry," I whisper. I swallow hard. I know that he's not him, and the fact that I was expecting him to be as rough with me as Robert is an insult to Deacon. Guilt hits me hard as my eyes find him. "Can we... maybe do that again? I-I wasn't ready."

"She wasn't ready," he muses, a smile pulling at his lips. The rough pad of his thumb glides over my bottom lip. "Are you ready now?" he asks in that deep timbre of a voice that has desire pooling between my thighs.

I bob my head.

"I need your words, sweetheart."

"Y-Yes."

He leans in a little closer. The hand gripping my thigh tightens. "Are you sure?"

The way he's asking for permission sets my anxiety at ease. I trust Palmer, and Deacon is her older brother. My best friend is standing three feet away from us. He's not going to hurt me. That curbs my anxiety, but then I remember Palmer is watching, and it rises again.

"She's watching us." My words are whispered. I know my best friend, and she's going to dissect this entire day. She's going to see something that's not here. We're just pretending for the camera lens.

"That's the point of this, right?" His voice is low so that the conversation remains just between us.

"Yeah, but that's a lot of pressure," I confess.

He moves the hand that was gripping my thigh to rest on my cheek as well. On instinct, I lift both of my hands to cover his, holding him to me. It's not lost on me that his touch is soothing. I've never associated a man's touch as being anything other than unwanted.

Until Deacon.

"Pretend that it's just us. Don't think about her. Don't think about the camera. It's just you and me."

"Just you and me," I repeat.

"You have the control here, Ramsey." His tone is soft and delicate while being deep and gruff at the same time. He's being so tender with me. "You want to stop. We stop. No reasoning required."

"I-I want you to kiss me." A smile that can only be described as a blinding light crosses his face. There is something about him that gives me an immediate sense of trust.

"Yes, ma'am." His hands remain on my cheeks when he tilts his head just slightly and presses his lips to mine.

The kiss is slow and sweet. Over and over again, he kisses me with such reverence it brings tears to my eyes and causes a moan to slip past my lips. That seems to fuel him. One hand slides behind my neck, pulling me closer while the other remains on my cheek. When he nips at my bottom lip, I gasp in surprise, but I don't hate it.

All too quickly, he removes his lips from mine. Slowly, I open my eyes to see that his are closed. His hand still grips the back of my neck while the other rests tenderly against my cheek. His chest rises rapidly with each breath.

When his tongue darts out to lick his lips, his name falls past mine. "Deacon," I murmur.

His eyes pop open. Gold pools of desire stare back at me. I watch as he smiles and shakes his head. "Come on, darlin.'" With that, he moves his hands toward my waist. "I'm going to lift you from the wall."

"Oh," I say, surprised. "Okay."

"Hey." Once again, his index finger gently lifts my chin so my gaze meets his. "Not because I don't want to be standing here with you. Not because I don't want to kiss the breath from your lungs. But because I want to do those things. This isn't the place for that. Not with an audience."

His words are like a bucket of ice water being dumped over my head. Palmer is capturing all of this. My face heats. She's my best friend, and here I am, mauling her brother.

He smiles, and I feel my world tilt. "Come on, Ramsey. We have a show to put on." His smile is big, and his eyes sparkle, and I don't hate today. I don't hate it at all. "I'm going to lift you," he reminds me. His hands are back on my hips, and he effortlessly lifts me from the wall.

Instead of placing me on my feet, he lifts me higher over his head. His face is tilted back, smiling up at me. On instinct, I brace my hands on his shoulders for support.

"Oh, very *Dirty Dancing*, big brother," Palmer calls out. "This is gold." I don't bother to look toward my best friend. I already know she's circling us, trying to capture the moment from every angle.

Deacon's deep, throaty laugh sends heat between my thighs. Slowly, he lowers me, letting my body slide against his until my feet are once again firmly planted on the ground. He leans in close, his lips hovering next to my ear. "You're beautiful," he says, quickly pulling back.

"Tell us where you want us," he says to his sister.

"Um, y'all are doing fine on your own." Palmer makes a show of fanning her face with her hand.

Deacon turns to look at me. "I'm going to hold you," he says as his arm slides behind my back. He's still staring down at me. I barely come to his shoulders, and that's with my wedges that I'm wearing. "Swings?" he asks.

"I'm wearing a dress."

"Trust me, sweetheart, I'm well aware that you're wearing a sexy-as-fuck dress." He bites down on his bottom lip. "That's all that was between us sitting on that wall," he reminds me.

"I'm sorry?" It's posed as a question. I'm not sure how to read him.

"Darlin'," he drawls, bending to place his lips next to my ear. "Never apologize for your pussy being nestled against my cock." His voice is gravelly and deep and causes goose bumps to break out on my skin.

He clears his throat and adjusts his stance. I want to look down, but I can't do it. I already felt him on the wall, and when my body slid over his when he set me on my feet. Deacon is unlike any man I've ever met. He's open and polite and apparently, a little dirty too, if his most recent confession is an indication.

"Come." With his arm still wrapped around my waist, he guides us toward the swings. "I'll push you." He releases me and holds a swing for me to sit on.

"You're not going to swing with me?" I ask him.

He steps in front of me, where I perch on the swing. Tilting my head back, I peer up at him. He grips the chains and bends in close. "If I swing with you, I can't touch you."

I swallow hard. "Is that what you want to do?"

"More than I should," he replies, leaning in closer. "Can I touch you, Ramsey?"

"Yes." This time my voice is clear. There's no hesitation or stutter of my words.

"Ramsey."

"Deacon."

"I'm coming in close."

"Okay."

"I'm going to kiss you again."

This time I nod as my tongue peeks out, and I lick my lips.

"Killing me," he mumbles as his lips press to mine. It's just a peck compared to the kiss he gave me earlier. However, it's still his lips connecting with mine, which causes a thrill to race through my veins.

I would never have imagined this is how today would have turned out. I went from dreading the shoot and wanting it to be over to hoping that the moment never ends.

I trace his bottom lip with my tongue, needing more of him. However, Deacon pulls back and points his index finger at me. "Behave," he playfully scolds me.

I can't hide my smile.

I don't want to.

Deacon steps behind me and places his hands on my shoulders. He massages gently before he gives me a soft push. He does this over and over until I'm flying high, like a middle-schooler at recess. My hair is flying all over the place, and I'm thankful I thought to tuck my dress around my legs and between my thighs, or I'd be giving Palmer some X-rated material to shoot.

With each pump of my legs, my soul grows lighter, and the heaviness that seems to reside on my shoulders day in, day out fades away. "Higher!" I call out to Deacon, and his deep laughter fuels my own.

I don't know how long I swing, but when I glance over and see Palmer staring down at her camera, I know my time is up. I stop pumping my legs and eventually drag my feet so the swing will stop. Deacon is there, offering me his hand. I don't hesitate to place mine in his, allowing him to pull me to my feet.

His arm snakes around my waist, and his lips land on my temple.

"Wait!" Palmer calls out. "I need to snap that." She runs over to us and bends down, snapping picture after picture.

"I think you got it, sis." Deacon chuckles.

Palmer looks up at us with a blinding smile. "You two are pure gold. I cannot wait to start editing these and printing them."

"I get one of each."

"Sure. I'll print you copies. Both of you."

"Palmer." Deacon waits until she looks up at him. "One of every image."

Palmer's mouth drops open, and I think this is the first time I've ever seen her speechless. Well, unless she's standing in a room with all nine of my cousins. That's a lot for any woman to take in.

"Palmer?"

"Yes, of course," she says, looking at me, her eyes widening.

"Do you have what you need?" I ask her.

"This is so much better than I expected." She glances at her camera. "I did have one more scene idea."

"What's that?" Deacon asks.

She points behind us, and there's a quilt spread out on the grass. "Maybe just sit close to one another and talk? Or kiss? Or... whatever feels right." She grins. Her smile is full of mischief, and if I'm not mistaken, a little bit of hope.

Deacon steps in front of me, giving his sister his back. "What do you think, sweetheart? You up for me holding you on the old blanket?"

"I think I can suffer through it," I tease.

Who am I right now?

He steps closer. He raises his hand and waits for me to nod. He slides his palm behind my neck and leans in close. "Talking or kissing, Ramsey?"

"What?" I ask, confused.

"She said talk or kiss or whatever. You pick."

"All of the above."

He grins. The act has my heart doing flips in my chest. "Equal opportunist. I like it." He slides his hands down my arms and laces our fingers together. He lifts both to his mouth and kisses my knuckles.

I hear the shutter of the camera, and so does he if the groan that comes from deep within his chest is an indicator. "Palmer, I'm on a date here," he says. He winks at me, making me laugh.

"A date I arranged, big brother," she reminds him. "A date you didn't want to go on," she says as he turns and guides us toward the blanket.

"I'm glad I did," he whispers against my temple. "After you." He motions toward the blanket.

Somehow I manage to sit without showing my ass. Literally, I make sure to tuck my sundress beneath my legs to keep the wind from blowing it up. Deacon lies next to me. He's on his side, with his head propped up on his elbow.

"Lay with me."

I take two seconds to think about it before I'm maneuvering into a similar position with my dress tucked in tightly between my thighs. Deacon reaches out and tucks my hair behind my ear. "I've had fun with you today."

"It was definitely better than I expected."

"Yeah? What were you expecting?"

"Lots of awkward touches and a disappointed Palmer."

"Yet, you came anyway."

"She's my best friend. It took her a couple of days of begging, but in the end, she needed me, so here I am."

"I'm glad it was you." He runs his index finger over my jaw.

"It's hard to believe we've never met before now."

"I work a lot."

"I do too." I pause and then toss his words back to him. "I'm glad it was you too. You made today bearable."

"Bearable enough to steal another kiss?"

"Is it stealing if I freely give it to you?"

"Ramsey." He leans in closer. "I'll take anything and everything you're willing to give me."

It's on the tip of my tongue to say everything, but I know that's not possible. Deacon is my best friend's older brother. He's got his shit together, he's established in life, and he has a family who supports him. He doesn't need my baggage. So, instead of everything, I give him what I can.

"Deacon?"

"Hmm?" His hand that's not holding him up cradles my cheek.

"Kiss me."

A low growl erupts from his chest as his lips press to mine. This kiss is different from the others. His tongue swipes at my lips, and I open for him, allowing his tongue to peek in and taste me.

The next thing I know, I'm lying flat on my back, with Deacon hovering over me, kissing me like I've never been kissed before. I faintly hear the shutter of Palmer's camera, and did she whistle? I can't be sure about anything other than how it feels to be in his arms.

Cherished.

It's not a feeling I've ever experienced, and I want to get lost in the tenderness. I want to sit here on this old, faded quilt for the rest of my life as long as he's sitting next to me. That thought has me pulling out of our kiss.

We're both laboring to breathe. His golden eyes are locked on mine.

"Holy shit. That was hot!" Palmer exclaims.

That has me sitting up, which forces Deacon to do the same. My hand comes to my lips. They're swollen, and I can still taste him. I can't believe I just made out with my best friend's brother while she took pictures.

"Those are for our eyes only," Deacon tells her. His voice is no longer teasing.

"Hell no. That was photography magic."

"Palmer." There's an edge to his voice. "Ramsey and I get the final say on what you print."

"What? I'm the photographer. That's stunting my creativity," she argues. There's a twinkle in her eyes that tells me she's messing with him.

"Palmer Leigh," Deacon warns.

"Fine, you big baby." She sticks her tongue out at him like only a little sister can do. "You can have veto rights."

"Ramsey too," he adds.

"Ramsey too," she concedes. Despite the annoyance in her tone, she's smiling wide. "I have what I need. We can call it a day. Thank you both for doing this."

Deacon climbs to his feet and offers me his hand to help me stand. His eyes find mine. He opens his mouth to speak, but Palmer wraps her arms around him.

"Thank you, Deac." She kisses his cheek.

He hugs her back, kissing the top of her head. "You're welcome."

"Rams." Palmer opens her arms for me, and I meet her embrace. "You did amazing," she whispers.

She pulls back and reaches down for the blanket. "I'm going to pack up." With that, she scurries back to the park bench, where she left her bag.

"Come here, darlin'." Deacon opens his arms for me, and I don't hesitate to walk into his embrace. "I enjoyed today."

"Me too." I lean back and smile up at him.

He angles his head. "Just one more, Ramsey. I need one more," he says as he presses his lips to mine. I grip his shirt, holding him close, while his lips dance with mine. All too soon, he's pulling away and taking a step back. Disappointment courses through me. My time with him is over. I was dreading coming here today, and now I don't want to leave.

"Ready?" Palmer asks. She's standing next to us.

"You two drive safe," Deacon says, taking another step away from me—the opposite direction that I want him to go. He points at Palmer. "Call when those are ready to view."

"Oh, I'm all over that. I can't wait to start editing."

"Ramsey." His voice is thick with something I can't name. "Good to meet you."

"I'll say," Palmer says under her breath.

"You too." I give him a wide smile. It's real and honest, and maybe intentionally a little too wide to hide the sadness that my time with him is over.

I stand still and watch as he gives us a final wave and turns and walks away. I don't move until I see him climb behind the wheel of his truck and pull away.

"Ramsey!" Palmer jumps up and down. "He's into you."

"We were caught up in the moment," I say, downplaying the connection we shared.

"Oh, you were in the moment, all right." She bounces her brows. "Come on. I can't wait to get home and start working on these edits."

I follow her to her car in a daze. I was scared as hell to come to this photo shoot today. It was nothing that I expected and everything I needed.

Chapter Four

DEACON

Frustrated, I toss down the legal brief I've been trying to read for the past two hours. I can't concentrate, and that's my thing. I do well under pressure, and my concentration is rock solid. Well, it was. That apparently doesn't apply to a dark-haired, blue-eyed beautiful woman named Ramsey.

I can't stop thinking about her.

I left the park hours ago, and she's done nothing but consume my thoughts. I don't let women consume my thoughts, but with this one, I have no choice. She's there. So is the memory of her soft hands and her body pressed tightly to mine. The feel of my cock nestled against her pussy, and the taste of her kiss still lingers.

No matter what's going on in my life, I've always been able to focus on work. Patrick and Gordman is a small law office in Willow River. We work on all kinds of cases, from real estate to divorce, to estate planning and wills. Mr. Patrick and Mr. Gordman have both been tossing around the idea of retiring since I came on board seven years ago. From that moment, I knew what I wanted. I want to buy the practice from them. I've been busting my ass, learning everything that I can, sucking up the knowledge from their combined experience like a sponge.

That kind of dedication comes at a cost. Working way more hours than any one person should leaves no room for a social life. My sisters like to call me a workaholic. Hell, so do my friends. Friends that it's been months since I've seen for more than a passing hello, or a quick call and text message. I've sacrificed a lot for my career. I keep telling myself that it will be worth it. I'm still young. I'm only thirty-two.

My mind once again drifts to Ramsey. I don't know how old she is, but she's best friends with my little sister, who is twenty-two. They look to be the same age. She's too damn young for me, but that doesn't stop me from thinking about having her in my bed.

"Fuck," I mutter. I run my hands over my face. I just need a break. That has to be what it is. This morning's photo shoot has been the first breather I've allowed myself in months. I need a beer and to shoot the shit with my friends. Decision made, I reach for my phone and pull up my best friend Orrin Kincaid's contact, and hit Call.

"He's alive," my best friend says with a laugh.

"Fuck off." I snort. "What are you getting into tonight?"

"Me and a couple of my brothers are going to the Willow Tavern for a few beers. Maybe I'll kick their asses in a game of pool," he replies.

"What time?"

"Hold up. Are you coming out? For real?" There's excitement in his voice, and that makes me feel like an even bigger tool. I need to make more time for those in my life that I care about. It's not like I'm in jeopardy of losing my job. I've just been on go mode from the day I got the call that the job was mine. I don't know any other way to be.

"Yeah, I was thinking about it." Even more so now that he said that they're going to the Willow Tavern. Ramsey works tonight. Seeing her again is probably the worst idea in the history of ideas with how I can't stop thinking about her, but I'm going to do it anyway.

"Fuck me, it might be summer, but it's going to snow," he jokes. "This is a rare event."

"Yeah, yeah. What time are you meeting there?"

"Brooks is working. His shift is over at six. That's if he gets out on time. The plan was to meet at the Tavern around eight. He almost never gets out on time, and he'll need to go home and shower."

"I'll meet you there."

"You better not stand me up, Setty," he warns.

I let out a hearty laugh. "I'm not standing you up. My concentration is shit. It's time for a break," I admit.

"You good?"

If you count lusting after your cousin, who is also my little sister's best friend, then sure. I'm good. "Of course." I knew that my little sister's best friend was his younger cousin from out of town. I knew that she had some issues with her parents and was building a life for herself here in Willow River. What I didn't know was that she's drop-dead gorgeous, or that her lips taste as sweet as honey. I guess those are the kinds of things you miss when you're married to your job.

"You want me to swing by and pick you up?"

"Nah, I'll just meet you there."

"All right, man, see you soon."

"See ya." I end the call, tossing my phone on the couch. I close the document I was working on and shut down my laptop before placing everything in a pile on the coffee table. There is definitely no working happening for me today.

I need to get out of this house and out of my own head. I have to stop thinking about her. I should drop in on Palmer and see how the edits are going, but that defeats the purpose of me trying to stop thinking about her.

"Fuck it," I mutter. Standing, I head to my bedroom and change into a pair of dark jeans and a black fitted T-shirt. I may not get to socialize much, but I still hit my home gym at least five days a week. However, it's not often I get to show off the fruits of that labor. Tonight is not one of those nights. Tonight I won't be dressed in my normal suit. Sometimes even if I meet the guys after work for dinner or beers, I go straight from the office. It almost feels foreign to be in plain clothes anywhere other than my own home.

Making sure I have my wallet, I grab my keys and my phone, and I'm out the door. I have no idea where I'm going. I still have a couple of hours before I meet the guys at the Tavern. There's a part of me that wants to just go sit at the bar, but I know I can't do that for a multitude of reasons.

I promised Mom I'd come and visit this weekend, and there is no better time than the present. Turning right out of my driveway, I head to their house. It's dinner time, and my stomach growls. Some of my mom's home cooking is exactly what I need.

Fifteen minutes later, I'm pulling into their driveway. As soon as I climb out of my truck, I can smell the grill, and my growl is more of an intense roar at this point. I don't bother with the front door. Instead, I make my way around the side of the house and find my parents sitting on the back deck.

"Deacon!" Mom's face lights up when she sees me. "We didn't know you were stopping by. Are you hungry? We have plenty."

"You know there's no better steak than mine," Dad tells me.

Cliff Setty is a mean machine on the grill. He mixes his own spices and holds that shit close to his chest. It doesn't matter how many times I ask for the combination. He refuses. He claims that's what keeps his kids coming home to visit.

"It smells great," I say, laughing at him. "You ever going to give up that recipe, old man?" I ask, even though I already know the answer.

"It'll be in my will," he tosses back.

"I wrote your will," I remind him.

"Fine, it will be in the house. You'll have to search for it."

"You hear this?" I ask Mom.

She just shakes her head. "He won't even tell me."

"And she," Dad points his tongs at Mom, "is the love of my life."

"I'm your son. You made me."

"She did that." He points at Mom again. "I just came in with the assist."

He winks at Mom, and the smile that she rewards him with is the one I've seen a million times growing up. It's the look that tells him that he owns her own heart and the look that also shows that she knows she has his too.

My parents have the best relationship. Don't get me wrong. It's not all sunshine and roses. They argue like the best of couples. It's that they never give up. They work out whatever it is, and the love they have for each other always outweighs all the other bullshit. All the white noise. They're solid, and they gave my sisters and me a great example of what a healthy relationship looks like

"What brings you by?" Mom asks.

"I just needed a break. I'm going to meet Orrin at the Willow Tavern later for a couple of beers. I promised you that I'd stop by."

"Well, I'm glad you did. You can tell me all about today." She grins.

"Today?"

"The photo shoot. Palmer was so excited. How did Ramsey do? She was so nervous."

Ramsey.

Shit. I thought I could come here and get her out of my head, but I should have known better. My parents have always been involved in everything we do. They've supported our dreams, no matter how big or small, and I've heard her talk about Ramsey before.

"It was fine." I don't dare tell my mother that I'm still thinking about the dark-haired beauty. She'll want to play matchmaker. Then again, probably not. Ramsey is young. I'm more than likely to get lectured on how I need to find a nice woman my own age to settle down with. Either way, neither conversation is one that I want to have.

"You have to give me more than fine. Palmer hasn't talked about anything else for weeks."

"I still can't believe she convinced you." Dad smirks.

"Like you can tell her, Mom, or Piper no." I give him a knowing look, and he shrugs.

"They're my girls."

"Details, Deacon. I need details."

"It was fine. She blindfolded us. We took them off at the same time, and Palmer took a billion pictures. We posed in front of the brick wall at the park, I pushed Ramsey on the swings, and we had a pretend picnic. It was fine."

It was more than fine. It was... unexpected and hot as fuck, but I'm keeping that all to myself. I'm not going to tell them that I can still feel her body pressed to mine or that I can still taste her on my tongue. I don't tell them that I saw something lurking in her eyes. Something that called to me to hold her close and make sure she knows how beautiful she is.

I also don't tell them how she flinched when I touched her and that she told me her wrists were off-limits. I can't even think about someone hurting her without seeing red. There is no excuse for a man putting his hands on a woman in hate. None. I don't care if it's Ramsey, one of my sisters, or the woman I'm standing behind at the supermarket. There is no excuse.

"Isn't she the sweetest?" Mom pulls me out of my thoughts.

You have no idea. "She was fine."

"Fine?" Mom asks, appalled. "Do you know any other word than fine?"

"You would think that he would have a little better vocabulary after all that college," Dad jokes.

"I don't know what you want me to say." I grab a roll out of the basket on the table. "I did it for Palmer. She begged, and just like Dad, I can't tell her no, even though I tried. I showed up in what she told me to wear, and she took some pictures of us. Ramsey seemed nervous, but by the time we were done, she seemed to be relaxed."

"Was that so hard?" Mom asks, smiling.

"Excruciating." If she only knew how hard I was trying to get the beautiful, too-young-for-me Ramsey out of my head.

"Well, I think it was nice of you to do that for your sister. I guess this blind-date thing is all the rage, and she's hoping to get some traffic to her business."

"I know. That's why I did it."

"And the fact that you're a pushover when it comes to your sisters," Dad chimes in.

"You're one to talk."

"I'll own it." Dad chuckles. "It's the pouty lip and the batting of the eyes. Kills me every time."

"You're just soft," Mom teases.

"I can prove you wrong on that, darlin'," he says, wagging his eyebrows at her.

"Really? We're getting ready to eat." I pretend to shudder. Their antics are something that I'm used to. Dad just can't seem to help himself.

Thankfully, the subject changes to the renovations they plan to do on their master bathroom. I try like hell to keep my head in the conversation. I keep looking at my phone, watching the time. I know she's going to be there, which means with each minute that passes, it gets closer to me seeing her again.

I need to know if that spark is there. Surely, it was just the atmosphere and the way we had to touch for the photo shoot. It has to be the situation. At twenty till eight, I stand and help my parents start cleaning up.

"Thanks for dinner," I tell them.

"You're welcome. We should do it more often," Mom says, hugging me.

"What she said." Dad nods.

"I know. I'll do better. I promise." With another hug and a fist bump for Dad, I'm in my truck and headed toward the Willow Tavern.

Walking into the bar, I have to force myself not to look for her. Instead, I head to the back corner where Orrin told me he and his brothers would be.

"There he is!" Orrin holds up his beer in salute as I take the chair across from him. "I thought for sure you were going to bail."

"We just grabbed these from the bar," Brooks, one of his younger brothers, says, sliding a beer to me across the table.

"Thanks."

"So, how have you been?" Orrin asks.

"Working my life away. Nothing new to report. You know me. Boring as always." I bite the inside of my cheek to keep from talking. Orrin has been my best friend since we were kids. He's going to see right through me.

"How about you all?" I look around the table at Orrin, his brother Brooks, and his brother Declan.

"Shop's doing good. Can't complain," Orrin replies.

"Good to hear."

"I'm still working the ER over at Willow General," Brooks chimes in.

"Man, I don't know how you do what you do all day. Some of the things that you see..." I shake my head. It takes a strong person to be a nurse, and I applaud him for it.

"It's not so bad. I would never want to be a nurse in the inner city, but in our small town of Willow River, I can deal. Sure, there are times when it's tough, but there are just as many that aren't."

"What about you?" I ask Declan.

"Shop's staying busy, and Blakely keeps me on my toes." He smiles wistfully as he thinks about his daughter.

"How old is she now?"

"She'll be three soon."

"Going on thirteen," Orrin adds.

"She has us all wrapped around her little finger," Brooks tells me.

"I can only imagine. My sisters are both adults, and they still have me wrapped around their little fingers."

"Thank fuck we have all brothers," Declan says.

"Agreed, but we have Ramsey now," Brooks reminds him.

"Speaking of Ramsey, it's time for a refill. Anyone want one?" Orrin asks.

We all say yes, and he heads off to the bar to buy another round. I almost told him that I would go with him, but I don't really want him to be there when I see her again. I don't know how awkward it's going to be.

Hell, with as much as she's been on my mind, it's hard to tell what will come out of my mouth.

"Any exciting cases?" Declan asks.

"This is Willow River. Nothing exciting ever happens. Besides, even if there were, I wouldn't be able to tell you. There is a thing called client confidentiality."

"Come on, nothing?" he asks.

"Not unless real estate and wills tickle your fancy."

"Your job's boring." He laughs.

"I could say the same to you. No way could I tear an engine apart and put it back together again."

"Touché."

"Here you go. I told Rams to stop by on her break and check-in," Orrin says, passing us each a fresh bottle of beer.

I pretend that my body doesn't hum at the sound of her name. I block out this overwhelming need to rush to the bar to see her and force myself to remain seated. Today has been weird as fuck, and I don't need to add to that. I manage to push thoughts of Ramsey to the side and halfway focus on the conversation of my friends around me.

Chapter Five

RAMSEY

"Hey, Rams, I need two drafts," Hannah, one of the servers, calls out her order as she reaches over the bar and grabs a handful of peanuts. "I'm starving. I thought I'd have time to grab something, but it's packed tonight."

"It's a little crazier than normal. Is there something going on in town that I missed?" I ask as I pour her two drafts.

"Not that I'm aware of." She shrugs as I place the two drinks onto her tray. "Thank you," she calls over her shoulder as she bustles her way through the crowd.

"You ready for your break?" Hank, the owner, asks, stepping up next to me where I'm standing behind the bar. Hank is tall with dark salt-and-pepper hair and two full sleeves of tattoos. He's got muscles for days, and the ladies flock to the bar when he's here. He's in his late thirties and still living the single life.

"I can work through. It's busy."

"You know better than that. Didn't I see Orrin and a few of the guys walk in earlier? Go sit, grab something to eat."

"Let Hannah go first. She's starving."

"I'm sending you both at the same time. Chance and I will man the bar until you're back. They can walk their drunk asses up here to order drinks for thirty minutes."

"What about serving food?"

"Tabitha just got here. It will be fine. We can handle it. If I have to call out the order, have them come to the bar instead of us taking it to them, I will. That's why we give them an order number. Now, go."

"Fine, but if you need me…" My voice trails off because he's already shaking his head no.

"You work too hard, kid. Go grab some food and visit with your family. I don't want you back on the clock until your full thirty minutes are up."

I stick my tongue out at him, and he laughs. "Thanks, Hank." With a nod, he jumps right into filling drink orders.

Making my way to the back, I think about what I want to eat. We have your typical bar food like nachos and cheese, soft pretzels, potato skins, fried pickles, cheese sticks, wings, easy to order and prepare items. I settle for an order of mozzarella sticks with barbeque sauce to dip them in instead of pizza sauce. Don't knock it until you've tried it.

Walking back out to the bar, I pour myself a Dr Pepper before making my way through the crowd to the back of the bar where Orrin, my cousin, told me he and his brothers were sitting.

"There she is." Orrin smiles as he pulls the empty chair that's next to him out so that I can sit. "I was beginning to wonder if Hank was going to give you a break." He smirks, because we both know that's not Hank.

"It's crazy in here tonight," I say, taking the offered seat. I look up to greet my other two cousins that Orrin said were here and freeze. My gaze collides with honey-colored orbs that have been on my mind all day.

"Ramsey," Deacon's deep voice, which sounds like velvet wrapped around my name, greets me.

My hands are suddenly clammy, and my heart begins to race. "Deacon." I nod and force myself to look at Brooks and Declan. "Hey." I smile at my cousins.

"You good, Rams?" Declan asks.

"I'm good. Who has Blakely tonight?" I ask him. As a single father to a little girl, Declan always seems to be more in tune with emotions than the rest of his brothers.

"Mom and Dad. They're camping out in the living room." He smiles as if the thought alone is pleasing.

"Damn," Brooks mutters, "I remember doing that when we were her age."

"I'm sure they'd let you join them," Orrin teases.

Brooks points at his oldest brother. "Don't tempt me, my man. A night of Mom's cooking and Blakely's snuggles sound like a good time to me."

I can't help but smile at their banter. My cousins, all nine of them, are close. They're the brothers I never had, and when I called my aunt Carol two years ago, they accepted me into their fold as if it was second nature. As the only girl in a house full of boys, it was challenging to say the least. I'm an only child, so it was an adjustment for me. Even though most of them had long since moved out by the time that I arrived, they're still there all the time. The relationship they have with their parents is one I've never known, and to this day, it still astounds me how close they are and how much love they share.

I hope they realize how truly special and fortunate they are to have that bond. Not only with their parents, but with each other. They'll never know the loneliness I grew up with.

"How did the photo shoot go?" Brooks asks. "I know you were stressing over it."

"Fine." I keep my eyes on his and don't dare look at Deacon.

"Just fine?" he asks. I can hear the question in his voice. I can also hear the expectation. This is where I would tell them all about it. The good and the bad parts. Instead, I keep my mouth shut. I'm sure they don't want to hear how I kissed their friend, who is much older than me, and that I've thought of nothing but him since the photo shoot.

"It wasn't as bad as I thought it would be." That's the truth. I imagined torture, but instead, I got... Deacon.

"Who was the guy?" Declan asks. "I know you were worried about it."

"I shouldn't have been. Palmer had my back." Another truth. No way can I tell them it was my best friend's older brother and their friend. The guy who is sitting across the table from me, and makes my heart hammer in my chest. I knew they were friends. I've heard them talk about him, but I've never met him. Palmer says he works all the time, and the guys have said the same. However, so do I. If there was a time he was around, I was probably at work myself.

"Yeah?" Orrin asks. "So, who was he?"

"Me." My eyes dart to Deacon as he raises his hand. "It was me." His eyes are locked on mine, and it's suddenly hard to breathe with his attention focused on me.

"You?" Orrin asks. He chokes on the word, as if he can't believe that Deacon was my blind date.

"Yep," Deacon replies, his eyes still locked on mine.

"How did Palmer rope you into that?" Declan asks with a laugh.

Deacon finally pulls his gaze from mine. "Fuck, you know how she is. I've never been able to say no to her."

"So? How was it?" Brooks asks again. He's bound and determined to pull it out of me.

"Good." Deacon turns his attention back to me. "It was good."

"Rams?" Brooks asks.

"I told you. It was fine. It wasn't as bad as I anticipated." Instead, it was better than I ever could have imagined.

"When do we get to see the pictures?" Orrin's gaze bounces between his best friend and me.

"Ramsey and I get the first look. We get to veto any pictures we don't want to be shared."

"Is there something that happened that you don't want to be shared?" Orrin's voice is a little harder and a lot deeper than it was just moments before.

"No," Deacon is quick to reply. "However, I know Ramsey was nervous, so I made sure that Palmer agreed to only share what she approved."

"And what about you?" Declan inquires.

Deacon gives a slow lift of his shoulders. "I'd share them all."

I can feel my face flame with embarrassment, but also something I can't name. A swarm of butterflies surge to life in my belly at his confession. Maybe I wasn't the only one feeling… connected that way. That's the best way that I can describe it. The moment I laid eyes on him, his presence put me at ease.

"What about you?" Orrin's eyes hold mine.

"Honestly, I'm not sure," I admit. "I mean, if she got a shot where my face is all messed up from a silly laugh or something, I'd probably ask her not to share that." Deacon's eyes bore into mine, and I hope he understands what I'm saying. I'm not upset about the outcome of the photo shoot.

"Nice," Brooks says, draining the rest of his beer.

"Palmer is really talented. I'm sure the pictures are going to turn out great." I'm not just saying that to be saying it. My best friend is talented as hell, and I can't wait to see the end result.

"How long is your break?" I can feel Deacon's eyes on me as he asks the question.

"Thirty minutes." I look across the table at him, and he nods at my mozzarella sticks.

"You better eat something." His voice is soft, but it also feels like there might be a concern there.

"Yeah, these are getting cold." I pick up a mozzarella stick and dip it into the barbeque sauce.

"Is that barbeque sauce?" Deacon leans forward to get a better look at my plate.

"Yes." Again, I feel my face flush. "It's good. You want to try it?" I offer him the mozzarella stick I just dunked, and to my surprise, he leans just a little further over the table and opens his mouth.

On instinct, I place it in his mouth, and he takes a bite, sitting back while he chews. "Not bad." He smiles at me.

"Right?" I dip the remainder of the mozzarella stick back into the barbeque sauce before taking my own bite.

"You share food with just anyone?" Orrin's voice is thick, and unease settles over me. The last thing I want is this attraction I feel toward Deacon to come between their friendship.

"No. But Deacon isn't just anyone." He's the guy I can't stop thinking about. He's also the one who was kissing the hell out of me just a few hours ago. "He's my best friend's brother and your best friend."

"You don't know him," Orrin counters.

"Sure I do. He's Deacon." I shrug like it's not a big deal.

Thankfully Brooks changes the subject by talking about something to do with his car. Declan jumps right into the conversation. I can feel Orrin's stare, and even though I don't want to, I turn to look at him. "What's wrong?"

"Are you okay, Ramsey?"

I smile at him. It's not fake or forced. It's genuine. "I'm good, O. I promise." I don't dare look at Deacon, but I want to. Instead, I focus on eating the rest of my mozzarella sticks and listening to my cousins talk about cars.

"I should get back to work," I say a few minutes later. I stand and gather my now-empty basket and my cup of Dr Pepper. "I'll see you guys later." I wave to the table. I don't make eye contact with any of them before turning on my heel and rushing back to the kitchen. I toss my trash and place the red plastic basket back on the shelf before clocking back in.

Hank looks down at his watch and then smiles. I shake my head at him as I jump back into filling orders. The weekends are usually busy, but tonight takes that to an all-new level. I'm slinging drinks left and right, singing along to the jukebox when I see him approach the bar.

"Hey."

"Ramsey," Deacon greets me.

"What can I get you?" I'm proud I'm able to keep my voice calm.

"How about some of that root beer that Hank makes?"

"It's so good," I tell him, grabbing a glass from the freezer, adding some ice, and filling it with Hank's homemade root beer. "Here you go." I slide the glass across the bar toward him. "Three dollars."

"Thanks." He hands me a twenty and turns to walk away.

"Deacon!" I call out. He stops and turns to look at me. "You forgot your change." I hold up the twenty, letting him know he gave me such a large bill.

"That's yours."

"No." I shake my head vehemently. "That's too much."

His golden eyes study me before he replies, "You're worth it." He winks, turns, and walks away.

The Tavern is loud as hell, but his words hit me as if they were screamed. I stand frozen in time, replaying his words over and over in my mind.

"Hey." An arm lands on my shoulder, causing me to jump. "You good?" Chance, a fellow bartender, asks.

"Yeah. Yes. I'm good." I nod. I shake out of my Deacon trance and get back to work. I try like hell not to think about him, but it's hard not to. Not after the photo shoot and then tonight. I know nothing can come of this… whatever it is, I'm feeling for him. It's just because he was nice to me, and technically, my first kiss, the first I approved of anyway. That has to be it. I just need to finish the night and go home and get some rest. Everything will be better after that.

My feet are killing me. I finish wiping down the counters and toss the rag into the dirty bin in the supply closet. Once in the small break room, I grab my purse and pull out my Mace. One of the guys always stays to walk us out, and Hank makes sure the parking lot is well lit, but you just never know. Willow River is a quiet small town, but my past is always lingering in the back of my mind that people aren't always what they seem.

"You ready?" Chance asks.

"I've been ready. I'm exhausted."

"Tabitha, you ready?" Chance asks.

"Yes." She smiles and joins us.

"Hank?" Chance asks.

"I'm just going to sleep upstairs tonight," he tells us. "I have a new vendor coming early in the morning to meet with me, and it's just easier to stay here."

"All right, man. See ya." Chance waves, as do Tabitha and I, as we follow him out the door.

"Who's that?" Tabitha asks.

I turn to follow her gaze, and my heart stops.

"Deacon," I whisper.

"You good?" Chance asks me.

"Yes."

"You sure?"

"I am." I smile at him, hoping he can't see the tremble in my smile. I know, or at least I think I know, that Deacon would never hurt me, but being alone with him in a dark parking lot isn't exactly a smart move.

"Hi," I say, breaking away from my coworkers and slowly approaching him. He's leaning against the side of his truck that's parked next to my car. "What are you doing here?" I ask him with a quivering voice.

"I left a couple of hours ago," he confesses. "Then I got home and started thinking about you getting off work late and walking out alone, and well," he shrugs, "here I am."

"One of the guys always walks us out," I tell him. "And I have this." I raise my Mace to show him.

He nods. "Good. That's good."

I take a step closer. "You were worried about me?"

"Yeah," he says, running a hand through his hair.

"I'm good."

He stands from where he's leaning against his truck and takes a step toward me, bringing us toe-to-toe. "Can I touch you, Ramsey?"

My breath stalls in my lungs, making speech impossible, so I nod.

Lifting his hand, he tucks my hair behind my ear before letting his index finger trace my jaw. "I had to make sure," he whispers in a gravelly voice.

"You good, Ramsey?" Chance calls out.

His voice breaks our trance, and Deacon drops his hand. I turn to look at Chance. "Everything is fine. Thank you for walking me out. I'll see you tomorrow night."

Chance studies us for a few minutes before climbing into his car but doesn't drive away.

"He's not going to leave until I do."

"Is he your boyfriend?" Deacon asks with more edge to his voice than I've yet to hear from him. It's not mean, just... disapproving maybe.

"No. Just a good guy. Hank, my boss, insists that one of the guys is with us girls, and they stay until we drive off. They're good people."

"That's good to hear. You better get going." He steps next to me, places his hand on the small of my back, and leads me the few final steps to my car door. I unlock the door and toss my purse inside.

"Thank you for checking on me."

"I'm going to lean in close," he tells me. I nod, and he leans in, pressing his lips to my cheek. "Drive safe, darlin.'"

The blood is rushing through my ears, making it hard to hear anything but the thunderous rhythm. "Night, Deacon." I settle behind the wheel. He waits until I've fastened my seat belt before he closes the door and taps twice on my hood.

My hands shake as I start the car and put it into gear. Slowly, my foot presses against the accelerator, and I pull out of the lot. I think about Deacon the entire way back to my apartment. I don't know what tonight was. I'm so damn confused, but I can admit, even if it's just to myself, that his attention isn't unpleasant. Deacon seems like a nice guy. He's gorgeous and off-limits. He's my best friend's older brother, and if my cousin's reaction tonight is any indication, he's not impressed with the mere thought of something happening between his best friend and me.

Chapter Six

DEACON

THIS HAS BEEN ONE OF THE LONGEST DAYS OF MY LIFE. I didn't sleep for shit all weekend, and my concentration, it's vanished in the face of a blue-eyed angel named Ramsey. It's Monday evening, and I'm still at work because I can't stop thinking about her long enough to get my shit together and get through this brief. I've been working on it since Saturday, the day I met her and the day she infiltrated my mind without permission.

Thankfully, the office was mostly quiet today, and my bosses were too busy with their own caseload to recognize that I'm not on my game. I'm *never* not on my game.

Never.

At least not until the last few days. It's a little after eight, and my stomach is growling. I missed lunch today. I was determined not to leave my office until I was finished. It should have been done this weekend but working at home didn't happen. Nothing has happened except for my mind constantly thinking about her. There are a million reasons why thinking about her is wrong. She's too damn young for me. She's my sister's best friend and my best friend's little cousin.

I didn't miss the looks Orrin was giving me on Saturday night while Ramsey was sitting with us. He went on to tell me that she's been through hell and that he worries about her. I got the underlying message. Leave her alone. He didn't come out and say it, but I heard him loud and clear. And he's right. I need to leave her alone. I'm at least ten years her senior, and she's already too close to people I care about. That can only end in disaster. I'm a workaholic, and she deserves someone who is going to give her their time. The time that she deserves.

Reaching for my bottle of water, I see that it's empty. Fuck it. I'm going to go to the break room and grab a cup of coffee. I need to head home, I need food, but I also need to finish this. I have just a few more pages, and I'm bound and determined that I'm going to finish them tonight. I'm not leaving here until they're done.

Standing from my desk, I make my way to the door. My phone alerts me of a message, and when I glance down at the screen, I see that it's my younger sister.

Palmer: Deacon! These images!!

Her text is followed up with three fire emojis. Palmer doesn't need to tell me how hot they are. I was there. I lived the moment that she only witnessed through her lens. I had my hands on Ramsey, tasted her lips, and had my cock nestled between her thighs. Three fire emojis are not enough to describe what went down that day.

Not even close.

Sliding my phone back into my pocket, I continue down the hall to the small break room. When I push open the door, there's a woman standing with her back to me as she wipes down the counters. She reminds me of Ramsey. Nope. Not going there. I clear my throat to alert the woman to my presence. "I'm sorry. I just need to grab a quick cup of coffee, and I'll be out of your way," I assure her.

The woman slowly turns to face me, and my mouth drops open in shock.

"Ramsey?"

She lifts her hand in an awkward wave and smiles. "Hi, Deacon."

"What are you doing here?" I take two steps toward her and stop. I want to pull her into my arms and hold her tight. I want to kiss her lips and just… fuck! I can't have thoughts like this about her. This has to stop.

"I'm cleaning. This is one of my side jobs. The girl who usually cleans called in sick, and since I don't work at the Tavern, I told them I would work."

"Have you ever cleaned this office before?" Surely if she had, I would have noticed her. Ramsey isn't the kind of woman you forget. I'm an expert on this at this point.

She nods. "I have, but usually, it's just me. Everyone is typically gone by the time I start. What are you still doing here? It's late."

Is that concern I hear in her voice? "Working." I run my hands through my hair, which I know has to look like I've been on a bender. I've done that same motion countless times today. I just can't get this woman out of my mind.

"So Palmer's right? You are a workaholic?"

There's no judgment in her tone. "Yeah. However, coming from someone who has three jobs, I'm not so sure you can give me a hard time about it." I'm teasing, and I hope that my smile tells her so.

"Oh. I'm not. I'm sorry. I was just… making conversation."

I take another step closer to her. I shove my hands in my pants pockets to keep myself from reaching for her. "I know. It's not a bad trait."

She smiles warmly. "No. It's not," she agrees.

My stomach grumbles, and she laughs. The sound fills the quiet of the room, wrapping around me like an embrace. "I forgot to eat today."

Her eyes widen. "You forgot to eat? Deacon, that's not good. You have to take better care of yourself. You can't go all day without eating. Your body and your mind need fuel," she scolds. Her brow is furrowed, and she's cute as hell.

"I know. It's not something I make a habit of."

"Go. Your day is done. Go home and eat and get some rest."

"How much longer until you're done?"

"I just need to sweep and take out the trash in the offices." She tilts her head to the side to study me. "Why?"

"Have you had dinner?"

"No. I just figured I'd grab something when I get home."

"Ramsey." I place my hand over my heart as if I'm appalled. "Your body and mind need fuel." I smirk.

A slow, sexy smile crosses her face. "I deserve that."

"Have dinner with me?" Asking her to have dinner with me is the last thing I should be doing. The warnings of why I can't have her are still alive and well, but I'm choosing to ignore every single one of them.

"Oh. Um… I don't want you to have to wait for me."

"I'm not going to. I'm going to help you." The idea takes shape in my mind. I can help her with the trash, and she can sweep, and then I get her all to myself.

"No. I mean, you can't do that. I can't let you do that."

"You're not letting me do anything. I volunteered. Besides, we both still need to have dinner, and from the sounds of it, we were both planning on going home and eating alone. This way, we can keep each other company." And I can spend a little more time with her and maybe satisfy this craving I seem to have for her that I can't shake.

"Deacon, I," she starts but quickly closes her mouth when I take the final two steps that leave me standing right in front of her. Her blue eyes peer up at me under long dark lashes, and she's just as beautiful as I remember her.

"Please? Let me buy you dinner." She's quiet as she chews on her bottom lip, debating her answer. "I'm going to touch you," I warn her. Lifting my hand, I rest it against her cheek, and fuck me. Her skin is so damn soft. "I'd love your company." It's not a line. I would love nothing more than to spend a few hours with her over a meal. There's just something about her that I can't let go of. Time with her will give me the opportunity to figure out what that hold is and how I can stop it.

"I'd like that," she replies. Her voice is soft, and her breath warm as it touches my face.

"Yeah?" I lean in even further. I'm so close I could kiss her. There are just as many reasons I should as I shouldn't, but my conscience wins, so I force myself to drop my hand and take a step back.

"Yes."

I flash her a grin. "I'll get the trash." I turn on my heel and head for the office across the hall. We're a small firm. Three offices, two conference rooms, a break room, two small bathrooms, and a reception area.

I rush through rooms, pulling bags of trash and tossing them into a pile by the back door. Once I've replaced all the cans with a new bag, I gather them all and take them out to the dumpster. The light in the lot flickers, but it doesn't provide much brightness. I've never thought much about it before, but we need to get that fixed. It's not safe for Ramsey or any woman to be out here at night by herself if the lot isn't properly lit. This is Willow River, and the crime rate is low, but her safety isn't something I'm willing to risk. I make a mental note to talk to Mr. Gordman and Mr. Patrick first thing in the morning about getting the light fixed.

I'm closing the back door and making sure that it's locked when Ramsey steps out of the small supply closet. "Thank you for your help, Deacon."

"Thank you for having dinner with me. Are you all set?"

"Yes." She looks down at her black leggings and her Maid For You Cleaning Service polo. "I'm not really dressed for going out."

"I know just the place. You like pizza?"

"Doesn't everyone?" she counters.

"Everyone I know." I nod, smiling. "Grab your things and meet me in my office." I rush down the hall and close down my laptop. I don't bother packing it up to take it home with me. I know I won't be getting any work done. I'll be back bright and early in the morning before everyone else arrives and try to get something accomplished.

"You can ride with me. I'll bring you back to your car," I tell her, placing my hand on the small of her back and leading her out of the building.

"Oh, you don't have to do that. I can just follow you wherever."

It's on the tip of my tongue to tell her to follow me home, but I keep that request to myself. "Nope. Come on." I guide her to my truck.

"I expected you to drive a car or an SUV," she confesses.

"I have a car too, but I prefer my truck." Reaching for the door, I pull it open. She gives me a spectacular view of her ass as she climbs inside. I wait for her to be settled and her seat belt in place before shutting the door.

"So, I thought we could drive to Harris and eat at Momma Joe's Pizzeria," I suggest as I put the truck in Drive and pull out of the lot.

"Oh. I've never been there."

"Harris is only a twenty-minute drive."

"I've been to Harris, but never to Momma Joe's," she explains.

"You've been missing out," I tell her. "I don't know what it is, but it's my favorite pizza around."

"I'm excited to try it." She smiles over at me, and something happens in my chest. It tightens, and the feeling is foreign.

"So you're off tonight. When do you work again?" I ask. I don't know much about her, but I want to change that. I hope getting to know her better will ease this infatuation I have with her.

"I'm off tomorrow. I usually work two shifts a week with At Your Service Catering, but they had a party cancellation, so they don't need me."

"How do you manage three jobs?"

"The cleaning gig I just fill in from time to time. It's nothing that's consistent. The catering job was my first when I moved to Willow River. They took a chance on me, and well, I hate to give them up altogether. That's also where I met Palmer. I also work five days a week. Wednesday thru Sunday at the Willow Tavern."

She went over this a little at the photo shoot, but I feel as though I wasn't giving her my undivided attention. Not when my hands were all over her. "If you could have any job in the world, what would it be?" I ask. Surely working at the Willow Tavern isn't her ultimate job. There is nothing wrong with it if it is, but something tells me it's not.

"Well, I... um, actually, I have a bachelor's degree in political science.

I've just never used it." She swallows hard. "My father was strict and insisted I start college classes post-secondary while in high school. I didn't mind it. I preferred it actually. I'd rather stay in and study than have to pretend with my fake friends, and the guy they insisted I date. I graduated early."

"First, I'm sorry. I hate that you had to deal with fake people, and a guy you didn't like. I hate even more that it was at the hands of your father. Second, congrats on graduating early. That's awesome. Why have you never used your degree? If you don't mind me asking?"

"It wasn't something that I wanted." She doesn't give me any more than that, and I don't push her. I want to, but something tells me asking for more would just make her clam up.

"Did you always want to be a lawyer?" she asks, her body suddenly stiff.

"Well, to hear my parents tell it, yes." I laugh. "I was the king of arguing with them and my middle sister, Piper, when we were younger. Not so much with Palmer. She was eight when I left for college." Just another reminder that this woman is too damn young for me.

"So, you're ten years older than Palmer?"

"I am."

She nods. "That makes you what? Thirty-two?" she asks.

"Yep. I'll be thirty-three in October. You?"

"I'm twenty-two. I'll be twenty-three in August."

She just confirmed what I already knew. I'm too damn old for her. There's a devil sitting on one shoulder telling me that age is just a number, and the angel on the other telling me we can only ever be friends. It's exhausting the way my mind keeps floating back and forth between the two.

"So? Being a lawyer?" She steers the conversation back to her question.

"When I started college, I had no idea what I wanted to do. I knew that I wanted a degree. I wanted a career where I didn't have to live paycheck to paycheck. My parents worked their asses off to raise the three of us, and at times money was tight, and I knew I wanted better. I wanted to be able to support a family should my future wife decide she wanted to stay home and raise our kids."

"You were thinking about a wife and kids in college?" Surprise is evident in her voice.

"Yeah, I mean, I wasn't ready right then, but I knew I wanted a family like my own one day. What about you?"

"I... didn't grow up that way. My parents were not as lenient with my choices."

"Meaning they controlled your life?" I ask, reading between the lines.

"Pretty much." She sighs. "I've never really been allowed to think for myself. At least not until I moved to Willow River."

"How'd you convince them to let you do that?" I ask. She's quiet. When I glance over, she's wringing her hands together in her lap. On instinct, I reach over and cover them with mine. "I'm sorry. You don't have to answer that."

"No. I want to. I just don't really talk about them."

"Then you don't have to."

She turns to look at me as I pull into the parking lot of Momma Joe's. "My dad's a lawyer too," she says softly. "He's—You're not like him."

"I don't know if that's a good thing or a bad thing."

She swallows hard. "It's a good thing, Deacon."

"Good." I give her hand a gentle squeeze. "Sit tight. I'll get your door." I pull the keys from the ignition, climb out of the truck, and race around to her door. Once I have it open, I offer her my hand to help her down, and my palm again finds its way to the small of her back as I guide her inside.

I don't know what the deal is with her and her parents, but I hate the look that it puts on her face. It's my new mission tonight to bring her smile back.

Chapter Seven

RAMSEY

THE HEAT OF HIS PALM RESTING AGAINST MY BACK PENETRATES through the thin fabric of my company-issued polo. I can't believe that I agreed to have dinner with him dressed like this. He's quite possibly the sexiest man on earth. I'm feeling frumpy next to him with my hair piled in a knot on top of my head, my leggings, polo, and tennis shoes. Not that it matters. Deacon is just being nice. No way would a man like him be interested in me.

Not that I want him to be. I've had my fill of men, lawyers in particular. Although, I must admit that Deacon doesn't act at all like my father or my ex. Then again, I don't really know him. I like to think I'm a pretty good judge of character. I knew instantly that Robert was not a good guy, but never once have I gotten that vibe from Deacon. He reminds me of my cousins—just a laid-back guy.

I almost argued the fact that I couldn't ride with him, but instead, I sent a message to my aunt Carol. I didn't want to send one to Palmer, because I didn't know how she would feel about me having dinner with her brother. Oh, who am I kidding? She'd be thrilled and probably be planning our wedding. I'm sure Aunt Carol is right behind her, but I needed to tell someone where I was and who I was with.

Just in case.

Speaking of Aunt Carol, my phone vibrates in my purse. "I'm sorry, I need to make sure Aunt Carol doesn't need me," I tell Deacon as we take a seat.

"Of course." He smiles kindly, and it's a smile that I feel I can trust. Pulling my phone out of my purse, I read Aunt Carol's reply.

Aunt Carol: Thank you for letting me know. Have fun on your date. He's a good guy, Ramsey. You have nothing to worry about. However, it's always good to let someone know where you're going to be. Be safe, sweet girl, and have a good time.

Me: Thank you. It's just dinner. I think he's being nice to me because I'm Palmer's best friend. I'll text you when we are on our way home.

I go to put my phone back into my purse, but her reply is instant.

Aunt Carol: You're beautiful, Ramsey. I have no doubt that's why that young man asked you to dinner.

Aunt Carol: It's a date, Rams.

I don't reply. Instead, I take longer than necessary to slide my phone back into the interior side pocket of my purse to hide the blush that I'm sure is coating my cheeks.

"You've got to tell me who caused that hue of pink to coat your cheeks," Deacon says, his voice is commanding but still soft.

"Uh, it was Aunt Carol. I just told her we were out to dinner."

He nods. "And what did she say?"

"Nothing." I wave him off and grab a menu, using it as a shield.

"Ramsey?"

My face is still hidden by the menu, but I know I can't hide behind it all night. Slowly, I lower the menu to the table. "She just said to have a good time on my date, and I told her it wasn't a date. That you were just being nice taking Palmer's best friend to dinner."

"Did I ask you to dinner?" He rests his arms on the table and leans forward as if my answer is going to be riveting.

"Yes."

"And I drove us here?"

"Yes."

"It's a date, Ramsey." He sits back on his side of the booth and crosses his arms over his chest. He looks proud of himself, while I'm internally freaking out.

"You don't have to say that."

"Do I look like a man who says things he doesn't mean?" he asks.

"I don't know you."

He nods. "But you will."

"What does that mean?"

"Just what I said."

"Welcome to Momma Joe's. I'm Becky. Can I start you off with some drinks?"

Deacon nods toward me. "Sweet tea, please."

"I'll have the same," Deacon tells her.

I'm way out of my comfort zone. His intense gaze is causing all kinds of weird things to happen. My palms are sweating, my heart is racing, and there's this flutter in my belly I've only ever felt while reading one of my favorite romance authors. It's not lost on me that there is no fear or dread in sitting here with him. "What's good here?" I ask, picking up my menu.

"Everything," he says, grabbing his own menu.

Finally, I feel as though I can take a deep, even breath. "Want to just split a pizza?" I ask him.

"Yes."

"What do you like on yours?"

"I'll eat anything."

"Yeah, but you have to have a favorite?" I pull my gaze from the menu and place it on him. He is so gorgeous. The pictures I've seen of him don't do him justice. It's the eyes. They're mesmerizing.

"I usually get supreme and add mushrooms."

"That works for me."

"Are you always this agreeable?" he asks.

"What's wrong with being agreeable?"

"Tell me what you want, Ramsey. What is your favorite?"

"I'm good with supreme and mushrooms."

"That's not what I asked you."

I have to look down at the table. I can't take the intensity of his eyes as they bore into mine. I know what he's asking, and sure, I have a favorite, but years of being trained to go with the flow with others is hard to break. The only people that I don't do that with are my aunt and uncle, my cousins, and Palmer.

"Move over." His deep voice sends chills down my spine, as he stands next to me. I was so lost in thought I didn't notice him stand up.

Doing as he asks, I move over in the booth, and he takes the seat next to me. I feel my anxiety start to peak. I've pissed him off, and I don't know Deacon well enough to know how he's going to react. My gut tells me I can trust him, but it's my head that is in control right now. I move as close to the other side of the booth as I can, putting distance between us. Distance that Deacon closes, and he presses his body next to mine.

He then turns to face me. "I'm going to touch you." His warning comes only seconds before both of his hands land on my cheeks. "Never with me, Ramsey. When you're with me, you tell me what you want. I don't care if I hate it. If you love it, that's what matters to me. I never want you to hide who you are." His thumb traces my bottom lip. "I never want you to hide your needs, wants, or desires from me. Never."

I nod because I've once again lost my ability to speak when Deacon is in my presence.

"This is one of those times I'm going to need your words, darlin'," he says softly.

"I understand. I'm sorry."

"You have nothing to be sorry for, Ramsey. I don't want to know the woman who you think I want you to be. I want to know you. The real you. That includes what you like and don't like on your pizza." He smiles, and I swear it feels as though my heart has tripped over in my chest.

"Ham and pineapple."

His smile widens. "Then we can do half and half." He nods as if it was the easiest decision ever made.

"No, we don't have to do that. I was just telling you because you wanted to know."

"Thank you, but we are doing that. There are no rules, Ramsey."

"Are you ready to order?" Becky asks, appearing with our drinks. She doesn't seem to be phased that Deacon is now sitting next to me.

"We'll take a large, one side ham and pineapple, the other supreme with mushrooms, and a large order of breadsticks."

"Pizza sauce okay for dipping?" Becky asks.

Deacon turns to look at me, and I nod my agreement.

"Yes, that's fine. Thank you." He hands her our menus, and she's gone to put in our order.

Deacon rises and moves back to his side of the booth, giving me some breathing room. It's not until I can no longer feel the warmth of his body pressed to mine that I realize I wanted him to stay where he was.

I watch him as he opens his straw before placing it in his glass and taking a deep pull of sweet tea. He winks when he catches me watching him. His eyes are smiling, if that's even a thing, and the soft curve tugging up his lips makes me feel at ease.

"They cut me off."

His head tilts to the side. "Who did?"

"My parents. That's how I ended up in Willow River. They cut me off."

His jaw tenses. "Sounds like a story." He's not pushing me for details, even though I can see his need to ask written all over his face, and if that wasn't enough to tell me, the firm set of his shoulders would.

"One I won't bore you with." I reach for my straw, unwrap it, place it in my glass, and take a quick sip of my tea.

"Nothing that comes out of your mouth could ever bore me," he says, licking his lips.

Taking another sip of my tea, I decide to just tell him. Palmer knows, and so do my cousins, which are some of his closest friends. He might as well hear it from me. Besides, him knowing where I came from will make it easier for him to keep his distance.

"My dad was controlling. He's a powerful attorney in New York, and from the minute I was born, there was never a decision in my life that was mine. I never got a say about my hair, the style, or color. I never picked out my clothes, well, unless you count him sending me to his personal shopper and choosing items that were preapproved for me. I didn't get to choose the college I went to or my major. He even chose my boyfriend."

"Damn," Deacon mutters.

"Robert Barrington the Third," I say his name with disgust. "He was the son of one of my father's partners at his firm. They had a grand plan. Robert and I would marry, and when our fathers retired, he would take over."

"Which is why you also have a political science degree." He nods as if understanding.

"No. Not for the reason you're thinking. My place wasn't to be at the firm. I was to be a good little wife, sit on the boards of multiple charities, and make sure the nannies were taking care of our children. My father insisted on a poli-sci degree so that when I was with Robert or escorted him at a fundraiser or event, I could keep up and talk shop to fit in. That is, when I wasn't supposed to be seen and not heard."

"Jesus," he hisses. He reaches across the table and laces his fingers with mine. "I'm so sorry, Ramsey."

His fingers are warm and rough against my own. "You have nothing to be sorry for." I exhale slowly and continue, "The day I left was the day my father laid down the law. He was insistent that I marry Robert and put his plan into action. For the first time in my adult life, I told him no. He was angry. Things happened, and I still stood my ground. He told me that if I refused to do as he said, I was dead to him."

"Motherfucker." Deacon's face is drawn up in an angry expression, but it doesn't scare me. I know he's not mad at me, but for me.

"I left. I walked out of the house with nothing but my purse and my cell phone. I left my car and everything I owned. Everything he bought me. Everyone I knew that were supposed to be my friends were chosen by my father. I had no one. Scrolling through my phone, I saw Aunt Carol's name and called her. She told me to get to the airport, and she would have a ticket waiting for me. I called a cab, cleaned out the two grand I had in my bank account, tossed my cell phone, and hopped on a plane to Willow River."

"Regrets?" he asks.

"None. My aunt and uncle took me in as if I was their own. My cousins rallied around me, and I'm more like their sister than their cousin. We didn't see one another a lot growing up. My mom, she's… well, she's worthless if I'm being honest. She would stand by and watch as my father—She just didn't love me like a mother should love her child."

"I hate that you had to go through that. I hate that your childhood was full of control and not carefree happy memories, but Ramsey, I'm fucking ecstatic that your past brought you to Willow River."

"Here we are." Becky places a plate of breadsticks in front of us. "Your pizza should be right up."

"Thank you," Deacon says, never taking his eyes off mine. "Can I ask you a question?" he asks as he picks up a small plate and dishes up a breadstick for me and then for himself.

"Sure." I shrug, unwrapping my fork from where it's rolled up in my napkin.

"Why not your wrists?"

I try not to show my embarrassment. "You remember that, do you?" I ask. He nods. "My ex, he used to grab me by the wrist when I wasn't agreeable. He was rough and often left bruises. I guess I'm still not over the fear he instilled in me." I stare down at my plate. I can't look him in the eye and see pity for how weak I was when it came to Robert and my father.

"Ramsey?"

I shake my head. I can't look at him. I swallow past the lump in my throat as I fight back the tears that threaten to fall. I never should have told him, and definitely not here. I'm sure in his eyes, I'm this young, weak girl who needs to get her shit together. The thought of seeing any of that reflected in his gaze has my stomach in knots.

"I'm going to hold you." I hear him say, not a second before his arms wrap around me. He's once again moved to my side of the booth, and he's got both arms wrapped around me. "I want to find him, and I want to hurt him for what he did to you. Fuck, Rams, I'm so sorry."

His words cause the dam to break and the tears to fall. It's been two years since I've allowed myself to cry over my past. I spilled every bit of my past to Aunt Carol the day I arrived in Willow River and swore to never give my father or Robert that kind of power over my emotions ever again. That's been working well for me, well, until Deacon. I hear him murmur a thank-you, and I know I need to get myself together. We're in a damn restaurant. Sure, we're not in Willow River, but it's just a short twenty-minute drive, and he loves this place. I'm sure he knows people in this town. Some might even be his clients. I pull out of his hold, and he reaches for a napkin from a pile that wasn't there before my breakdown. I wipe at my eyes and offer him a watery smile.

"I'm sorry. I'm not usually this emotional. Just… telling you the story, it brought it all back."

"Never apologize when you're with me, Ramsey. Own how you feel. Let the tears fall, scream, yell, whatever you need to do. You do it."

My eyes roam over his face, looking for any signs of falseness to his words, but I find none. Just honey-colored eyes, willing me to just be me for him. "You're a good man, Deacon."

"You wouldn't be saying that if you could read my mind." He slowly raises his hand, giving me time to tell him no, and tucks my hair behind my ear.

"Tell me."

"You're sitting here crying, your heart cracking wide open, and all I can think about is kissing you. Well, I want to kill the fucker who hurt you, but the kissing you part is just as strong."

"I'm a crying snotty mess." I shake my head, unable to believe what he's telling me.

"There are several reasons I shouldn't be thinking about kissing those sweet lips of yours, but that's not one of them. You're beautiful."

"Stop. You don't have to say those things to cheer me up." I know he's just trying to be nice. I wish I could believe his words, but I'm scared to allow myself the chance to hope or even dream of a man like Deacon taking a permanent place in my life.

He leans in close. "I only say things that I mean, Ramsey." Then to my complete surprise, he presses his lips to the corner of my mouth. He pulls back far too soon for my liking. He stands and moves to his side of the booth just as Becky arrives with our pizza.

Deacon serves me a slice of my side first before serving a slice for himself. "Now," he says, smiling across the table at me, "let's forget about all of that. I don't want to talk about anything for the rest of the night that removes that smile from your face."

Not wanting to make a mess of myself, hearing my father's voice in my head, "Ladies don't eat with their fingers, Ramsey." I nod and grab my fork and begin to eat. The conversation turns to the photo shoot and how excited we both are to see the final images. I tell him stories about my cousins and their antics, and he does the same. I didn't realize it, but he and Orrin have been best friends for years and a few of my other cousins by association. They're all really close in age, so it doesn't surprise me.

"Can I get you anything else?" Becky asks.

"Ramsey?" Deacon asks.

"No. I'm fine. Thank you."

"Just the check, please," he tells her. She reaches into her pocket and produces the check, handing it to Deacon.

"How much is it?" I reach for my purse and pull out my wallet.

"What are you doing?" he asks incredulously.

"Paying for my part of dinner."

He points his index finger at me, furrowing his brow. "Never with me. Put that away." He points at my wallet as if it's a snake or something.

I match his stare, furrowing my brow at his demand. "Please," he adds, his tone lighter.

"Deacon-" I start, but he gives me a look that tells me this isn't up for negotiation.

I never want to be dependent on a man or anyone really ever again. I don't expect him to pay for me, but it's obvious he wants to. He's not being mean about it, more like I've offended him by even offering. There were times in my past when I was expected to pick up the check. Granted it was my father's money, but still, this is just different for me. I put my wallet back into my purse. "Thank you for dinner," I tell him. He nods, and the scowl is gone with my acceptance of him paying for our meal. I make a mental note that if I ever get the chance to have dinner with him again, I'll slip away to the bathroom and pay the bill before he has a chance to.

We exit the restaurant the same way we entered, with Deacon's hand on the small of my back, guiding me. He opens my door for me and helps me into his truck, and my heart quickens in my chest.

I have a crush on Deacon Setty, and I don't know what to do with that.

Chapter Eight

DEACON

It's been four very long days since I've seen Ramsey. At least seen her in person. She's on my mind every day, all day, and at night when I'm home alone, she's there too. She's there when I close my eyes and try to sleep. She's just… there—all the time. I can't stop thinking about her. I have somehow managed to get some work done after our dinner date Monday night. However, like a toddler, I had to make a deal with myself. I had a brief to review and two sets of adoption papers to be filed, as well as a handful of wills and trusts to work on.

I told myself that if I got through all of it, I could reward myself with dinner Friday night at the Willow Tavern. I'm basically rewarding myself with Ramsey. The self-motivation worked because it's just after eight on Friday night, and I'm leaving the office with my to-do list much smaller than it was late Monday night when I made a deal with myself. I managed to get everything on my bargaining list done and then some. I call that a win.

I don't waste time by going home to change out of my suit. Instead, I drive straight to the Willow Tavern. I drive straight to Ramsey. Pulling into the lot, I see that the crowd is not what it was last Saturday night, and I'm grateful. Maybe I'll be able to do more than see her. Maybe she can take a break and eat with me or at least have a conversation.

Pulling open the door, I'm hit with the low hum of Lee Brice as I make my way to the bar. I know she never waitresses, so the bar is where I need to be. Feeling as though luck is on my side, there's an open stool at the very end of the bar. The same end that Ramsey is currently working. Picking up my pace, I snag the stool, removing my suit jacket and hanging it on the back.

"What can I–" She looks up, and a slow smile greets me. "Deacon. Hi."

"Ramsey," I greet her with a gruff voice.

"What brings you by?" She places a napkin on the bar in front of me.

You. "Dinner."

"Let me grab you a menu." She stretches her arm out to grab a menu, and my eyes go to her belly, where her Willow Tavern T-shirt rides up just a little. My mouth waters at the sight. "Here you go." She places the menu in front of me. "Can I get you something to drink while you decide?"

"Sure, uh, water is fine for now."

She smiles, and it makes me want to lean over this bar and kiss the hell out of her. "Coming right up." She walks away to grab my water while I realize I'm sitting at a bar ordering food and water just to get a glimpse of her. That's how far I've fallen where Ramsey is concerned. I know it's wrong, but fuck if I can find it in me to care. She's consuming my thoughts. I had to see her.

"Here you go. Just wave me down when you're ready to order." She places my water in front of me and skips off down the bar to fill orders. I pretend to be looking at the menu when really my eyes are trained on her. That's how I know she keeps glancing my way. I smile at her when our eyes connect, and I'm satisfied to see her lips tick up in a grin as she serves her customer.

"Ready to order?" she asks, making her way toward me.

I look up from where I've been forcing myself to read the menu. "Cheeseburger deluxe and fries."

"Anything else to drink?"

"Nah, water's fine."

"I'll go put this in for you." She turns on her heel, and I watch her and her ass in those jeans as she disappears behind the swinging doors to the kitchen.

"Well, if it isn't, Deacon Setty. It's been a long time," Sarah Sanders, a girl I graduated with, says, moving to sit on the stool next to mine.

"Sarah." I nod, barely sparing her a glance. Sarah has been married three times and is, I'm sure, looking for husband number four, and I'm not interested. I am not even tempted to dip my dick where so many before me have gone.

"You should let me buy you a drink." She places her hand on my arm, which is followed by her moving in close and rubbing her tits there too.

"No thanks."

"Come on," she coos. I think it's meant to be sexy, but it's anything but. "We're both single. What's the harm?" She runs her pointed blood-red fake fingernail down my arm, and I shiver at the contact. Not because it turns me on, but because she keeps fucking touching me. There is no part of me that's even remotely attracted to Sarah.

"I'm not single," I blurt.

"Oh, really? Who's the lucky girl?"

"I am." Ramsey's sweet voice wraps around me, and it takes me a few seconds to comprehend what she just said.

Slowly, I turn my head to look at her. She's glaring at Sarah and her hand that still rests on my arm. I watch as she forces herself to look away and lay eyes on me. There's something in her expression I can't name, but it has me opening my mouth to agree with her.

"Hey, babe," I reply gruffly. This time I'm watching closely as her eyes soften and her body relaxes. Was she afraid I was going to reject her?

"You expect me to believe that you're with her?" Sarah asks. "Isn't she like best friends with your sister and way too young for you?" Sarah sneers.

"She's Palmer's best friend, and her age is of no relevance when it comes to being able to hold my attention. She has all of it. All the time."

"So you're robbing the cradle?" Sarah laughs humorlessly.

"In case you missed it, I'm a grown woman who is, in fact, old enough to serve you the drink you're holding. Which also means I can make my own decisions, and I can kick your ass out of this bar."

"Me?" Sarah gasps. "What did I do?"

"You're breathing," Ramsey mutters under her breath, and if I wasn't so in tune with her, I probably would have missed it. "Hitting on my man."

Something happens to me with those four words. I sit a little taller on my stool and my chest does this crazy tightening thing. "I was just telling Sarah I wasn't interested." I ignore Sarah altogether and keep my eyes on Ramsey.

"Yeah?" Her smile does things to me, and I'm glad that I'm sitting down.

"Yep." I reach for my water and take a long pull, wishing it was beer.

"Why didn't I know about this?" Sarah asks.

"Because what we do is none of your concern," Ramsey says, crossing her arms over her chest.

"Whatever. When you want a real woman, you know where to find me." With that, she stands, and turns on her heel and walks away.

"I'm so sorry," Ramsey blurts.

"What are you sorry for? You saved me just now."

"I just—You looked uncomfortable, and I've seen her charade one too many times, and I-I just reacted."

Her hands are now braced on the bar, so I reach out and slide one of mine over hers. "Thank you, Ramsey. You read the situation correctly. I wasn't the least bit interested." She flinches at my touch, and I curse myself for not warning her. I knew I was supposed to warn her.

Quickly, I pull my hand from hers. "I'm sorry. I know you like to be warned." I nod to where her hand still rests on the bar.

My mouth falls open in shock when she reaches across the bar and places her soft hand over mine. "I'm okay, Deacon."

"Why?" The word falls from my lips before I have a chance to stop it.

"I think-" She looks down, and I don't push her. I give her the time that she needs to process what she wants to say. When she looks up, her beautiful blue eyes lock with mine. "-because it's you. You've shown me kindness." She shrugs. "I know I can trust you." She pauses. "I can trust you, right?" She chuckles nervously.

I swallow the words I want to say. The ones that tell her that I feel this connection to her that I've never felt before and that it's slowly driving me insane. I want to tell her I can't stop thinking about her, her floral scent, or the taste and feel of her lips. Instead, I go with the words that I'm hoping won't scare her away. "Yes, Ramsey. You can trust me. Always," I add, my eyes boring into hers, willing her to believe the conviction in my voice.

"Hey, cutie, can I get a beer?" some drunk asshole calls out.

Ramsey removes her hand from mine and stands to her full height. She doesn't spare me a single glance as she makes her way down the bar to fill orders. I wait patiently for her attention while she does her job. It's as if nothing else exists for me when she's around. I know she's working, and I need to stop monopolizing her time.

I need something to do other than stare at her, so I pull my phone out of my pocket and scroll through my calendar. Just as I'm about to switch over to my email, I get a text message from my sister.

> **Palmer:** The images are ready! I want to reveal these to both of you at the same time.

That's when I notice she's sent a group message. It's Palmer, me, and one other person who can only be Ramsey. I glance in her direction and see she's also looking at her phone, and there is a small smile playing on her lips.

> **Me:** When and where?

> **Palmer:** How is your place? Tomorrow?

> **Palmer:** Ramsey, what time do you have to be at work?

I turn to look at Ramsey again, and she's looking at me instead of her phone. I motion for her to come to me, and she does without question. "You okay?" I ask.

"Yeah, I just need to double-check the schedule to make sure I have my shift right for tomorrow."

"What's going on tomorrow?" Hank Morrison, the owner of Willow Tavern, asks.

"Oh, uh, I was just telling Deacon that I need to double-check the time I'm scheduled tomorrow."

"You got plans?" he asks.

"Yeah, we uh, kind of. We helped Palmer with a photo shoot, and she wants to show us the images tomorrow." She's not telling him the whole truth, but she's not lying either. I wonder if there's a reason she doesn't want him to know.

Does she like him? Do they have a thing going on? No, he's too old for her. Fuck. I sit up a little straighter as I watch the two of them together, looking for signs. He can't have her. She's mine.

"I was actually coming out here to see if anyone wanted the night off tomorrow. It's dead tonight, and tomorrow is going to be worse. The music festival is going on over in Harris, and the headliner is a big up-and-coming artist. I don't expect us to have much business other than a few hardcore regulars." Hank glances at a small table of four older gentlemen who have been a staple at the Tavern for as long as I can remember. Two are widowed, and the other two have never been married. They made their life about partying and look at where that got them. Here drinking with their buddies on a Friday night, and no one to keep them warm at night. I might not get out much, but Willow River is a small town, and word travels fast.

"Oh," Ramsey replies.

"I know you work a million jobs. I was going to offer it to you first. Why don't you take the night off?" Hank suggests.

"Are you sure?"

"Ramsey?" I wait for her to turn and look at me. "Say yes." She studies me like she can't quite figure out why I'm asking her to take the night off work. "Palmer wants to meet together. We can throw some burgers on the grill at my place," I suggest. I'd much rather have her all to myself, but being around her will have to do. I'll take anything I can get when it comes to Ramsey.

"It's settled then. You're off tomorrow night. I'll see you for your shift on Sunday." With that, Hank turns and walks back through the door he emerged from.

"Did that just happen? Maybe I should go talk to him?"

"Why?" I blurt.

"Because that doesn't happen."

"Did the two of you have a fight or something?" I'm digging for information. I'm dying to know if the two of them have something. I know she's single, but they're way too familiar with each other. I realize this could be all in my head because that's where she lives. In my head. I can't stop thinking about her, and the thought of another man having her, in any way, causes a possessive side I wasn't aware I had to make itself known.

"No. Of course not. Hank is a great guy. I just… wasn't expecting that conversation."

Our phones both go off again.

Palmer: Hello? You can't ignore me, you know?

I smile at my sister. "Why don't you want to take the night off work?" I ask Ramsey.

"I just—It's nothing."

"Is it Hank?" I have no claim to her, but the thought of her with him has my blood boiling. "Is that why you work so many hours? To spend time with him?"

"What?" Her head rears back as if I slapped her. "It's nothing like that. Hank is my boss. He's a good guy, and I work because I have to. I have no one to lean on but myself. My aunt and uncle helped me get back on my feet, and I never want to feel that way again. I never want to feel dependent on another person for my basic needs. I work my ass off to ensure I'm never in that situation again. I take care of me," she adds.

Her chest is rapidly rising and falling with each ragged breath she pulls into her lungs. Her blue eyes are dark as midnight, burning with determination, and if I'm not mistaken, shame. My gut twists. I let my unwarranted jealousy get to me and, in turn, upset her.

"Ramsey, order up!" the cook calls out.

Without a word, she turns and walks away. I want to chase after her, but she'll be back with my food, and I can apologize. In the meantime, I text my sister back.

> **Me:** Ramsey is off tomorrow night. You pick the time. I'll throw some burgers on the grill.

No way am I going back on my offer. I want to keep Ramsey there as long as possible. Quickly, I tap on the group message and save Ramsey's number to my contacts. I tell myself it's just in case, but I know it's more than that. I like knowing I can get ahold of her whenever I need to. If and when I would ever need to. Damn, she's making me sound as if I've lost my damn mind.

> **Palmer:** What?? Are you sure??

"Here you go." Ramsey sets my plate of food in front of me on the bar, reaches underneath the bar, and produces a bottle of ketchup.

"I'm sorry." She's not looking at me, and I'm desperate for her to. "I was wrong." She's still not looking at me. Her hand is still on the bottle of ketchup. She's staring at it as if it is the most fascinating thing she's ever laid eyes on. She's avoiding me, and it's all my fault. "Ramsey, will you look at me?" At my request, she gives me those baby blues. "The thought of him or anyone else touching you drives me mad. I was wrong. I let my mind get away from me."

"I-I don't understand."

"You're all I can think about." It's a confession I wasn't planning on making, but at this point, I'll do whatever I can to get that smile back on her face.

"Deacon-" she starts, but she's once again called by another customer.

"Go. I'm going to be right here." She still looks uncertain. "I'm not leaving this bar until you do, Ramsey. Go do your thing. I'm going to eat my dinner and try not to stare at you like a creeper." That's what finally does it. One corner of her mouth ticks up just a fraction, but I see it. With a nod, she rushes off to fill her orders.

Me: She's really off. Hank just told her it would be dead and that she's not to come back until her shift on Sunday.

Palmer: How do you know this?

Me: I'm having dinner at the Tavern.

Palmer: Interesting.

Palmer: Ramsey, I'm picking you up at four thirty. Deacon, have the burgers ready to go on at five.

Me: So bossy.

Palmer: The perks of being the baby of the family. Love you, big brother.

Me: Love you too, little sister.

Palmer: Ramsey?

Ramsey: I'll be ready.

I can't help but smile when I read her reply. Glancing down at the other end of the bar, I see her watching me. I hold my phone up in the air and wink. Even from here, I can see the slight blush on her cheeks. Never in my life has a woman blushing turned me on.

Not until Ramsey.

Chapter Nine

RAMSEY

When Deacon said he wasn't leaving the Tavern until I was, I didn't think much of it. Now, here we are several hours later, and he's still perched on the same stool. There's a beer that's barely been touched sitting in front of him. I dropped it off to him about an hour ago when I realized he really wasn't leaving. He's taken a couple of sips at best. I'm sure it's warm and nasty as hell by now. I've kept his glass of water full, and each time he smiles at me.

It's not just a "thank-you for the refill" smile. No, this smile is one he only seems to be giving me. It makes me feel things I've never felt before. I know it's more than just the smile responsible for those feelings. It's the man behind them who gets full credit. He said he can't stop thinking about me, and I so badly want to tell him that I know exactly how he feels. I've done nothing but think of him since the photo shoot, and then after our dinner on Monday night, he's my first and final thought each and every day. The in-between is filled with thoughts of him too. So, yeah, I understand what he's saying.

"Favorite color?" Deacon asks.

"Blue. You?"

"Blue."

I nod. "Are you happy being a lawyer?" I know that my father, and even Robert, became lawyers for the money and the power. I don't see that in Deacon, and I'm honestly curious to know if he enjoys his job.

"I do enjoy it. I like helping people. Being a small town lawyer means I deal with more than just one subject matter." He pauses and then tells me more. "We weren't poor growing up, but there were definitely times of struggle. I wanted a career that would allow me to provide for my future family, and hopefully not have to struggle financially. I also always knew that I wanted to come back to Willow River after college. This is my home, and while some run from small-town life, I missed it. I wanted a career that would allow me to do that."

"One of the good ones," I mutter softly.

"Why the Willow Tavern?" he asks, taking a sip of his water.

I lean forward on the counter, resting my weight on my elbows. "It's not anything near as inspiring as your reasoning. When a job came open, Hank assured me tips would be good, especially on the night shifts, and weekends, in addition to my regular salary. Palmer and I were actually here having drinks. We'd both just turned twenty-one." My face heats at the confession, reminding us both of our age differences. "I saw the sign, asked one of the waitresses, and Hank interviewed me on the spot. I started the next night, requesting the nights he claimed would bring me more tips, and here I am."

"So you requested this shift?"

"I did. At the time it made sense. I could work my other job during the day and work here at night. I was determined to build a nest egg for myself."

"And have you done that? Built your nest egg?" he asks.

"I have. I don't ever want to rely on someone else to take care of me."

He nods and opens his mouth to speak, but a customer comes to the bar for a refill, and I walk away before he can, feeling raw and exposed.

"What's going on there?" Tabitha, my coworker, asks. It's just the two of us left tonight. Hank wasn't exaggerating when he said this weekend was slow. Hank is still in his office. He never leaves any of us here on our own, and that's one of the reasons I love working here. He ensures we are all safe.

"What's going on with what?" I pretend I have no idea what she's talking about. We both know I'm full of shit.

"What's going on with the fact that that man sitting at the end of the bar has been here for hours and only has eyes for you? I've seen several women try to talk to him, and he wants nothing to do with them."

She's not wrong. Every time another woman approaches Deacon, vying for his attention, I heave a sigh of relief when he sends them on their way. Every time, his eyes find mine, and he gives me a smile, a nod, and this most recent time, a wink. I can feel his eyes on me no matter where I am in the room. It's both unnerving and exhilarating at the same time.

"I didn't notice."

"I call bullshit." Tabitha laughs. "He's waiting for you, and everyone in this bar knows it."

She's not wrong, but what I can't figure out is why. There are all the heated looks, and his declaration that he's not leaving until I do, and then the whole "I can't stop thinking about you" confession. I'm surprised I can even function with having his eyes on me all night. Thankfully it's been a very slow night, and almost everyone here is ordering draft. You can't really mess up draft.

"I don't know what you want me to say. He's my best friend's older brother. He's just being nice."

"Oh, sweetie, if you call the looks that man has been giving you nice, then we need to sit down and have a talk."

"I-I don't know. I know he's here for me. I know he says he's not leaving until I do. After that, I just don't know."

"What do you want?" She must see the confused look on my face and takes pity on me. "Do you want him? Do you like the idea of him staying until you get off work? Do you want to go home with him? Do you want him to walk you to your car and send you on your way? What do you want?" She points a long, manicured nail my way.

"I want… I'm not really sure." I don't bother to tell her I've never been given the choice before. I was never allowed to choose who I dated, or hell, even what I wore on those dates. This is all new to me.

"How long has it been since you've been on a date?" she asks.

"Well, uh, Deacon and I had dinner on Monday night, but before that? Two years. Then I don't even really think you can consider them dates since they were arranged and chosen by my father."

"Ouch." She winces. "You don't talk much about your life before you came here, but something tells me it's not something you want to relive."

"You would be right."

"So you need to think about what it is you want. Are you interested in him?"

"He's Palmer's older brother."

"So? He's still a man, a gorgeous one at that, and you're still a woman. I'm not going to try to pretend that I know what you went through, but I do know that you work all the time. You barely ever take time for yourself. Maybe you should consider that when you're deciding how far you want things to go with the hottie at the bar."

Glancing at her wrist, Tabitha smiles. "Last call!" she yells. There are only the four regulars who close us down almost every night we're open, a group of five ladies, who have all tried their luck with Deacon, and the man himself left at the bar.

I move behind the bar to start closing procedures and paying out tabs. The four regulars pay easily and tip me well, something they do each night they're here. The group of ladies all eye me suspiciously as I take each of their cards and run it through our system.

"Deacon, do you need my number for that date?" Sarah calls out. She's almost to the door and stopped to turn and look at him.

"Nope," Deacon calls back.

"Come on, handsome," Sarah slurs.

"You know that I'm spoken for, but in case you've forgotten, let me remind you." He stands from his stool and moves behind the bar. He wraps his arms around my waist and rests his chin on top of my head. "I'm taken. Happily taken, and I'm not interested now, nor will I ever be. I don't need your number. I'm not going to call you, and no, I would never consider anything behind Ramsey's back. Just stop."

My mouth falls open in shock, but I quickly close it when I make eye contact with Tabitha, and she motions for me to do so. His arms are warm, and instead of feeling worried or anxious due to his touch, I feel safe and content, and I'd like more of it. More of him.

"I think it's time for you ladies to go." Hank's deep voice startles me.

I try to pull out of Deacon's hold, but he's not interested in letting me go. "I've got you," he whispers, his hot breath fanning across my cheek.

"My boss," I whisper back.

"He's fine. You're fine. We're fine," he assures me.

"What? It was your employee who started this mess," Sarah accuses.

"I won't tolerate any kind of drama or bullshit when it comes to my staff. I've been in my office all night. The music was turned off, and I heard it all. Ramsey didn't start a damn thing."

"Well, what about him?" Sarah points at Deacon.

Hank steps up next to us and crosses his arms over his chest. Did I mention that Hank is built? We're talking bouncer kind of built, and he doesn't look anything close to his thirty-eight years of age. "Deacon is standing up for my staff. He stays."

"I'm going to tell everyone how you treat your customers," Sarah declares.

"You do that. Now get out." Hank's tone is firm and to the point. He couldn't give a shit what Sarah says about him or his bar. He wants her gone. With a stomp of her foot, Sarah and her minions scurry out the door. Tabitha is there to lock the door behind them.

"You two have been keeping up on the cleaning all night. Cash out the register, and you can go. I have the At Your Service crew coming in for a deep clean tomorrow. Let me know when you're ready to leave, and I'll be sure to walk you out." Hank nods at Deacon and heads back to his office.

Once Hank is gone, Deacon releases his hold on me. "What can I do to help?" he asks.

"Nothing. I'm going to cash out the register while Tabitha cleans up the last few tables, and then we can go home."

"I'll help with the tables." He walks away and begins to clear one of the two tables and follows Tabitha's lead taking the glasses to the back and loading them into the dishwasher. By the time they reappear, I have the drawer cashed out and the money in the small safe underneath.

"Yo, Hank!" Tabitha calls out. "Let's roll."

Hank's laughter is loud within the walls of the now quiet Tavern. He appears out of his office, spinning his keys around his finger. "Is the front door locked?"

"Yep."

"Let's do this." He nods toward the back door that leads to the employee lot, and we all follow suit. It's weird that Deacon is still here, but when he places his hand on the small of my back, I forget about the fact that he's not an employee, and all I can think about is that he's here for me.

Me.

Once we're outside, Hank locks up and turns to Deacon. "You got her?" he asks.

"Yes." It's a simple answer, but the tone of his voice holds so much conviction, almost as if Deacon feels like I'm his to protect. I know that sounds crazy, but I have the feeling all the same.

His hand remains on the small of my back until we reach my car. "This is me," I say lamely. I'm so bad at this dating thing. Hell, I'm bad at just liking someone. I've never had that privilege. This is all new to me. I'm on an uneven playing field.

"I'm glad I got to see you tonight," he says, shoving his hands into his pockets.

"Me too. I'm glad you stopped by. You didn't have to waste your night sitting and waiting for me to get off work."

"That's just it. It wasn't a waste. I got to know you a little better, and anytime I get to see you is worth the time. I know you said Hank and the guys make sure you get to your car safe each night, but I was here, and I wanted to do it."

"You do know I work five nights a week, right?" I ask, hiding my amusement.

"Don't remind me," he grumbles.

"I've worked here for going on two years, Deacon. Willow River is a small town. I'm safe." I think that's the first time I've ever said those words out loud. I've repeated them over and over again in my head since arriving in Willow River, but that's the first time I've given a voice to them.

"Yeah, I'd like it to stay that way."

"Should I tell Hank that seat is reserved? Maybe I can order you a plaque that has your name on it so that everyone knows it's yours," I tease.

"Hmm, that's not a bad idea." He smiles, and I wish I could take a picture of him right now to always remember this moment.

"So, your place tomorrow?"

"Yeah. Are you excited about seeing the pictures?" he asks.

"Nervous is more like it."

"Nervous? Why are you nervous?"

"Well, I'm me." I look down at my jeans and Willow Tavern T-shirt. "And you're... you." I point to his suit.

"These are just clothes, Ramsey. Pieces of fabric. They're not at all who we are."

"That's not how it works where I come from."

"Well, wherever you might have lived before isn't Willow River. I do believe your driver's license says Willow River is your home, right?"

"It does." I peer up at him.

"Then this is home, Ramsey. This is where you are from. It might not be where you started, but it's where you're from. This town is your home."

"I still feel as though I'm an outsider."

"You have family here. Lots of family." He laughs.

"I do," I agree. "I didn't really know them when I moved here. I hadn't seen any of them in years, but my aunt Carol was the first and only person I could call. She's the only one who wasn't connected to my father and the life I was trapped in." I don't know why I tell him all of that, but the words just seem to fall out in a rush when Deacon is around.

"You have Palmer," he reminds me.

I smile. "I do. Your sister has been there for me and refused to let me hide and remain in my shell. I'm grateful she chose me to be her best friend."

"Don't sell yourself short. She needed someone loyal like you as well."

"How do you know that I'm loyal?"

"I like to think I'm a pretty good judge of character. Also, I know my little sister. If you were not worth the time, she wouldn't be giving it to you."

"She's not afraid to speak her mind, that's for sure."

He takes a step closer. "I'm sorry about earlier."

"Sorry?"

"I didn't warn you that I was going to touch you."

"No, but it was okay." He studies me. "When it's you, it appears to be okay."

He nods. "So, do I still need to warn you if I'm going to touch you?"

"No. But my wrists," I say at the same time as he takes my hand in his and his thumb traces over the bottom of my wrist.

"You didn't flinch this time."

"No. Not with you."

"Never with me." He takes the final step that has me tilting my head back to look at him. "Ramsey?" His hand makes its way up my arm, and he slides it behind my neck.

"Yeah?"

"I'm going to kiss you now."

I don't have time to process his words before his lips descend on mine. His lips are firm yet soft, just how I remember them. The kiss is gentle, but something tells me that it's for my benefit and not his. I don't know how long we stand here under the parking lot lights, kissing, as I grip his shirt, trying to get closer. However, when we both need to come up for air, he slowly breaks away and rests his forehead against mine.

"Tell me that was okay."

"That was okay."

He pulls back to look at me. He must like what he finds because he nods and then pulls me into his arms, hugging me. It's the best hug I've ever received. My parents were never affectionate. I didn't really know that's how families were until I moved to Willow River. Out of all of the hugs I've ever received in my lifetime, this one is my favorite.

"I should let you get home. It's late." He makes no move to release his hold on me. "Will you text me when you get home? No, call me when you get home."

"I'll be fine, Deacon. I just live in the apartments a few blocks away."

"I'll follow you home then."

"That's really not necessary."

He raises his hands and moves them toward my face. I flinch, not because of him but because it's hard to let go of my past. "I'm going to cradle your cheeks," he whispers. I nod, and he moves in slow, pressing a warm palm to either side of my face.

"We're going to work on that, baby. I never want you to worry that I will ever hurt you. You never have to worry about that with me. I just wanted to feel your soft skin and explain to you that although you might feel as though it's unnecessary for me to follow you home, for me, it is. I need to know you're safe."

"You don't have to worry about me."

"I don't have to, Ramsey. I choose to. There is a huge difference between the two."

"I guess we should get going?" I don't know what to say. I can't tell him that he makes my heart race. I can't tell him that I love that he's concerned about my safety. I can't tell him that even though I flinched, I crave his touch.

"I'm parked around front. Drive me to my truck?"

"Sure."

My breath hitches when he leans in and presses his lips to my forehead. He then drops his hands and reaches for my door, pulling it open. He waits until I'm inside before jogging around to the passenger side and slipping into the seat.

I drop him off at his truck, wait for him to get settled, and pull out onto the road. Willow River is a small town, so the traffic at this time of night is nonexistent. We make the short drive to my apartment with me glancing in my rearview mirror every ten seconds. Deacon parks next to me and rolls down the window.

"Call me when you get inside."

"Deacon, I'll be fine."

"I know. Just humor me."

"Okay. Thank you for looking out for me." He nods, and I turn and walk away before I do something like beg him to stay with me. Once I'm inside, I turn on the lights, make sure the door is locked, and pull up the text message thread from earlier. I quickly save his name and number into my contacts and hit Call.

"You good?"

"Yeah, I'm good. The door is locked and deadbolted for the night. I'm taking a shower and going to bed."

"I'll see you tomorrow then?"

"I'll see you tomorrow. Good night, Deacon."

"Night, Rams," he says, and the line goes dead.

Chapter Ten

DEACON

I'M PACING MY LIVING ROOM FLOOR AND HAVE CHECKED FOR messages on my cell phone so many times today, I'm surprised the battery isn't dead. I scan my house to make sure everything is in its place and there are no dirty socks lying around. I'm a pretty clean guy for a bachelor, all things considered. Never in the past have I ever worried this much. Hell, Ramsey has been here before. Multiple times, in fact. She and Palmer have used my pool on several occasions, but I've never been here. I've always been at the office.

My sisters both call me a workaholic, and I used to brush them off. I was working on building my career and being someone that Mr. Patrick and Mr. Gordman wanted to sell their practice to when they retired. I've been working more hours a week than any one person should, and sure I have my career, but nothing else to show for it.

I never really noticed that until I met Ramsey. Since I have, I can't stop thinking about her and how she would fit into my life. I don't date, I don't have time, but now I might want to start. I always thought it would be difficult to visualize a woman fitting into my life. My work can be long hours, and that's not fair to anyone. However, now that I want to have someone to share my life with, I realize that I brought it all upon myself. I work because that's all that I have.

I want more.

I want Ramsey.

I shouldn't want her. Not only am I ten years her senior, but she's my little sister's best friend. She also has a troubled past, and her cousin is my best friend. The list of reasons why I shouldn't make her mine is long, but not nearly as long as all the reasons why I want her.

I've asked myself countless times if I'm willing to harm those relationships to be with her. Is the age difference too much for us to overcome? When I'm around her, it doesn't feel like our age is a divide. No, the only divide I feel is the fact that she's not mine. That I can't yell from the rooftops that she's my girl. I feel protective and enamored. Our age difference is nonexistent when I'm with her.

Finally, I hear a car door slam, and my heart rate kicks up just knowing I'm about to lay eyes on her. Palmer texted me about an hour ago and said she was getting ready to leave her place to pick Ramsey up before heading here.

She's here.

I want to rush to the door, pull it open, and tug her into my arms. I want to taste her lips and hold her body next to mine. Instead, I make my way to the living room and take a seat on the couch. I pull my phone out of my pocket and pretend to be interested in what I'm looking at when I hear the front door open. I knew Palmer would make herself right at home.

"Deacon!" Palmer calls. "Where are you hiding?"

"In the living room," I call back.

"Oh, no!" Palmer's arm flies out beside her to block Ramsey. "He's sick. Quick, call for help," Palmer says, barely containing her laughter.

"What?" Ramsey asks, and she sounds almost panicked.

Palmer loses control of her laughter. "He must be sick. He's not working. It's been well… years since I've seen my brother just sitting on the couch without his laptop and a million files surrounding him," she teases.

"Oh." Ramsey's shoulders drop as if she's relieved.

"You're hilarious," I deadpan.

"Seriously though." Palmer sobers. "You're not working today?"

"No." I don't give her an explanation because telling her that I can't stop thinking about her best friend long enough to concentrate isn't something I want to reveal just yet.

"For real, are you feeling okay?" Palmer asks.

I barely, just barely, stop myself from rolling my eyes. It's the concern in her voice that stops me. "I'm fine. Just taking a much-needed day off."

"Huh." She nods. "Well, all right then. Let's get down to business." She places her bag on the coffee table. Reaching inside, she pulls out an iPad. "Sit." She points at Ramsey and then to the couch.

My eyes follow Ramsey as she moves to take the seat next to me on the couch. She's not as close as I'd like her to be, but she's close enough I can smell her floral scent.

"So, I normally wouldn't edit this many, but this shoot was pure gold. You two were the perfect subjects," Palmer explains as she taps the screen. "Seriously, some of these were just hot. I fear I'm going to have a hard time convincing my customers that the two of you were strangers. Here." My sister thrusts her iPad toward me. "Just scroll to the left."

"You said we have veto power, right?" I clarify.

"Yes, but I'm telling you, you're not going to want to veto any of them. See for yourself." She nods toward the iPad in my hands.

I look over at Ramsey. "Are you ready for this?" She nods, but her teeth have her bottom lip held hostage. Something tells me she's not much on telling anyone how she really feels. I want to let her know she can tell me anything, but instead, I do one better. I move a little closer, holding the iPad between us. Her toned, tanned legs are pressed against mine, and my cock takes notice.

Tapping on the screen, the first image pops up. It's the two of us, smiling at each other, still standing a few feet apart. It's our initial introduction, and it's hard to believe since that very moment, she's consumed my every thought.

I keep scrolling. I'm giving us both time to study each image. When I come to the images of her leaning against the wall and me caging her in, I hear Ramsey suck in a breath.

"I need to use the restroom. I'll be right back," Palmer says, moving swiftly down the hall.

"You want to veto this one?" I ask Ramsey.

"Do you?" she asks.

"That's not what I asked you."

"I know, but I'm just curious as to what you want?"

"I don't care who sees these images, Ramsey. My insistence that we could hold veto power was for you."

"For me?" Her big blue eyes show her surprise.

Unable to help myself, I reach over and place my hand on her bare thigh. Her jean shorts are so damn short they leave me plenty of smooth skin to grip beneath my palm. "For you. I could tell that you were really uncomfortable at the start of all of this. I wanted you to know that you had that control."

"It's sexy," she says softly.

"Of course it is. It's you."

"Deacon…" She breathes my name. It's a sound I want to hear with her lying beneath me or even straddling my thighs. I'm not picky. Not when it comes to Ramsey.

"You're beautiful." That light pink that I love so much coats her cheeks. "If you see one that you don't want to be shared, you tell me. I'll take care of telling Palmer."

"Okay."

Slowly, I begin to click through the images once more. She's right, they're sexy as fuck, and I agree with Palmer. It's going to be hard to sell this as a stranger photo shoot. The chemistry between us is glaringly obvious.

These images only prove what I've been feeling since that day, is real. The connection between us isn't some made-up notion from a fun day at the park. From dinner earlier this week to the shared looks and the kiss goodnight last night, all of it is more than what I ever could have considered would happen when I agreed to do this. Now, here I am, sitting next to the woman who I'm positive that I want to make mine. I don't know how she feels about it, and then there's my sister and my best friend to consider.

"Wow," Ramsey breathes. It's the shot of us kissing. I have one arm around her waist while my other hand is resting against her cheek.

"You like this one?"

"My first," she mumbles.

I freeze. No way did I hear her correctly. "What was that?"

"Nothing. It was nothing."

"Hey." Palmer comes rushing back into the room. I forgot she was here. She holds up her phone. "I forgot I have a wedding consult that I need to get to. I'm going to go."

"Wait!" Ramsey calls out. "You're my ride. I'll go with you."

"No." Palmer quickly shakes her head. "It would look unprofessional. Besides, you're not done looking," she says, peering down at the iPad. "I can give her a ride home."

"You don't have to do that," Ramsey speaks up.

"We have to get through all of these," I tell her, holding up the iPad. I watch as she wavers with herself. "Besides, I have burgers ready for the grill, and I can't eat them all on my own."

"How about this? How about you two do your thing," Palmer points at the iPad, "I'll go do the consult and come back? I'll text you when I'm on my way, and you can fire up the grill," she tells me.

I want to say no. I am perfectly capable of taking Ramsey home, but this needs to be Ramsey's decision. She's the one who will be here alone with me. "Ramsey?"

"Are you sure you don't mind if I stay?" Her voice is quiet, as if she's not sure asking is the right thing to do.

"Absolutely."

"Perfect. I'll see you later." Palmer waves over her shoulder and rushes out the door.

Ramsey is shaking her head, and I wish more than anything that I could read her mind. "What's going on in that pretty head of yours?"

"Nothing." She waves me off.

"Hey." My hand settles back on her thigh. "Tell me."

She hesitates before saying, "I think she made it up."

"Made what up?"

"The client consult for a wedding. Palmer is meticulous with her schedule. She either made it up or planned this all along. She chose the time for our meeting."

"I hadn't really thought about it." I was too busy thinking about kissing her. "But you're probably right. She doesn't lie, so my guess is she planned to leave you here. She decided on the time and that she was picking you up."

"Yeah," she agrees.

"How do you feel about that? Being stuck here with me?"

"We do have to finish looking at all of the pictures."

"Here." I hand her the iPad. She takes it while giving me a confused look. "You flip through them. I've only got one hand." As if she needs a reminder, my thumb traces the silky soft skin of her outer thigh.

She swallows hard and begins to slowly flip through each image. My thumb continues to caress her thigh. When she wiggles in her seat, I know I should ease up, but I don't. Instead, I turn and place my lips just below her ear.

"Deacon." There's a quiver in her voice.

I immediately pull away and find her eyes. "I'm sorry. I should have warned you." I start to move my hand, but she places hers on top of mine, preventing me from moving.

"No. I'm not mad."

If she's not mad, then she's turned on. Damn if my cock doesn't throb just from the thought. "You hold all the cards here, Ramsey. You have to tell me what you want."

"What do you want?" she asks.

I take the iPad from her hands and place it on the table. We're at the images where we're lying on the blanket. We've seen all that we need to. "I want to know what you want."

"I-I want you to kiss me."

"Here?" I place another kiss just below her ear.

"Yes."

My mouth trails across her cheek, where I kiss the corner of her mouth. "Here?"

"Yes."

Sliding my hand behind her neck, I turn her to face me. Slowly, so I don't scare her, I brush my lips against hers. Once, twice, three times. "You want me to kiss you like this?" I ask. I don't even recognize the huskiness of my voice.

"Please."

"Tell me what's off-limits, Rams." She hesitates. "There is nothing you could tell me that would make me not want you. Nothing. I just need to know, so I don't scare you."

"You don't scare me like that."

"What do you mean, like that? Do I scare you?"

She nods, and her teeth once again attack her bottom lip. "Yeah," she confesses.

"How do I scare you?" I pull away, dropping my hands from her body. Fuck me. I don't want to scare her into kissing me.

She reaches for my hand and presses it to her cheek. "I'm not afraid you will hurt me physically, but emotionally..." Her voice trails off.

"Never," I promise, my voice holding conviction. "I will never hurt you."

"But you could."

"You have the power here, Ramsey. I've done nothing but think of you since the moment I laid eyes on you. I've battled with myself over wanting you. Our age difference, my best friend, my little sister, we have so many connections, but yet I just now found you. Why do you think that is?"

"I think," She pauses, closing her eyes. I give her time to process what she wants to tell me. "I think maybe I wasn't ready for you before now."

Damn. "And now?"

"I've never been with someone who wants to hear my thoughts and opinions. I've never been able to choose. My first kiss was stolen from a guy my father insisted I date. He wasn't my choice, and it wasn't my choice to kiss him. He just took it."

"Did he?" I can't even ask the question. The fear that she was sexually assaulted holds my voice hostage.

"No. He was rough and mean, but he didn't do… that."

"Thank fuck," I say, pulling her into my arms. I need to hold her right now, and by the way her body sinks into mine, she doesn't mind.

"I've never been on a date with someone I chose. I've never kissed someone I wanted to kiss. My life wasn't my own."

"I'm so sorry." I press my lips to the top of her head.

"I ran away from all of it. I swore off dating and men, and I just wanted to do me. I wanted to work and save money and get my own place. I wanted to save more money because I never wanted to have to depend on someone to take care of me ever again."

"I can understand that." Her three jobs make much more sense to me now.

"I didn't know I needed you or someone like you until I met you."

"Me," I correct her. "Needed *me*. Not someone else. Just so we're clear," I say, making her laugh.

Pulling away from my chest, her eyes lock on mine. "You were the first kiss that I wanted."

Her words have my heart beating faster. "Have dinner with me?"

"I thought we already were?"

"Not here. A date. Go on a date with me?" I'm more than asking for a date, and we both know it. I'm asking her to choose me. Regardless of all the obstacles that could stand in our way, I still want her.

"When?"

"You pick the day, and I'll make it happen."

"Is this where I'm supposed to pretend like I have to look at my calendar?"

I move in close. Our lips are barely a breath apart. "No, baby. This is where you choose me. This is where we stop worrying about anything that could complicate this and choose to be with each other."

"I think Palmer is on board." She smiles.

"And Orrin, well, he's just going to have to deal with it."

"I'm twenty-three next month."

"I'll be thirty-three in October."

"Ten years isn't so bad." The words are barely out of her mouth before I'm kissing her.

How can I not kiss her when her statement has been my biggest hurdle in all of this? Sure, my best friend might be pissed, but this is Ramsey we're talking about. I'd be a fool not to see where this goes, and if he can't understand that, then so be it. As far as my sister goes, Ramsey's right. Palmer is on board. In fact, it wouldn't surprise me if she planned this from the very beginning. She's always telling me I need someone to share my life with and has begged me for a couple of years now to let her fix me up. I can't help but wonder if the person she wanted to fix me up with was Ramsey all along.

"I work on the weekends."

"I don't care when."

"Monday night? I don't work Monday or Tuesday next week."

"Both."

"What?" She laughs.

"I want both nights."

"What if I'm terrible company?" She grins.

That simple act has me standing a little taller and puffing out my chest. She's comfortable here. With me. "Not possible. Monday and Tuesday."

"Okay."

"Okay?"

She nods and leans in close. Her eyes find mine asking for permission. I nod, and she kisses me. It's soft and quick, and it was her choice. That fact alone makes me want to beat against my chest like a caveman.

"Are you hungry?"

"Yes. I was too nervous to eat before I came over."

"And now?"

"Now, I'm not."

"Good." I kiss her once more before standing and pulling her to her feet. "Come keep me company while I cook for you." She allows me to link our hands together and lead her into the kitchen. I can't help but think about life with her, lazy Saturday afternoons. Sundays in bed making love. The vision is clear and so real.

I want that.

I want her.

Chapter Eleven

RAMSEY

"Nothing fancy," Deacon says, leading us into his kitchen.

"Can I help with anything?" I ask him.

He turns to face me and grins. "You can. You can keep me company."

Before I know what's happening, he grips my hips and lifts me onto the island. He leans in and pecks my lips with a kiss before pulling away. I watch him as he begins to remove items from the refrigerator.

"You sure you don't need any help?" I ask.

"I'm positive. We're having burgers on the grill, and I have a couple of different kinds of chips, and I picked up a fruit tray for dessert."

"The perfect summer meal." I smile. I find that I do that a lot where Deacon is concerned. I feel comfortable with him. And we're going on a date! I don't know what it means, and I'm not going to ask. For once in my life, I'm rolling with it, because I want to see what happens, not because I'm being forced to. Deacon is definitely someone I want to get to know better.

"I thought so too. I already sliced a tomato and cut up some lettuce, so really, I just need to grill the burgers."

"Aren't we supposed to wait on Palmer?"

He closes the fridge and turns to face me. He's holding a plate of hamburger patties. He's really prepared for this. "She told us to, but I have to do something. If I just sit next to you, I'm going to kiss you."

"Is that so bad?" I quickly place my hand over my mouth. I can't believe I said that out loud. "I-I'm sorry."

Deacon places everything in his hands on the counter and steps between my legs. "Can I touch you?"

I nod. I'm so embarrassed I just blurted that out. I hate that suddenly he feels as though he has to ask again. I was doing so well.

He places his index finger beneath my chin and lifts it until my eyes are level with his. "Never with me. Never sensor yourself. If you're pissed off, I want to hear it. I don't care if you're screaming and yelling at me. I want to hear it. If you want me to kiss you, I want you to tell me. If you want my hands on you," he leans in even closer, "I want you to tell me. There is nothing that you could do or say that would cause me to put my hands on you in anger. I might get pissed off, and we're going to argue, Ramsey. We're human and emotional creatures, but I promise you, baby, I will never hurt you."

His words have my eyes growing misty with tears. "I was never allowed to… my ex and my father, they would get angry, and it was easier just to bite my tongue."

"Nah, none of that," he whispers huskily. "I can think of so many better things to do with that tongue," he says as his lips press against mine.

I feel bold and brazen and more alive than I've ever felt in my entire life. I wrap my legs around his waist, holding him to me while my hands lock behind his neck. This time I'm the one who takes things further, swiping at his lips with my tongue, begging for entrance.

Deacon wraps his arms around me and opens his mouth, letting me take the lead. I'm nervous. I've never had the opportunity to do so before. Not only that, but I want to kiss him. I enjoy kissing him. I could kiss him for hours. His hand slides up my back and cradles the back of my neck, holding me close. His hot breath mingles with mine as everything around us fades away. It's just the two of us, sharing a kiss that lights my body on fire, and soothes the ache in my heart.

"Rams, baby, we have to stop." He pulls out of the kiss, resting his forehead against mine. "I owe you dinner."

"Meh," I say, making him laugh. We're both breathing heavily, our chests rising rapidly as we try to recover from the passion that ignites between us.

"As bad as I want to kiss you, I also want to feed you." He gives me a quick, chaste kiss before stepping away from me. He points his finger at me. "You and your lips are addictive."

This time it's me who's laughing. Deacon tilts his head to the side, a look I can't decipher on his handsome face. "What?"

"I like the sound of your laugh filling my home." He steps in close and kisses me one more time. "Now, I have to focus on dinner." He winks, grabs the burgers from beside me on the island, and disappears outside to the patio.

I can't take my eyes off him as he places the burgers on the grill once it's heated up. That's probably why I don't hear Palmer.

"Earth to Ramsey." She chuckles, waving her hand in front of my face.

"Oh. Sorry." I blush. I'm busted, and we both know it. There is no way that I can get out of this one.

"Like what you see?" she teases.

"She better." Deacon winks as he comes back inside with an empty plate in his hands. He strides over to the sink and rinses it before placing it in the dishwasher. He washes his hands and pulls another from the cabinet.

"Started without me, I see," Palmer comments.

"You were supposed to call, and we were hungry," Deacon tells her.

"Oh, I know." Palmer leans against the island and bumps her shoulder into mine.

Deacon just smiles, grabbing the salt and pepper shakers and heading back outside. "You're into him." Palmer smiles.

"He's a nice guy." I stare down at the floor.

"He is. He's also single. You're single, so…" She lets the words just hang there.

"He's your brother."

"Right? We could be sisters." She's excited by the prospect. There is no mistaking that by the sound of her voice.

"He's Orrin's best friend." Not that I need my cousin's permission, but he and his brothers and my aunt and uncle saved me. I don't want to do anything to disrespect them, but I feel as though there's a string tied to me, and it's locked around Deacon. It's as if I'm tethered to him, and I'm okay with that. He reminds me a lot of my cousins and uncle—men who respect women and let them have a voice.

"I'm sure he would agree that Deac is a great guy," Palmer counters.

"He's ten years older than me." The age difference doesn't really bother me. When he's kissing me, or even when we're talking, the age difference isn't there. He's just Deacon.

"Age is just a number. Besides, ten years isn't that bad. When he's fifty and you're forty, you can still get the senior discount. Win-win." She cackles with laughter.

"What's so funny?" Deacon asks, closing the patio door.

"Nothing." I'm quick to send this conversation on a detour.

"I was just telling Ramsey here that age is just a number. For example, say the two of you got together. When you're fifty, and she's forty, she can benefit from your senior discount." Palmer is smiling like a loon, proud of herself.

Me, I'm blushing. I can feel the heat in my cheeks. I don't know what this is with Deacon. Sure, he asked me out on a date. Two dates if I'm getting technical. We've shared a few kisses, but that doesn't mean he wants to date me.

"She's right, babe." Deacon grins. "Think of it as a perk."

Palmer's mouth drops open in shock.

"What's wrong, little sister? Cat got your tongue?" Deacon goads. He takes it a step further, striding toward me and stopping next to me. "I'll give you all my discounts, darlin'," he purrs before placing his lips against my cheek. "The chips are in the pantry, and the fruit salad is on the counter. Palmer, make yourself useful and grab the condiments from the fridge. There is lettuce and tomato cut up as well." He winks at me and walks back outside, shutting the patio door behind him.

"What. The. Hell. Was. That?" Palmer is vibrating with excitement.

"Nothing."

"Oh, no you don't, Ramsey Smithfield. That was not nothing. I need details, and I need them now."

"It was nothing."

"Fine, I'll just ask Deacon. I can get it out of him. I've had years and years of practice getting my big brother to fold to my ways. Just ask Piper. She taught me everything she knows." She smiles smugly, crossing her arms over her chest.

Before I can answer her, Deacon is stepping back into the kitchen with a plate of grilled burgers. They smell delicious and make my mouth water. His eyes find mine. "Hungry?"

"Yes." Not just for the burgers.

"So, Deacon, what was that kiss about?" Palmer asks him.

"Can I not kiss my girl?" he asks, setting the plate of burgers next to where I'm sitting on the island. My heart stalls in my chest at his words. I don't know what I expected him to say, but it wasn't that.

"Ramsey!" Palmer scolds me. "You didn't tell me."

"That's because I didn't know," I counter.

"Deacon?" Palmer asks.

He shrugs. "We're going on a date next week."

"That makes her yours?" she asks, barely containing her smile.

His eyes find mine. "That means I want her to be mine. The rest is up to Ramsey."

"Me?" I croak.

"I won't take the choice from you. You decide."

My heart melts into a puddle of goo, and I'm glad I'm still sitting on the island. Why do his words affect me so much? Is this really him? Are the sweet words just a show? How do I know if I can really trust him?

I know the answer to that. I don't. At least not when it comes to my heart. I'm going to have to take the chance. I've never had to worry about losing my heart before. This is new to me.

"Can I just make it known that this was my idea and that your firstborn should be named after me?" Palmer boasts.

"I think one Palmer is all we can handle." Deacon laughs.

Something flips in my belly. I assumed he would tell her she was crazy and there were no babies in our future, but instead, he just refused the name. Am I in some kind of alternate universe?

"Oh, how many babies are we talking about?" Palmer asks, reaching for the package of hamburger buns and making herself a plate.

I move to hop off the counter, but Deacon is there before I can. He places his hands on my hips and lifts me. "I can handle jumping off the counter," I tell him, ignoring the catch in my breath.

"Yeah, but then what excuse would I have to put my hands on you?" he asks quietly.

"Do you need an excuse?"

"Not as long as I have your permission."

"You didn't ask for permission," Palmer chimes in. Deacon rolls his eyes, but there is a playful smile tugging at his lips. He lifts me from the counter, and I take a step away from him.

"So, how many?" Palmer asks again.

"Did you get everything out of the fridge?" Deacon asks her.

"Nope. This conversation is too riveting."

He chuckles and moves to start pulling items out of the fridge. "Ramsey, what do you like on your burger?"

"Oh, um, whatever is fine."

He stands and pins me with his stare. "I'm going to need your words, sweetheart, and they need to be yours. Your wants, not whatever."

My heart races. "Mayo, mustard, ketchup," I reply. My hands are clasped together, waiting for him to tell me that it's gross and that's not how a lady eats. That's for sure what my father and Robert both would have told me. Hell, they wouldn't let me have a burger. It was salads only.

"There she is." He winks and goes back to digging in the refrigerator. He rises with his hands full of condiments, as well as a plate of lettuce and tomato. He sets them on the counter and reaches for a plate, handing it to me. "Make yourself a plate."

Palmer leans into me, bumping her shoulder with mine. "You've bewitched my brother," she teases.

"Stop." I shake my head at her.

"No, I'm serious. He's being all sweet and whatnot. I've never seen him that way with anyone else. Not unless it was me, our sister, or our mom. What happened while I was gone?"

"Nothing." I keep my voice low, my eyes darting to where Deacon is pulling chips out of the pantry.

"You've been holding out on me." She gives me a look that tells me I'm not getting out of telling her all the details.

Thankfully, she lets it go, and the three of us sit down to eat. Palmer controls the conversation about the photo shoot, and Deacon and I agree that all the pictures are good for her to use. They're intimate, but that's the point of the project.

"We want you to be a success," I tell her.

"I love you too." She grins. "Thank you both, really. This was a better outcome than I ever could have expected. Behind the lens, I was excited, but once I started to edit them, I was elated. I can't wait to start posting them on my social media. This shoot alone is going to boost my career. I can feel it."

"I'm glad," Deacon says, tossing his napkin on his now-empty plate.

"It worked out for all of us." Palmer smirks.

"The images are great. You did a wonderful job."

"Ah, thanks, bestie." She grins. "What are we doing the rest of the night?" she asks me.

"I'm not sure. I'm not used to having a Saturday night off. It's weird."

"We can swim or watch a movie here," Deacon suggests.

Before we can even talk about his suggestion, his phone rings. Pulling it out of his pocket, he smiles and shows me his screen. My cousin Orrin's name pops up. "Hey, man," Deacon greets him. He listens. "I'm not working tonight. Palmer and Ramsey are here. We're talking about swimming or a movie." He listens again.

I can hear Orrin's deep voice, but I can't make out what he's saying.

"Hold up," Deacon tells him. His eyes seek mine. "How do you feel about Orrin and a few of his brothers coming over to join us?"

"I vote hell yes. Those Kincaid boys are F-I-N-E," Palmer answers, even though he was asking me.

"How do you feel about that?" I ask Deacon.

"O, I'm going to call you back." He doesn't wait for a reply before he ends the call and places his phone on the table. He pushes back his chair and stands, offering me his hand. "Come with me for a minute."

I glance at Palmer, and she waves me off, encouraging me to go with him. Slowly, I stand and place my hand in his. The warmth of his skin instantly calms me. With his fingers linked with mine, he leads me down the hall and into what appears to be his home office. As soon as the door is shut, he pulls me into his arms.

"I didn't realize it would be this hard keeping my hands off you."

I don't say anything back. I'm not sure what I should say. I know I want to tell him that he doesn't have to, but I keep that to myself.

"Ramsey, tell me how you feel about Orrin and the guys coming over. I want to spend time with you, so if that's going to make you uncomfortable, then I'll tell them no."

"This is your home, Deacon. I can't make that choice for you."

"That's where you're wrong. This is our day. I don't know when I'll have you for another Saturday night, and I don't want to waste it." He presses a kiss on my forehead. "Tell me what you're thinking."

"What do we tell them?"

"What do you mean?"

"I mean this. You holding my hand, and hugging me, and kissing me, and lifting me on and off counters."

He smirks. "I'm taking any excuse I can to touch you."

"They're my family."

"And Palmer is mine."

I'm beating around the bush, and so is he. He wants me to say what's on my mind. "What if they ask about it? About the touches or the looks? What do we say?"

"What do you want to say?" he asks.

"Ugh. Stop answering my questions with questions."

"I'm sorry, I just don't want you to choose what I want. I want you to speak your mind. Don't worry about me and my answer. Just speak yours. I promise I'll give you my honest truth. I want yours in return."

"Fine." I nod, take a deep breath, and give him what he wants. "I don't know what we are, and I know it's too early to put any kind of label on us in the first place. However, I don't want to lie to them. I don't want a relationship built on secrets and lies. I left that world, and I never want to go back."

"I agree with you. Honesty is always the best policy. As for us, to me, there is an us. You're the first woman to capture my attention like this in well... ever. I know it's been a very short time, but I don't want to see anyone but you. I don't want to share you." Those last five words are more of a growl, and it's so hot.

"I would never... I'm not like that. I would only see you if that's what we choose to do."

"Good. So, we're dating then. Are you good with that explanation?"

"Yes." I don't even have to think about my answer.

"Tell me what is okay in front of others and what's not."

"What do you mean?"

"Can I kiss you? Hold your hand? Hold you? What's okay for me to do in front of other people?"

"I want you to be you." Again, I don't have to think about my answer. "I come from a world of fake and deception, and I left for a reason. If we're dating, it's to get to know each other better, and we should be us, who we are all the time for that to happen. If you feel like kissing me or holding my hand or holding me, then I want you to do it."

"Tell me what I need to ask permission for?"

"Nothing. I've been around you enough that I feel as though I can trust you. You've proven that in the short amount of time that I've known you. Just maybe, try to refrain from gripping or holding my wrists, and when you touch my face, just… be gentle."

"Always, baby." As if he needs to show me, he cradles my cheek in his warm palm and presses his lips to mine. "Am I allowed to call you my girl?" he asks, a grin tilting his lips.

"Do you want to?"

"Damn right I do."

"Then that's what you'll call me."

"Come on. Palmer's probably pacing the floors by now." He places his hand on the small of my back and guides me out of the room.

"Everything good?" Palmer asks.

"Perfect," Deacon tells her. "Swimming, and we can order pizza or something later. I'm going to call Orrin back."

"Well, we need to go get our suits." Palmer points toward me.

"Okay. Hurry back," Deacon says. He then leans in close and whispers, "You should leave one here so that I don't have to lose time with you next time we want to swim. On second thought, never mind. We can skinny-dip."

I have to shift my weight to alleviate the ache his words cause between my thighs. "Yes. That, we should do that." I pull out of his hold and stride toward Palmer. His eyes heat at my confession, and he winks.

"We'll be back," she calls out, grabbing my hand and pulling me toward the door. As soon as we are in her car and on the road, she speaks. "Spill."

So I do. I tell her about running into him at his office and then dinner after. I tell her about him coming to the Tavern last night, and I tell her he wants to see me exclusively. She's quiet the entire time, which is unlike her. When we pull into my apartment complex, she turns off the engine, removes her seat belt, and turns to face me.

"I need to confess. Deacon is the one I've been trying to fix you up with. You were both too stubborn to let me even try. The blind-date shoot was just an excuse to get the two of you in the same place at the same time. Sure, it's great for my career, but I could have chosen any random stranger. I'm so happy for you."

"It's new," I remind her. Although I suspected Deacon was the guy she's been begging me to meet for the last few months, I can't help but wonder if I had met him sooner if we would be where we are now. I firmly believe that I wasn't ready for him yet. That we weren't ready for each other.

Now we are.

"Nah, this is the start of something incredible."

I can't help but hope that she's right.

Chapter Twelve

DEACON

I wait until they're gone before I call Orrin back. "Everything good?" he asks.

"Yeah, it's all good. I wanted to make sure Ramsey was good with the plans before I made them." My girl wants honesty, and I plan on giving her nothing but. I figured I might as well spill the beans with my best friend before he gets here. I know I'm not going to be able to control myself, and she doesn't want me to.

"Why is Ramsey there?"

"She just left with Palmer to get their suits." He doesn't need an actual explanation, and he's not getting one.

"Why did you need to check with my baby cousin?"

"First of all, she's a grown woman, who is younger than you, but she's not a baby. Second of all, that's usually what you do when you're dating someone." I let the words fall. No point in easing into this conversation. He's either going to accept it, or he's not.

"You want to repeat that?" Orrin asks.

"You heard me the first time, but since you're so old and all, I'll repeat myself. Ramsey and I are dating."

"Dating?" I can hear the disbelief in his tone. "She's my baby cousin."

"She's also a very beautiful woman."

"How long has this been going on?"

"It's new."

"Fuck, I was not expecting you to say that."

"Well, she and I talked, and there are no secrets, so I thought I might as well tear off the Band-Aid, so to speak, so that when you get here, you don't cause a scene and upset her."

"Would that bother you?"

"Of course it would bother me. What jackass wants to see their girl upset?"

"Your girl?" he asks.

"What part of we're dating do you not understand?" I laugh.

"You're claiming her? That's a hell of a lot more than just dating."

"She's mine, Orrin. Look, I understand she's your cousin. I know she's been through some shit, and you want to protect her, but you don't have to protect her from me. Hell, if anything, I'm the one you should be worried about. She's torn into my life like a tornado and has me thinking and feeling things I've never thought or felt."

"Damn," he mutters.

"Yeah. I'm into her, man. This isn't just some 'get my dick wet' scenario. I really like her." I more than like her. I'm starting to care about her. It's too soon to be saying that, but I challenge anyone to spend time with Ramsey Smithfield and not harbor feelings for her. Friendship or otherwise. No wonder she and Palmer hit it off so well. My sister is the same way. Hell, both of my sisters are that way. You can't help but want to be around them.

"She's ten years younger than you."

"And? She's an adult. She's twenty-two, I'm thirty-two. Yes, there are some years between us, but I don't notice them when I'm with her."

I'm not just blowing smoke up his ass. I know that the ten years are there, but I don't feel it. At least not yet. Besides, there isn't anything he could say that I haven't thought of myself. I've fought an internal battle from the day I laid eyes on her, and I've come to the conclusion that I just don't give a fuck. I don't care what anyone has to say about our relationship. The only people who matter are Ramsey and me.

"Fine. You treat her right, and we won't have any issues. I'm telling you, man, she's blood, and if you fuck her over, you're going to have my brothers and me to deal with," he warns.

"Trust me, that's not going to happen, and the last thing I want is nine Kincaids after my ass. Even the younger ones."

"They're closer to her age than you are," he quips.

"Fuck off."

He roars with laughter, the sound ringing in my ears through the cell phone. "So, what's the plan?"

"The girls went to get suits, and we already grilled out, so I figured I'd just order pizza."

"I'll pick up some beer. Brooks and Declan are with me. Sterling is hemming and hawing around and can't decide what he's doing tonight, so he might be with us too."

"They're all welcome. You should warn them about Rams and me."

"Yeah, yeah. I'll tell them."

"Later." I end the call, sliding my phone into my front pocket. That went better than I anticipated. I knew the age difference would be an issue for others, and I know it should be an issue for me as well, but I just can't seem to find it in me to care. Not when I'm kissing her.

Walking into the kitchen, I clean up our dinner and head upstairs to change into some swim trunks. I take the stairs two at a time as excitement courses through me. It's not just the time I get to spend with my little sister and my girl, but also the guys. I need to make more time for life outside of work. I don't want to wake up in another ten years and have nothing but my job. I'm settled within the practice, and I'm the obvious choice to buy them out. If they don't choose me to do that when they retire, then I'll just start my own practice.

It's time to start living.

Orrin and his brothers show up before the girls get back. The four of them file into the room, and although they're all smiling, I can feel the tension all around us. "Just say what you have to say."

"She's family," Brooks speaks up.

"And too damn young for you," Declan adds.

"Too sweet to be tossed away," Sterling comments.

I turn to Orrin. "Let's hear it."

"Nah, I think my brothers did just fine."

I expel a heavy breath as I face the firing squad. "Look, I already told Orrin," I start, but the front door opens.

"Honey, I'm home," Palmer calls out. All five of us turn toward the door and the sound of her voice.

They walk into the room, and my eyes immediately lock on Ramsey. She's wearing the same cutoff jean shorts and top as before, but there's a bag now hanging off her shoulder. I want to go to her and wrap her in my arms. I want to kiss the breath from her lungs, showing her overprotective cousins that she's mine.

But I don't. Instead, I wait her out. I want to see how she's going to handle this situation. I'm already feeling things it's way too soon to be feeling. I'm more than willing to stand up to them, to fight for this, whatever it may be. We're dating, it's new, but it feels old. However, I need to know it's not just me. I need to see how she handles this. She's younger than me, and there's a nagging voice in the back of my head telling me she might not be ready for all the things racing through my mind where Ramsey is concerned.

"Rams." Orrin opens his arms, and she doesn't hesitate to walk into his embrace and return it. She steps out of his hold and repeats the process with Declan.

"Why does she get all the hugs?" Palmer teases. Orrin opens his arms for her, and she laughs as she gives him a hug.

They both hug all four of the Kincaids standing in my kitchen, and then there's me. Ramsey releases Brooks and turns toward me. Her steps are slow, but she takes them. When she's standing close enough, she wraps her arms around my waist and rests her head on my shoulder.

My hand settles on her hip as I wrap my arms around her. Unable to stop myself, I press a kiss to the top of her head. I feel her body relax, and I have to fight to hide my grin.

"So this is really a thing?" Brooks asks. He has his arm slung over Palmer's shoulders, and she doesn't seem to mind.

"Is what a thing?" Ramsey asks.

"The two of you." Sterling points at us. "A thing," he clarifies.

"If by the 'thing' you mean that Deacon and I are dating, then yes, this is a thing." Her voice is strong and clear, and my chest swells with pride, knowing she's using her words and that she's open with them.

The room is quiet, which causes Ramsey to nervously shuffle her feet. I want to whisper in her ear that no matter what they say, this is between us. I want to encourage her that we can do this. We don't need permission. We're both consenting adults, but I don't. A whisper in the quiet state of the room would sound like I was shouting.

I stand tall next to her, not letting any of the doubts that have plagued me show. I don't have the words to explain how I feel when I'm with her. I don't think about work. I don't care about what's going on around me. I keep my focus on her, and that's a first for me. I've never met a woman who could hold my attention like Ramsey does. When it's the two of us, even in a crowded bar, it feels like we're alone. As if she's the only other person in the world. It's some kind of voodoo magic or something, but I crave it. I crave her and how she makes me feel.

Grounded.

Settled.

Content.

I'm all those things and more when I'm with her. One afternoon with Ramsey Smithfield changed how I view things. I'm a workaholic, and I put work before everything else. I never realized how much I was missing out on. My friends and family have tried to tell me. I've heard countless lectures about working my life away, but nothing resonated with me until the beautiful dark-haired, blue-eyed beauty walked into my life.

The four of them stare us down, but it's Declan who breaks the silence. "When are we ordering pizza? I'm starving."

"We just ate," I tell him.

Declan pulls his phone out of his pocket. "It's pizza. It's good hot or cold. What does everyone want?" he asks.

"No anchovies." Palmer shudders. "Other than that, I'm good."

"Ramsey?" Declan asks.

"Oh, I don't," she starts, and I squeeze her hip. She freezes and tilts her head up to look at me.

"Your words, sweetheart." I keep my voice soft, just for her. Not that I care if the others hear me, but my words are for her. To give her the courage and encouragement she needs to speak her mind.

I want more than anything for her to understand that her wants and needs are important, just as much so as anyone else's. For far too long, she's just gone along with what everyone else wants. I want the real Ramsey. The good, the bad, and every fucking thing in between.

"Ramsey?" Orrin asks.

She pulls her gaze from mine, and I do the same. I can see the contemplation on his face. My eyes scan to Brooks, Declan, and Sterling, and they're all hanging on her every word.

"I'm not really a fan of black olives, but I can pick them off," she adds.

"No black olives." I leave no room in my tone for arguments. She's not going to pick them off. We're just not getting them. If they want them that damn bad, they can order a special pizza with black olives.

Declan opens his mouth, then quickly shuts it. I'm on high alert, waiting for someone to say anything negative to her. They don't realize they're going to have to answer to me. I'm a pretty laid-back guy, but there is something about Ramsey that reveals the protective side of me.

Declan gives a slow nod, looking at Ramsey as if she's a stranger to him. "No black olives and no anchovies. Got it." Placing his phone next to his ear, he steps out of the room to make the call.

"Rams, we need to get changed." Palmer grabs Ramsey's hand, and they disappear upstairs.

"How the fuck did we not know she doesn't like black olives?" Sterling asks.

"How did you know?" Orrin asks me.

"How did I know what?"

"That she didn't like black olives?" he clarifies.

"I didn't until she said it."

"But you knew there was something she didn't like." His gaze is intense.

I shrug. "It was a feeling."

"A feeling?" Brooks asks in disbelief.

"You wouldn't believe me if I told you." Not that I would know how to explain it. I just feel like I know her. There's an intense connection between us, and it's as if we've known each other and been together for years.

All three nod their acceptance and take my words at face value. "It's hot as hell. Let's hit the pool." Brooks throws an arm over my shoulder, and we all file outside.

"Last one in pays for the pizza!" Sterling shouts as he takes off running and cannonballs into the water.

Soon after, we're all rushing to shed our shirts and make sure our phones are out of our pockets before diving in.

"Too slow, big brother," Sterling boasts, pointing at Orrin. "Looks like dinner's on you."

"I hope things are going well at the body shop," Declan calls out. "You should never let me order when I'm starving."

"Like I'm not used to it. Hell, the five of us can eat a large all on our own, and then the girls will probably split one. That's six."

"I ordered eight, just to be safe." Declan smirks.

Orrin grumbles under his breath, but it's all in good fun. He's the oldest of nine, and you would never know it when they all get together. Even the twins, Maverick and Merrick, who just graduated this year, all seem so close in age when they're together. I spent a lot of time at their house growing up. Carol and Raymond Kincaid have more patience than any other parents I've ever met.

"Incoming!" Palmer calls out as she comes running toward the pool. We barely have time to move out of the way before she's splashing into the water. "Ramsey, get your ass in here," my sister calls out for her best friend.

I turn and see Ramsey smiling, shaking her head at my sister's antics. She makes it to the edge of the pool and sits, sticking her feet in the water. I swim to where she's sitting and run my hand over her leg that's underwater.

"Are you not getting in?" I ask her.

"Oh, uh, yeah, maybe later."

"Ramsey."

"Deacon," she sasses, and my cock is instantly hard.

"Tell me why you're not swimming."

"I just," she starts to feed me some bullshit line, but that's not who we are. She set the rules, and now she has to abide by them.

"I need your words, sweetheart. Your truth," I remind her.

"I'm not used to swimming in crowds. I've gained a little weight since I've been here, and I just… don't want to take my cover-up off just yet."

"No." I move in closer, positioning myself between her legs, and wrap my arms around her waist. "You're perfect. They played with your emotions, but baby, that's not going to happen here. Your family is here, and Palmer, and it's just me. If you think there is anything underneath this sheer piece of black fabric that I don't want to set my eyes on, you are sorely mistaken."

"It's hard to push them out of my head. I'm doing better. It's just times like these that I remember words that were said, and I revert to that girl."

"You were never that girl. That's who they wanted you to be. The only person I want you to be is Ramsey. You have to decide who that is. If you truly don't feel comfortable, I won't pressure you, but don't let something those assholes said to you keep you from having a good time."

She nods and gives me a smile that's forced and doesn't reach her eyes.

"You're beautiful, Ramsey. Not just your body, but your heart and your mind. Don't let them keep holding you back. Be you." I pause, giving her time to process what I just said. "Now, tell me, do you want to swim?"

"I do. I love to swim." This time her smile is brighter.

"Take this off," I say gruffly, pulling at the sheer black cover-up hiding her body from me. "I want to see you." I move back, giving her the space she needs. I dip under the water to cool myself off. Not from the heat of the sun, well, that too, but from being so close to her. When I emerge, she's sitting on the edge of the pool in a black bikini.

I'm moving before I can think better. I grip her hips and pull her into the water with me. Luckily, it's only about five feet where we are, and I can stand because she wraps her legs around my waist.

"So fucking sexy." My voice is raspy even to my own ears.

"They're watching us," she says, burying her head in my neck.

"Does that bother you?" She doesn't answer, so I ask her again, "Ramsey, does it bother you that they're watching us?"

Slowly, she pulls away and lifts her head. Her blue eyes are brighter than the sky over our heads. Instead of giving me her words, she leans in slowly and presses her lips to mine. The kiss is brief, and it speaks volumes. She took what she wanted. She made a choice for herself. Not because she thought it was what I wanted, but because it was what she wanted.

"Not when it's you." Her soft reply is only for me, and I don't know if she means for the words to wrap themselves around my heart, but that's exactly what they do.

Chapter Thirteen

RAMSEY

I'VE BEEN ON DATES BEFORE BUT NEVER WITH A MAN I ACTUALLY wanted to be on a date with. Tonight is my first official date, and it's with Deacon. We texted back and forth all day yesterday, and most of today, and the more time I spend talking to him, the more I like him.

For me, that's scary and exhilarating at the same time. I feel like a sixteen-year-old girl all over again, only this time, I get to make the decisions. I'm getting to choose the boy, well, in this case, the man, and I'm giddy. That's the only way to describe myself.

I've changed my outfit three times already, and I'm desperate enough to break down and call my best friend. "Help," I beg as soon as she answers the video call.

"What am I helping with?"

"I don't know what to wear."

Her eyes soften. "Ramsey, take a deep breath," she instructs, and I do as she says. "Now, slowly exhale." Again, I do as I'm told. "There. Now, he's going to like you in anything. He's into you. Don't think too much about this."

"How can I not, Palmer? This is the first time I've gotten to choose my date. This is a big deal. I don't have much to offer him. He's older, successful, and handsome, and he has his shit together. I'm a twenty-two-year-old who works three jobs and ran from her parents and her abusive ex-boyfriend." The truth of my anxiety tumbles freely from my lips.

"Let's dissect that, shall we?" She holds up one finger. "First of all, so there are a few years or ten between the two of you. Who cares? You're mature, and you're both into each other. That's inconsequential. Second," She holds up a second finger, "you are the epitome of successful. You left the only home you'd ever known, moved to a new town to stay with family you barely knew, and look at where you are. You have your own place, a nice dependable car, and money in the bank. You've done all of that, Ramsey. You're a hard worker, dedicated, and you're a fighter." She holds up a third finger. "Third, you're beautiful. I hate that what they did to you made you think otherwise, and I hate that you're too caught up in shying away from others that you don't see the way men look at you. I hate that you don't see the way that my brother looks at you."

A month ago, I would have pushed her words to the back of my mind, not allowing myself to believe them. Today, however, they hit differently. They cause hope to bloom in my chest and warmth to fill my soul. When will I let myself realize that this is my life? I'm not what my father wanted me to be. I'm so much more.

"This... Well, Deacon. He's the first thing I've wanted for me, and more than stability, for a very long time. I have all these emotions coursing through me. I've never had a guy affect me this way. I've never had them want to spend time with me and me with them in return."

"Show me what you have on."

Propping the phone up on my nightstand, I take a step back. "This is my third attempt."

"You know I love that dress. Shoes?" she asks.

"I was thinking of my brown strappy sandals." Walking away, I grab them from my closet and hold them up. The dress I'm wearing has a high neck and cutouts for the arms. The pattern is paisley, in dark blue, oranges, reds, and cream. It goes well with my dark hair, and the brown sandals match it perfectly.

"Ramsey, you look beautiful. I'm confident that the other two outfits were perfect too. Don't try too hard. Just be you. If Deacon doesn't see how incredible you are, then you don't need him. I don't care that he's my brother. If he's too blind to see what's in front of him, then good riddance."

"I really want him to see what's in front of him," I whisper, but I know she hears me.

"Just be you, Ramsey. It's impossible not to want to be around you." As soon as she says the words, there's a knock at my door.

"He's here."

"Go. Have fun. And I want to hear all about it."

"Thank you." I blow her a kiss, end the call, grab my phone and sandals, and rush out of my bedroom. Pulling open the door, my breath escapes my lungs. Deacon is dressed in a black button-down, which is rolled up at the sleeves, and a pair of dark-washed jeans that appear to be made just for him if the way they're molded to his thighs is any indication. His hair looks as though he's run his hands through it multiple times. It makes me want to reach up and do the same.

"You're beautiful." The words come easy to him, and he takes a step forward. Slowly, he slides his arm around my waist and presses his lips to my cheek.

"Thank you. You too. I mean, you look handsome."

He smiles, and a swarm of butterflies takes flight in my belly.

"Are you ready to go?"

"Yes. I just need to put these on." I hold up my sandals. "Come on in." I back away, giving him room to enter my apartment. Taking a seat on the edge of the couch, I make quick work of strapping on my sandals. I grab my small clutch and make sure I have everything I need, adding my cell phone before closing it. "Ready." I glance up to find him watching me. He just stands there, staring at me. "Deacon?"

"Sorry, I'm just trying to tell myself that devouring you is off the table tonight. You really do look incredible, Rams, and it's been too long since I've laid eyes on you."

"You saw me Saturday."

"It's Monday. That's too long." In two long strides, he's once again standing in front of me. He tucks my hair behind my ear. "I told myself I was going to be a gentleman. I want more from you than your kisses, but I also crave them."

"You want to kiss me?"

"Very much."

"I'd like that," I confess.

That's the only encouragement he needs. His lips are soft and warm yet firm at the same time. His hand glides behind my neck as he pulls me closer. His scent surrounds me, and I have to grip the front of his shirt to keep from falling over. His kiss literally makes my knees weak.

Too soon for my liking, he's ending the kiss. "We should go. If we don't, I can't be held responsible for my actions."

His words cause a tingle to race down my spine, yet it's not from fear but from the heat behind his words and the need that I have for him racing through my veins.

I want to tell him that we can stay in, and I would be fine with that. However, a bigger part of me wants this date. I want this experience, and I want to share it with Deacon. "I'm ready," I tell him.

He nods and, with his hand on the small of my back, guides me out of my apartment. We stop just outside the door so I can make sure it's locked before he leads me to his car. "Where's your truck?"

"I started to drive it. The thought of you climbing up in it in a dress was both torture and pleasure. Torture won. No way am I risking any other man seeing you but me."

"You could have helped me," I tease. It's not something I've done with dates in the past, and it feels foreign, but then again, with Deacon it feels right. I'm a walking contradiction.

"Yeah, I thought about that too, but I was missing you and knew I needed to keep a level head. My hands on you won't help with that."

"You seemed to separate from me okay at my place," I say as he opens the door for me.

"Trust me, darlin', there was nothing easy about it." He waits until I'm strapped in before shutting the door and rounding the car.

"So, where are we going?" I ask once we're on the road.

"I thought we could drive over to Harris, have dinner, and see a movie. You mentioned that dating wasn't really something you got to do or choose, and something tells me that the fuckstick you were dating didn't plan outings to please you."

"I've never done dinner and a movie. Not on a date. With friends, but looking back, they were never my true friends, not like Palmer is to me. They wanted to be with me because of my last name and my parents' money."

He reaches over and places his hand on my bare thigh. "I'm here for you, Ramsey. Just you."

We manage to have easy conversation the remainder of the drive to Harris. We talk about college, and it's easy to say that his experience was different than mine. We talk about our families, his and mine. Both the ones I left behind and the ones I have in Willow River.

"So tell me, what do you see yourself doing? If you could have any career, what would it be?"

This is the second time he's asked me this question, and I still don't have an answer. I need to give my future some real thought. I need to look past the security that I've built for myself and think about what else lies ahead. "Honestly, I'm not sure. I've always known that the choice wasn't mine to make, so I never let myself dream of anything different."

Deacon is sitting across from me at the restaurant. We've ordered our meals and are just waiting for our drinks. "I think you should give yourself some time to consider what you really want. Not just as a career but out of life. I know meeting you has put things into perspective for me."

"How so?" It's hard for me to wrap my head around the fact that meeting me could have that kind of impact on his life. That dating me has given him any kind of new perception on life and his career.

"I'm a workaholic." He flashes me a grin. "You can even tell Palmer that I admitted it. I was so focused on making something of myself. My parents lived paycheck to paycheck growing up, and I didn't want that. Don't get me wrong, we never wanted for anything, and my sisters and I all went to college, but I still just wanted more. When I was hired at Patrick and Gordman, they were talking about retiring in a few years. I wanted to prove to them that I was someone they could trust their years of hard work with. I wanted to be the only logical candidate when it came time for that to happen."

"And now?" I take a drink of my sweet tea.

"Now, I realize that what my parents, and my sisters, and even my buddies have been telling me is true. I'm working my life away. I don't want to wake up in another ten years and have nothing to show for my life but a career. I want a family of my own."

"You want kids?"

"I do. And a wife." His eyes hold mine, and I try really hard not to squirm under his gaze. "Do you want kids? A husband?"

"It was always just assumed that I would marry Robert and give him an heir. It wasn't something I wanted with him, but that was what my parents would have demanded if they'd managed to get me down the aisle with him. The choice was never mine. When I told my father that I refused to marry Robert, things got… heated, and that's the night I left."

"And now?"

"Yeah, I want kids. I want to be better than my parents. I want to show my kid or kids that they're loved and that the sky is the limit to what they can do."

"And the husband?" His voice is gruff.

You.

A vision of life with him by my side flashes through my mind. "I want a man who will love me and honor me. I want someone who will stand beside me and let me make my own choices. I want someone who is in my corner always but still not afraid to tell me when I'm wrong." I quickly clamp my mouth shut when it dawns on me that I've basically just described Deacon.

"Do you plan on staying in Willow River?" he asks. There is a slight tilt to his lips, and at first, I worry that he knows I was describing him, but then I remember I've asked for honesty and have vowed to give it in return.

"I am. This is my home now. There's nothing for me to go back to in New York."

"Here you go. A pizza burger and fries." The waitress sets a plate in front of Deacon. "And a bacon cheeseburger and cheese sticks for you. Can I get you all anything else?"

"Rams?" Deacon asks.

"No. Thank you, this is perfect." I smile at the waitress.

"I'll be back to check on you," she says and scurries away.

"I can't believe we're eating at a place that serves burgers and fries for a date."

"Were you hoping for something fancier?"

"No. Not at all. This is… everything I ever wanted. I just wanted to be normal. I didn't like having to be 'on' all the time. Image was everything to Donald and Angela Smithfield."

"I was hoping you would like this place. I went back and forth about where to take you and what we should do, but from our conversations, I just wanted to give you a little piece of what you missed out on."

"Thank you, Deacon. This is perfect. I can't think of a better night. Ever."

A lazy smile tilts his lips. I avert my gaze and focus on my food before I just sit and stare at him the rest of the night. It's so easy to get lost in his gorgeous honey-colored eyes.

"Well, what did you think?" he asks.

"I loved it. I've not seen any of the others, but I need to."

"My girl has been sheltered," he teases, wrapping an arm around my waist and guiding us to his car.

"I work three jobs," I remind him as he opens the door for me. Always the perfect gentleman, even when no one is watching. He waits for me to be belted in before closing the door.

"Is that a 'need to' thing? Or just a 'security' thing?" he asks once we're on the road.

"A little of both, I guess. I have a good nest egg, but I never want to be in the position of needing to rely on someone else for my basic needs. If Aunt Carol and Uncle Raymond hadn't taken me in, I don't know what I would have done."

"I hate even thinking about the way you were treated and the life you were living, but I can't hate that it brought you here to Willow River. To me," he adds, glancing over before putting his focus back on the road.

"I know this sounds terrible, but I don't even miss them. My parents, I mean. Or Robert, for that matter. I just… They were never good to me. No matter how hard I tried to be what they wanted me to be, they just didn't care about me."

"You know you're not alone, right?" he asks. "Ramsey, you will never be alone again. I know with absolute certainty that the Kincaid clan will never let that happen. They're good people. I'm not sure where the relation comes in. I don't know if it's your mom's side or your dad's, but they are nothing like the family you left behind. You have Palmer, and you have me."

I nod because there is a lump in my throat. I know it's dark in the car, and he can't see me, so instead, I reach over and place my hand on his arm, giving it a gentle squeeze. Without taking his eyes off the road, he links our fingers together, placing a tender kiss on my knuckles before resting our joined hands on his muscular thigh.

The remainder of the drive is quiet but comfortable. In fact, I've never felt this overwhelming sense of calm with anyone else.

When we pull into my apartment complex, he rushes around the door to open mine. It's weird to have a man do it when no one is watching. The only time Robert ever did anything remotely nice for me was when it was for show. I shouldn't compare the two, but they're light-years away as far as their differences go. It's just going to take some getting used to.

"Thank you for tonight," I say when we reach my door. "Do you want to come in?" I offer. I'm nervous, but I'm not ready for the night to end.

"Yes. But I won't," he quickly adds. "I don't trust myself to not want to take things further, and we're not there yet."

"What if I said that we were?"

He leans in and kisses just below my ear. "You're making it really hard for me to be a gentleman."

"Is that what you are?" I ask.

"That's what you deserve."

"It's okay if you don't want me or if you've changed your mind," I blurt.

"Ramsey, baby." He takes my hand and places it over his very hard cock. Heat pools between my thighs. "I want you. I've never wanted a woman the way that I want you, and I'm so proud of you for asking me in, but I want to do this right. You're not a sleep-with-the-guy-on-a-first-date kind of girl, and I know that anything worth having is worth waiting for."

"What if I want to be?" I challenge. I'm not sure where this confidence is coming from. The only explanation I can come up with is that it's him. Deacon gives me strength.

"Do you?"

"I had such a good time. I'm not ready for the night to end."

"Tomorrow night."

"What about it?"

"Instead of going out, we can have dinner at my place. That will give us more time together, just the two of us."

"That's a long time from now." I don't know what I'm saying because he's right. I'm not the kind of woman who jumps into bed with her date on the first night. I'm also not the type to be so vocal about what I want or how I'm feeling. All courtesy of the man standing before me.

He smiles. "I know, but it gives us something to look forward to." Slowly, he lifts his hand and places it on my cheek. "Good night, sweetheart." His kiss is soft and slow, and it leaves me wanting more. "Lock up behind me."

His kiss has stolen the breath from my lungs. I take a minute to regroup before saying, "Thank you for tonight."

His eyes soften. "You're welcome. Go in and lock up."

"Will you… will you call me when you get home? Or just text me? I-I want to make sure you make it home okay."

"I'll call you," he agrees. "Night, Rams."

"Night, Deacon." I step behind the door and quickly close it, clicking the lock into place. My fingers touch my lips, and I can still feel his pressed to mine. I don't have to look in the mirror to know that goofy, happy smile that only Deacon can pull from me is lighting up my face.

Chapter Fourteen

DEACON

"Is everything okay?" Palmer answers.

"Yes. Why wouldn't it be?"

"Because you're calling me when you're supposed to be working."

"I left early."

"What? What happened? Are you sick? Is it Mom and Dad? Piper?" I can hear the panic in her voice.

"Palmer, calm down. Everyone is fine. I'm fine." I'm quick to reassure her.

"Then what are you doing off work at," I imagine her looking for a clock, "four in the afternoon?"

"Ramsey is coming to my place tonight for our second date. I want to make sure my house is on point. I need a shower, and I need to figure out what we're going to eat."

"And you left work early? For that?" she asks for clarification.

"I did." I know what she's thinking. I never leave work early. Never. Unless it's a family emergency. There was also the one time I had the flu and was forced to go home, not that I was getting much done at the office anyway. Otherwise, I'm there past normal quitting time on most days.

"I knew the two of you would hit it off," she boasts.

"We are. We went out last night and decided tonight we would stay in. That's why I need your help. What should I make or order for dinner?"

"Aw, you're nervous."

She's right. I am nervous. I want tonight to be a good night for Ramsey. For both of us. I want her to see that staying in can be just as fun and that I don't need to show her off. Sure, I'd love to do just that, but I'm also good to keep her all to myself. Her ex used her as arm candy, and I'm not that guy.

"Are you going to help me or not?"

"Just be you, Deacon. What do *you* want to make?"

"Well, we had burgers on the grill Saturday afternoon, and we had burgers last night. I don't want to order pizza again like we did Saturday night."

"What's something that you enjoy making that won't stress you out?"

"I know how to cook lots of things. I have lived on my own for years now."

"Old man," she teases.

"Palmer," I growl.

"Fine. I was just kidding. You know that, right? Ten years isn't the end of the world, and you make her happy, Deac. That's all that matters. She needs and deserves all the happiness after the life she's lived."

"How about lasagna? Does she eat lasagna?" I ask my sister.

"Why don't you ask her?" she inquires.

"I-I don't know. You're right. I'll call her now."

"Deacon…" She rushes to get my name out before I hang up. "Just be you. She really likes you. And you don't have to tell me that you really like her. Your actions speak volumes. Be happy, big brother."

"Thanks, kid," I say, getting my own dig in about her age. However, it's a little creepy now that I think about it since she and Ramsey are the same age. I shake out of my thoughts and focus on her laughter.

"Love you, big brother."

"Love you too, little sister. Hey, when do I get copies of those pictures?"

"Is there one in particular you want?"

"All of them."

"Do you want any prints?"

"Yes. Can you make that happen?"

"Sure. I'll email you the link. I'll get 4x6 copies of all of them, but if you want one blown up or on a canvas or something, let me know."

"Thanks, Palmer." I end the call and start typing out a text to Ramsey, but a text won't do. While I get to see her in a few hours, the thought of hearing her voice wins over, and I back out of the message and hit Call instead.

"Hello."

I exhale a heavy breath at the sound of her voice. "Ramsey," I murmur.

"Is everything all right?"

I guess me acting out of character is stumping everyone in my life these days. "I just needed to ask you something, and I wanted to hear your voice, so I called instead of texting you."

"You wanted to hear my voice?"

"Yes."

"What did you want to ask me?"

Right. Get to the point, Setty. "Do you like lasagna?"

"Oh, um, yeah."

"Ramsey." It's not meant to be, but it comes out as part growl. "I need your words, sweetheart."

"I like lasagna. I'm not really a fan of ricotta cheese or cottage cheese."

"Me either. I make it with meat, sauce, noodles, parmesan, and mozzarella. Does that sound good? Maybe some garlic bread to go with it?"

"That sounds perfect, Deacon. What can I do?"

"I'm sitting outside the grocery store now. I'm going to run in and grab what I need and then head home. You can come over anytime." I need a shower and to straighten up the house, but I'm a pretty tidy guy, so I'm not too worried about that. Besides, she needs to know the real me, just like I want to know the real her.

"Okay. I'll grab something for dessert."

It's on the tip of my tongue to tell her that she's dessert, but I refrain. "You don't have to do that."

"I want to. It's just after four now. How about I come over around five or so? I can help you cook."

"I'd like that. I'll see you soon."

"See you soon." Grabbing my keys from the ignition, I climb out of my truck and head to the grocery store. Grocery shopping is usually a task I hate, but I don't mind it since it's because Ramsey is coming over to make dinner with me. She's quickly becoming a bright spot in my life

As soon as I walk through the door, I dump the grocery bags on the counter, not bothering to put any of them away, and sprint off to the shower. Ten minutes later, I'm in a pair of gym shorts and a Kincaid's Body Shop T-shirt that I stole from Orrin when he was fixing a small dent in the door of my truck.

Rushing through the house, I check the half bath that guests use to find it's sparkling clean. I never use it. I always go to my bedroom. I purposely don't do anything to straighten my room or my bathroom. I'm hoping that will keep me from taking her up there.

Don't get me wrong, I want her there, but we're not there yet. She needs to know that it's her. Her company and her time that I'm after. Anything else she gives me is just a bonus. After all the stories she's told me, I refuse to be another man who takes from her. Not if it's something she's not willing to give. In the meantime, I'll keep jacking my cock like fifteen-year-old me.

At exactly five, there's a knock at the door, and if I wasn't living it, I wouldn't believe that my heart actually skipped a fucking beat just knowing that Ramsey is standing on the other side.

Abandoning the groceries, I rush to the door and pull it open. She smiles and holds up a small container. "I made cookies."

"You didn't have to do that. I picked up a chocolate cake at the grocery store, but homemade cookies sound much better. Wait, what kind of cookies?"

"Peanut butter. Oh. You're not allergic, are you? Crap, I should have checked," she mumbles the last part.

"No. I'm not allergic, and peanut butter cookies are my favorite."

"You're just saying that." She laughs.

"Come on in. I can prove it." I step back, allowing her room to enter my house. With my hand on the small of her back, because I have to touch her, I lead her into the kitchen. When we reach the island, I grab her hips and lift her up, causing her to laugh.

"A chair also works," she says with a giggle. The sound wraps around me like a warm embrace, and it fills the silence of this big empty house. It's a sound that I could find myself craving if I'm not careful.

"Maybe." I shrug. "But if you're sitting in a chair, I'd have to bend to do this." I lean in and press my lips to hers. It's just a peck on the lips, but it lights me up inside all the same.

"Hmm," she responds. "I think I can see the merit."

Playfully, I squeeze her side before stepping away from her. I have dinner to cook. "How was your day?"

"It was good. I ended up covering a shift for an early morning meeting in Harris for the catering company. It was just eight to noon. After that, I came home and showered and read a book."

"Today was supposed to be your day off."

"Yeah, but they needed me, and I didn't have anything going on. I didn't mind."

"You work too hard."

"Hello, pot." She laughs. I just nod and laugh as well, because she's right. "How was your day?"

"Good. Short, which is new for me."

"You don't leave early often, huh?" she asks.

"Never really."

"And yet you did today?"

"I did. I was excited to see you, and I wanted to stop at the store to get what I needed." Reaching into my back pocket, I pull out my phone and dial my sister Piper. I was going to call Palmer, but I don't need her gloating. My mother is out of the question. I keep waiting for her to get wind that I'm seeing someone. She'll have our wedding planned in no time, so my middle sister is the winner.

"Hey, everything okay?" Piper greets me. Her voice is loud over the speaker. I made sure I used the speakerphone so Ramsey can hear our conversation.

"I'm fine. Everyone is fine. I have something to ask you, and I need you to just roll with it and answer honestly."

"Have you been drinking?" she asks. "Have you finally worked yourself to the brink of alcoholism?"

"No. I'm not drinking, and I'm fine. I just need you to answer something for me."

"Okay." There's caution in her tone.

"What are my favorite cookies?"

"Peanut butter. Why? Are you planning on having Mom make you some and then hide them from us again?" She laughs.

"No, although that's not a terrible idea," I tease. "I'm on a date, well, dinner at my place, and she made cookies. I told her they were my favorite, and she thought I was just telling her what she wanted to hear."

"Hold up. You're not at work? You're on a date? Dinner at your place? Who are you and what have you done with my brother?"

I start to smart off but decide to answer her rapid-fire questions. "No. I'm not at work. Yes, I'm on a date. Yes, we're having dinner at my place, and I'm still your brother."

"What's gotten into you? I'm impressed."

"Ramsey."

"What? Ramsey? Palmer's Ramsey?" she asks, confused.

"She's my Ramsey now, and yes, she's one and the same. Now, I need to get off here so I can make dinner for her and eat some of her cookies."

"I hope you literally mean the cookies she made you." Piper cracks up laughing.

"For now. Love you," I say, hitting End on the call and placing my phone on the counter. "Do you want something to drink?" I ask her.

She's still, so still I'm not sure she's even breathing, and her mouth is hanging open. Her gaze searches mine, looking for what I'm not sure. Finally, she clears her throat. "No. I'm okay for now." Her cheeks are tinted pink, and I smile inwardly. Good. She got the meaning behind my words.

I nod and begin to unpack the groceries.

"You're not like them."

"Like who?" I open the pound of ground beef and place it in the pan.

"My dad. Robert. They're both lawyers too. You're not like them."

"No," I agree. "I'm not like them."

"I know it's wrong, but I guess I always thought all lawyers were like them. Ruthless. Heartless."

"Not this one."

"Every lawyer I've ever met has been like them. Until you."

"Are you trying to tell me I'm special?" I glance over my shoulder at her and wink.

"Maybe. To be honest, I'm not sure. I guess I just wanted you to know that I know you're not like them. My father never once in my entire life ever treated me with an ounce of the respect that you do. And

Robert, he was my father's golden boy. He was allowed to do whatever he wanted."

Turning the burner down on low, I move to stand between her legs. I lift her hand and press my lips to one wrist and then the other. "They didn't deserve you. Neither of them." I kiss the corner of her mouth and step away, back to the stove before I say fuck dinner and carry her to my room. I'd show her how she deserves to be treated.

"What can I do to help?"

"Nothing. I bought the noodles that you don't have to boil. So once the meat is done, all I have to do is assemble it and pop it in the oven."

"I feel bad just sitting here while you do all the work."

"Fine. You can grab the lasagna pan. It's in the cabinet beneath the island." I hear her feet hit the floor as she hops down, and the sound of the pan being placed on the island. She comes to stand next to me, leaning her back against the counter.

"Palmer texted me earlier. She said you're getting some prints from our photo shoot. She wanted to know if I wanted any."

"Yeah, I asked her to send me copies of each and that I might want to make a few bigger versions. I just need to decide where I would put them."

"Deacon?" She waits for me to give her my attention. "You're really going to hang pictures of us in your house?"

I shrug. "Why not? We're dating."

"*Dating*, Deacon." She shakes her head as if I've lost my mind.

Maybe I have.

"Am I not allowed to have a picture of the girl I'm dating in my home?"

"This is so new."

"But it feels right."

"What if it jinxes us?"

"Are you worried about that?" I ask her. She shrugs, and when I start to tell her I need her words, she gives them to me freely before I can.

"Maybe. I don't know. I know you're unlike any man I've ever met, excluding Uncle Raymond and my cousins. I know I think about you before I go to sleep and again when I open my eyes each morning. I know that being with you causes butterflies to flutter here." She places her hand over her stomach.

"Okay." I can give her this. Easily. "I won't make enlargements yet. However, I am getting copies of all of them."

Another smile and shake of her head. "What am I going to do with you?"

"Kiss me." My body leans into hers, and she dutifully presses her lips to mine. I go back to the ground beef, and she keeps me company. Fifteen minutes later, and with a mess on the counter, the lasagna is in the oven.

I grab two bottles of water and lead her outside to the patio. This is my normal routine, to sit outside and relax after a long day. She barely has her ass in the chair next to me, and I already know it's better with Ramsey.

I have a feeling life and everything in it is better with Ramsey.

Chapter Fifteen

RAMSEY

I feel him before I see him. It sounds creepy as hell, but it's the truth. It's been four weeks and a handful of days since our first official date. Since then, we've been inseparable. Monday and Tuesday nights are my only evenings off, and I spend them with Deacon. We're either at his place or mine, and sometimes we venture out, but mostly, we both prefer to stay in. Palmer jokes that we're already an old married couple, and I don't hate it.

In fact, I love it. I enjoy spending time with him and he with me. He's such a great guy, and with each passing day, I fall a little more than the day before. Deacon Setty is just one of those guys who's the total package. He's charming, handsome, sexy, and yes, they both are worth mentioning. He's got a great job, owns his own home, loves his family, and he wants to be with me.

Some days it still feels as if I'm dreaming.

"Yo, Ramsey, your man is here," my coworker, Tabitha, calls out.

I nod and continue to fill the order I'm working on. Two Sex on the Beach mixed drinks for girls my age, according to their IDs I just made them present. After I cash them out, I allow myself to let my eyes search for him.

I don't have to look long. He's sitting at the very far end of the bar. The same seat that he always occupies when he's here. He eats dinner here most nights that I'm working, and if he's not eating here, he's bringing me dinner. From the looks of the container set on the bar, I'm guessing tonight is one of those nights.

"Hey, handsome," I greet him. I want to lean over the bar and press my lips to his, but I refrain. Hank is a cool boss, but it's unprofessional and immature. I already have our ages working against us. I don't need to add fuel to the fire. We've had a few odd looks when we've been out around town, but neither one of us seem to care. I was worried about my aunt and uncle and Deacon's parents, but they all seem fine with it. We've not been together with our families as a couple, but Deacon grew up here and is best friends with Orrin, so my family knows him and his family and vice versa. I have met Deacon's parents and his other sister with Palmer, but not as Deacon's... whatever I am. We're dating, and it's glorious, and I'm fine with not putting a label on it.

"Darlin'," he drawls. "How is your night going?"

"So far so good. How about yours?"

"Boring without you. I made chicken stir-fry for dinner." He slides the container toward me. "Have you taken your break yet?"

"It's time," Hank says, sliding up next to me. He offers Deacon his hand, and they shake. "Thirty minutes, Ramsey. Not one-second sooner." He gives me a warning look that holds no heat whatsoever.

"This should still be warm." Deacon grasps the container he just pushed toward me. "Let's go sit outside while you eat."

"Let me get a drink." Reaching into the cooler, I grab a bottle of water and walk toward the opposite end of the bar, where Deacon is waiting for me. "Oh, I need something to eat this with," I say. Rushing back around the bar, I grab a plastic cutlery set. When I make it back to where Deacon is standing, he offers me his hand, and I don't hesitate to take it.

Hand in hand, he leads me to his truck. Dropping the tailgate, he sets the container down and then lifts me to sit, stepping between my legs. His hands frame my face as he kisses me as if today could be our last. "I missed you," he says, dropping his hands and reaching for the container. He pulls off the lid, snatches the utensils, opens them with ease one-handedly, and forks up a bite, feeding it to me.

"So good," I say, covering my mouth with my palm.

"I'm glad you like it. I made way too much, so we'll have this to eat tomorrow too."

"I thought you had to help your dad move stuff around in the garage tomorrow?" I ask before opening my mouth to accept another bite.

"I do. I told him I would be over later after you go to work. I only get you two nights a week and two days. I'm not taking our time away."

"He's your dad."

Deacon shrugs. "He understands," he says, offering me another bite.

"You can't just put your life on hold because of my work schedule."

"Watch me."

I take the container from his hands and place it next to me on the tailgate. "What's going on?" I lock my arms around his neck. In turn, he wraps his arms around my waist, locking his hands at the small of my back.

"I miss you. Don't mind me. I'm cranky."

"You see me all the time."

"No. I see you four days a week. That's not enough for me. I get glimpses of you Wednesday thru Friday, and a few hours each day on Saturday and Sunday, and the same Monday and Tuesday nights, if you don't have a later catering gig."

"I've been turning them down."

"What?"

"I'm just a part-time, as-needed employee for At Your Service Catering. After that one Tuesday night that I had to cancel on you, I've been turning down any jobs that are going to have me working after five. This," I point to the Tavern behind us, "is my main job."

"I know you enjoy working here, and I would never ask you to quit for me, but I miss you. I dread the middle of the week because I know I'm only going to see you while I'm here eating or not at all."

"I'm sorry." I hug him closer.

"You have nothing to be sorry for. I'm being selfish. There's a part of me that wants to demand you find a day-shift job. However, there's a bigger part of me that knows you're a grown woman who can make her own choices. I won't take that away from you like they did. I might be pissy about it, but I would never demand that of you. No matter how bad I want to."

"I miss you too," I confess. "I've been thinking a lot about how I could use my degree. Well, just about what I want to do for the rest of my life. The Willow Tavern isn't forever."

"As long as I'm still in the forever column, we're all good," he assures me.

He has no idea that his words set off an explosive tidal wave of emotions in my chest. He just basically told me he wanted me forever.

"Eat up. You have to go back to work soon. Unless you're willing to let me tell them that you have food poisoning from my awful cooking and need to take the rest of the night off," he offers.

"Stop. We both know you're an excellent cook, and they already know that because this isn't the first meal you've brought me while I'm working."

"Damnit. Why do I have to be one of the nice guys?" he teases.

"I'm glad you're one of the good ones, Deacon. I'm also glad you're in my life."

"Me too, baby. Me too." He presses his lips to my cheek and moves to sit beside me on the tailgate while I finish my dinner.

Six hours later, we finally lock the doors and call it a night. My feet are killing me, and I've been distracted by my conversation with Deacon earlier. It bothers me too that we only have two weeknights that we can go out, and it's something I've been thinking about a lot. When I first accepted this position, I was fine with the nights. The tips were better, and if Palmer was busy, I just sat at home alone anyway. Now I have someone other than my best friend in my life who I want to spend time with. I used to spend Sundays at my aunt and uncle's, and I've been missing that lately too. Every spare minute I spend with Deacon and it's not enough.

I'm not sure that any amount of time with him will ever be enough.

"Hey, Ramsey, can you grab some napkins from the supply closet?" Tabitha asks.

"Sure." I drop the dirty glasses I just collected off at the bar and head down the hallway to the supply closet. I pass Hank's office, and instead of passing it like I would any other time, I knock on the door frame.

"Ramsey. Come on in." He smiles kindly. "What's up?"

"Well," I say, wringing my hands together, "I was wondering if we could talk about my schedule."

"Sure, you need a day off?"

"Kind of. I was hoping I could have fewer nights on the weekends. I know that I said I could work with them when you hired me, but my situation has changed."

"Deacon." He smiles.

I nod. "I work every Friday, Saturday, and Sunday night. That doesn't leave much time to grow a relationship."

"Trust me, I know." He nods. "So what are you thinking?"

"Maybe one weekend night a week? Out of those three days?"

"That's a big ask. That's going to disrupt the entire schedule."

"I know. I'm sorry for asking." I turn to walk out of his office.

"Ramsey," he calls out to me.

"Yes?" I turn to look over my shoulder.

"Let me see what I can do. You're a hard worker and very dependable. I'd hate to lose you. I've been thinking of adding another employee anyway. It's always nice when someone calls off to have options. It would take some time to get them trained."

I try to hide my smile, but I can't. "Yes. Of course. I'm happy to help and pick up shifts during the day, whatever I need to do to help train them."

He chuckles. "All right. I'll keep you posted."

"Thank you, Hank." He waves, ending the conversation. I quickly grab a couple of packs of bar napkins from the supply closet and take them back to Tabitha.

"I thought you got lost," she teases.

"No. I was talking to Hank."

"Well, we're all set here. Are you cashed out?"

"Not yet. Give me five." I move toward the register and quickly count my drawer before taking it to Hank, where he's still sitting behind his desk. "We're ready to go."

"Good deal. I'm beat. You ladies grab your things and meet me by the back door."

"Hank's meeting us at the back door," I tell Tabitha.

"My feet are killing me," she groans.

"Tell me about it. It wasn't even that busy tonight. We've had worse."

"I know. Maybe it's because we did more standing, and when we're moving, it's not as bad?" she suggests.

"Possibly." Grabbing my purse from underneath the counter, I turn off the lights and follow her down the hall.

"Have I told you I love you for hiring a cleaning crew permanently?" Tabitha asks our boss.

"You have, but you can keep telling me. I like getting out of here at a decent hour. I was here early anyway to let them in, so the cleaning crew made sense."

"Good call, boss man." Tabitha pats him on the back as he pushes open the back door.

"Where do I find me one of those?" Tabitha asks.

I look to where she's nodding and see Deacon sitting on his tailgate. He's casually scrolling through his phone as if he's not sitting in a parking lot at nearly two in the morning waiting for me to get off work. My heart does a somersault in my chest. He's here for me.

I don't reply to Tabitha. I manage to lift my hand in the air to wave at the two of them, but I can't be sure if they see me, and right now, I don't care. All I want to do is hug him. I need Deacon's arms around me. Even more so, I need my arms around him.

I don't know what I did to have this incredible man come into my life, but I'm grateful, and I just pray that he's always here with me. He jumps off the tailgate, and he must read the expression on my face. He opens his arms wide, and I walk straight into them.

"I don't know why you're still here, but I needed this," I tell him after a few minutes of clinging to him.

"I'm here for you, Ramsey."

I open my mouth to thank him, but the words that come out of my mouth are different than what I intended. "Stay with me tonight." Four words that are sure to move our relationship to a new level, and I do not regret them.

Deacon frames my face with his large hands and studies me for what feels like hours but is only seconds. "My place or yours?"

"Yours." It's not because I don't like my place. I do. It's more that Deacon's house feels more like home than my tiny one-bedroom apartment. Right now, I need him and the comfort that his place brings me.

"I'll follow you." He kisses me quickly and then leads me to my car. Like the gentleman he is, he opens the door for me and waits for me to be settled before closing it.

My gaze follows him as he climbs into his truck and flashes his lights, letting me know he's ready to go. This isn't the first time he's followed me home. However, it is the first time he's followed me to his. It's the first time either of us has ever mentioned spending the night with the other. Prior to meeting Deacon, I never imagined asking this of a man. Ever. He makes me feel strong and beautiful, and I need more of that tonight. I needed his hug.

I need him.

As I drive to his place with his headlights in my rearview mirror, I don't stress about what's to come. I don't worry about spending the night at his place. I know I'm safe with Deacon. He said he missed me, and I missed him too—more than I can ever relay with words.

A bolt of excitement lights me up inside, thinking about falling asleep next to him. At least I hope I get to fall asleep next to him. I should be nervous. This will be a first for me. One that Robert never stole. However, I'm not the least bit worried. Even if he doesn't want to sleep next to me, I know he'll be just down the hall. That beats being across town from him any day.

Chapter Sixteen

DEACON

"Are you hungry? Thirsty?" I ask Ramsey as we step into the house from the garage.

"I'm good." There is a slight tremor in her voice, telling me I need to ease her fears.

"Come here." I open my arms, and she walks into them without question. "This is one of those times I'm going to need you to use your words, Ramsey."

She tilts her head back to look at me. "I have been."

I smile and lift an arm from around her waist to smooth her hair back out of her eyes. "I know you have, but I can feel the nervous energy rolling off you in waves. It's just me. There is nothing to be nervous about."

"You're wrong," she counters.

"Explain that. Are you worried about staying here with me?"

"No. I'm not worried about staying with you." She pauses, and I know she's trying to find her voice to tell me what's bothering her. "I am worried about staying."

"You're confusing me, sweetheart."

"I've never spent the night with anyone."

"You don't have to sleep in my bed with me. I have two spare rooms that you can pick from, or you can take my bed, and I'll sleep in the spare room. Whatever you need to be comfortable." I mean it. I want her to feel comfortable and safe here. What I don't tell her is no way in hell am I sleeping knowing she's just down the hall, but she's still here, and that's worth a night of no sleep. It's worth a lifetime of no sleep, and I refuse to think about what that means.

"What do you want, Deacon?" she asks.

"This isn't about what I want. This is about what makes you feel the most comfortable."

"No. I know that." She's quick to assure me. "I know I'm safe with you. What I mean is, I'm nervous because I don't know what you want."

I feel as though we're talking in riddles, but I understand why. She's nervous. "I'm going to tell you, but only because I think your fear is getting the best of you. I need you to know that where you sleep tonight is your choice, regardless of what I want. The choice is yours, and I will gladly accept your decision. I'm just happy you're here." My lips find their way to her temple.

"The suspense is killing me." She chuckles nervously.

I guide her to the kitchen island and lift her like I've done countless times before. I like being able to move in close and look at her without bending my neck. Stepping between her thighs, I wrap my arms around her. "I want you. I want you in my bed and in my arms. That's how I want to fall asleep, and that's how I want to wake up." My palms are sweaty as I wait for her reply. She makes me feel like a damn teenager.

"But just to sleep?" Her cheeks go pink, the adorable shade that causes my cock to harden.

With my arms around her back, I pull her to the edge of the counter. My cock is nestled against her pussy. Sure, there are layers of clothes between us, but I know from the way her eyes widen that she can feel what she does to me.

"I feel like this is a trick question." I chuckle.

"Stop." She swats at my chest playfully. "I'm being serious."

"I told you that I want you. But you know as well as I do that you hold all the cards here, Rams. I can't give you what you want unless you tell me what that is."

"What if once I tell you, you don't want to give it to me? I mean, give me what I want."

I know what she wants, at least I'm pretty sure I know. But there is the off chance I could be wrong, and that's why I'm going to need her to spell it out for me. There is zero room for miscommunication when it comes to sex.

"Trust me, sweetheart. There is nothing you could ask of me that I would say no to."

"You don't know that."

"Try me."

She hesitates. "What if I told you that I wanted you to touch me?"

Fuck yes. "I am touching you." I hug her a little tighter to prove my point.

"Other places."

Fuck. She's killing me.

"Where do you want me to touch you, Ramsey?"

"Everywhere," she confesses in a rush, burying her face in my neck.

Everywhere.

Every-fucking-where.

My hand easily finds its way up the back of her shirt. My fingers caress her soft skin as I trace her spine. "Here?" A shiver races through her at the contact, and my cock twitches behind my zipper.

"You've already touched me there," she whispers huskily.

She's right. I have touched her there. It's been over a month since we've been dating, six weeks since the day I first laid eyes on her, and I've kissed the breath from her lungs more times than I can count. I've also let my hands roam up the back of her shirt like I am now. Over her belly, up her sides. Anywhere I can touch her without taking it there, I've done.

I'm not usually this slow to close the deal, but Ramsey isn't just a quick fuck. The more time I spend with her, how special she is imprints into my soul. Not to mention she's come from a background of never getting to choose.

As bad as I want to take control and slip her out of her clothes, all those times I was kissing her, I held strong. I've been waiting for this moment. For the time when she's ready to make the next move. She's an adult, but she missed all the dating and the buildup you get as a teenager. She was thrust into a relationship with a guy she hated who forced her to kiss him when she said no, and she swears that's all; he was just really rough with her when she would deny him. I hate to think of his hands on her.

I want to hunt him down and beat his ass, but I know that's not going to help her. It's only going to help me. Instead, I'm trying to give her everything he stole, making out like teenagers, sending her home with my balls tight and aching. I've jacked off more times in the last six weeks than I have in all my thirty-two years.

I'd do it again.

For her.

For Ramsey.

"You're right," I answer, pulling out of my thoughts. "I have touched you there. Are you thinking somewhere new then?" I ask coyly.

"Yes."

"Will you show me?"

"Deacon." She laughs. "Just… do it."

"Do what? Do this?" My hand moves around to her breast under her shirt, and I trace her hard nipple through her silk bra.

"That. Yes, that." She nods as her eyes close.

"Open your eyes, Ramsey." I wait for her to show me those baby blues. "I need to see you. If you won't tell me with your words, I need to see your eyes."

"Everywhere, Deacon," she reminds me.

"Fine. I just like it when I know you're watching me." I wink at her. "Can we get rid of this?" I tug at the Willow Tavern T-shirt she's wearing.

She swallows hard and nods. I wait patiently, and she rolls her eyes. "Yes."

"Thank you." I reward her with a peck on the lips before pulling the shirt over her head. I discard her shirt on the counter before my hands test the weight of her breasts. My thumbs trace her nipples, and she moans.

"Deacon."

"What, baby?"

Her blue eyes lock on mine. "More."

"Are you sure?"

"Stop asking me if I'm sure," she pants. "Touch me. Please."

"It's important to me to know that this is what you want."

"I want. I *so* want," she breathes, as my thumbs continue to rub over her peaks.

"Take it off." My voice is gruff, and I'm barely maintaining my composure as it is. I've thought about this since the moment I laid eyes on her.

I stay right where I am, my hands resting on her thighs as she reaches behind her and unclasps her bra. Slowly she lowers one strap and then the other, holding the material to her chest as if she's not sure this is what she wants to do. I lick my lips and open my mouth to tell her we can stop, but the words won't come. I try again, but before I can get the words past my lips, she drops her hands and pulls the fabric away from her body, letting it fall to the counter.

I tear my shirt over my head and let it fall to the floor. I need to feel her skin against mine more than I need my next breath. Moving in closer, I place my hand behind her neck, beneath her hair, and guide her mouth to mine. Her hands reach under my arms and grip my back. Her tits press against my bare chest, and it's the best damn thing I've ever felt in my entire life. If skin-to-skin contact is this good, I can't imagine what her pussy is going to feel like wrapped around my cock.

Her tongue slides against mine with practiced ease. My free hand travels to her breasts and captures her nipple between my thumb and forefinger. I roll the pebbled bud, and her nails dig deeper into my back.

"Deacon," she mumbles against my lips.

This time I don't ask her if she wants more. We're both too far gone to think otherwise. Tearing my lips from hers, I trail kisses across her cheek and over the length of her slender neck. My lips follow a trail to her breasts, where I suck a hard nipple into my mouth. Her skin is so fucking soft, yet her nipple is hard enough to cut glass. I nip at her with my teeth and quickly soothe her with my tongue.

"Oh, god," she moans. Her head falls back, and I'm sure her eyes are closed, but I can't focus on that right now. It's better that she just feels. I want her to feel all of this. Her legs lock tighter around my waist, and my cock nestles even closer to her pussy. She's panting now, and I'm on the brink of losing my ever-loving mind.

"Can we go to my room?" I ask. She lifts her head, and her blue eyes are so dark they're almost black, and the desire I see there almost brings me to my knees. "I want to lay you out on my bed and explore you. Please?" I add, because I'm a desperate man where she's concerned.

"Yes."

"Hold on." She wraps her arms around my neck, and we're moving. I don't bother with the lights or our clothes that are scattered haphazardly around my kitchen. Instead, I take the stairs two at a time. Her face is buried in my neck, and the way she clings to me has something tripping over in my chest. It's not the first time that feeling has happened when I'm with her, but this time it feels different. Maybe it's because her body is wrapped around mine, and her bare tits are pressed against my chest.

Maybe it's just Ramsey.

We reach my room, and I make my way to the bed in the darkness. I don't set her down. Instead, I grip her tightly with one arm while I find the switch to the lamp and turn it on, bathing the room in a soft glow.

I sit on the bed with her still wrapped around me, and she's now straddling me. "Ramsey." My voice is gravelly. "Look at me, baby." She lifts her head and gives me a shy smile. "Tell me where you want this to go? There is no wrong answer here. I'll give you whatever you want. I just need your words."

"Make this ache go away."

"Here?" I place my hand over her chest, over her heart.

"No. You already fixed that ache," she whispers.

It's a good fucking thing I'm sitting down. Her confession would have knocked me on my ass. As it is, I'm stunned speechless. I wrap my arms around her back and hug her tightly. So tight I'm probably crushing her, but fuck, she takes my breath away.

"Deacon?"

"Yeah?" I answer gruffly.

"This ache," she says, rocking her hips against mine.

A few things happen at once. My cock pulses painfully against my zipper. My shy girl finds her voice and tells me exactly what she wants. And lastly, and probably the biggest, is that something happens inside me. Something shifts. It's a feeling not only in my chest but in my gut. It tells me that she's different, something I've known all along, but it's more than that. I care about her. I crave her and this new sensation. It's soul-capturing and all-consuming. It's unlike anything I've ever felt before.

It feels a lot like… love.

I've never been in love. Sure, I had relationships in the past. There was a woman in college who I thought was going to be the one, but it didn't work out. We wanted different things. I was torn up for a couple of weeks when we broke things off, but I got over the pain and her with ease. I know with absolute certainty I would not get over losing Ramsey.

Never.

I also know that what I felt for my college girlfriend is nothing compared to the woman in my arms.

As badly as I want to strip her down and fuck her, this feeling, this realization, changes things. I don't want our first time to be after she's been on her feet all night and exhausted. I want it to be… more. I don't know what more is or how I make it that way, but I'll find a way. Right now, my girl has an ache that I need to take care of.

Standing, I kiss her softly before resting my forehead against hers. "I need you out of these jeans," I tell her.

"Capris," she corrects me.

"They're denim, and they're in my way," I counter. She giggles, and the sound wraps itself around my heart. Slowly, I let her body slide down mine. When her feet touch the floor, she steps back. She maintains eye contact as she reaches for the button of her *capris* and pops it open before lowering the zipper—the sound echoing through the room.

"Why am I the only one getting naked?" she asks.

"Because I can't trust myself not to fuck you into next week."

"What if I want you to?"

"Is that what you want? A hard fuck?" To prove my point, I lower my zipper and shuffle out of my jeans, kicking them to the side. My cock is peeking out above my boxers, and I squeeze it tightly to ward off my ache.

"I want to make you happy."

I'm glad she's found her voice, and she's telling me what she wants, but those six words confirm that my cock will not be going anywhere near her pussy. Not tonight. I don't want her to want me inside her to make me happy. I want her to want it because it will make her happy. Call me a pussy, or take my man card or whatever, but she's lived her life for everyone else. I won't let her make decisions like this because she thinks that's what she needs to do to make me happy.

Her breathing makes me happy.

I just have to prove that to her.

"Wow," she breathes. I find her eyes, and they're locked on my cock.

"Rams," I growl. "Baby, you can't look at me like that. I'm barely holding on to my control."

"Tell me what to do."

"You want the ache to go away?"

"Yes."

"On the bed."

She drags her panties over her thighs and lets them pool at her feet. Stepping out of them, she does as I ask and climbs on the bed. "Where do you want me?"

"Head on the pillow, beautiful." She shimmies until her dark hair is splayed out, and the sight gives me pause.

"Are you all right?" she asks softly.

"I'm just memorizing this moment."

"Please." She presses her thighs together. It's as if my words have caused the ache in her pussy to grow. Maybe they did. I know my cock is weeping for her.

I move to the bed, my boxer briefs still on. "Open for me," I instruct in a voice that does not sound like my own. Her legs fall open, and her pussy glistens for me, calling my name. She's bare, and that surprises me. "Is this for me?" I ask, running my finger through her folds.

"For both of us, I guess."

"I approve," I tell her. Then I move, letting my legs hang off the bed, and kiss her bare pussy. When my tongue takes its first taste, she bucks off the bed. I slide my hand up to hold her still as I drink my fill of her.

"Deacon," she pants. "Oh, shit."

Her cry of pleasure is all the incentive I need. I suck on her clit while sliding a finger inside her, making her thighs squeeze my head. Placing my hands under her ass, I lift her to get a better angle, and her legs completely trap me.

Fuck yes.

The only way I can describe the next few minutes is an out-of-body experience. I eat at her like she's my last meal. Her legs grip me tightly, and she buries her hands in my hair. She's moaning my name, and "more," and "please," and I give her what she wants.

What she needs.

When her pussy grips my fingers, I know she's close. My mouth closes over her clit, and she erupts like a rocket. I don't stop until her legs fall open, her hands release from my hair, and her body relaxes into the mattress.

This is a night I will never forget.

This moment with her has changed me.

My heart is no longer my own.

Chapter Seventeen

RAMSEY

My heart is racing. My limbs are weak, and I'm lying naked on his bed. I should move to cover up or thank him for tilting my world on its axis. However, all I can do is lie here and try to catch my breath and calm my heart before it pounds out of my chest.

The bed dips beside me and I peer over. Deacon is on his side, his large hand resting on my quivering belly as he watches me. "There she is," he whispers.

"Thank you." I manage two words in my catatonic state.

"You thanked me when you came all over my tongue. Otherwise, I don't need your thanks." He leans in and presses his lips to mine. It's a chaste kiss, and after where his mouth just was, you would think that I would shy away, but I want anything he's willing to give me.

"That was worth a thank-you. That's the least I can do." I'm very aware that I sound like the inexperienced woman that I am, but I can't seem to find it in me to care. "I've never," I start but then shake my head, keeping my confession to myself.

"You've never?" He slides his hand over my pussy, and traces through what I'm sure is a sticky mess, but again, I don't seem to have the energy to care. I'm sure once I feel like myself again, I'll be mortified.

"It's nothing."

"Rams, come on now. Don't get shy on me. Tell me. There is nothing you can say that's wrong. Just tell me the first thing that comes to your mind."

"I've never done that. Or had that done to me," I blurt.

"That's because he was a selfish asshole," he grumbles.

He leans in for another kiss, and his erection presses against my thigh. "What about you?"

"I'm not a selfish asshole." He winks.

"Oh, trust me, I know. What about you?" I nod to his erection.

"I'm fine. Tonight was about you."

"I want it to be about you too."

"We'll get there," he promises.

"That has to be uncomfortable, right?"

"I'll take care of it."

"How?"

He raises his hand and winks. "I'm good, sweetheart, I promise."

"Can I watch?" I ask.

He sputters and coughs. "You want to watch me jack my cock?"

"Yes." I don't know why, but suddenly I have no problem telling him what I want. I might be embarrassed when I come off my orgasm high, but right now, I'm rolling with it.

I watch as he removes his hand from where he was leisurely exploring my pussy and rolls to his back. He lifts his hips and removes his boxer briefs. He takes his cock in his hand and strokes slowly from the base to the tip. His head turns to me, and the corner of his mouth lifts in a grin. "I'll never be able to say no to you."

"Nothing?" I ask, a plan already forming in my mind.

"There is nothing that you could ask for that I wouldn't try my fucking best to deliver."

"So what if I said I want to do it."

"Do what?"

"That." I point to where he's fisting his cock. "Can I touch you?" I ask, just as he has asked me so many times before.

"Always. You never have to ask for permission with me, Ramsey. There is no one else but you." His gaze is intense, so I look away and reach for his cock. He grabs my wrist, and I flinch but don't pull away.

"Fuck. I'm sorry, Rams. I didn't mean," he starts, but I lean over and kiss him to shut him up.

"It's okay. I'm okay. I flinched a little, and I might always, but there was no panic or fear. Not with you."

"Doesn't matter. I knew better. You made the boundaries clear."

"Fuck the boundaries," I say, surprising both of us. "I don't want boundaries. Not with you." I stare him down, willing him to see the truth in my eyes. "Never with you."

He swallows hard. "Never with me." He nods, letting me know he hears what I'm saying.

It's the best I can do without telling him that he owns my heart. I'm not ready to bare that truth just yet.

"Can I?" I reach for him. My hand is suspended in the air.

He nods and lets his hand fall away, and mine takes its place. When I move to rest on my elbow so I can get a better angle, he slides his arm under me and pulls me close. "I'm yours," he whispers huskily.

I tear my gaze from where my hand is gripping his cock. "And I'm yours." The confession rolls off my tongue with ease. His lips press to mine, and I can taste myself on him. It's more of a turn-on than I thought it would be. "Show me what you like."

"There is nothing you can do that I won't like."

"I don't know what I'm doing, Deacon. I want this to be good for you."

"Your hands are on me, baby. Trust me. It's good for me."

"Tell me."

He reaches over to the nightstand and opens the drawer.

"What are you doing?"

"We need lubrication."

"Like this?" With a move bolder than I ever thought I could be, I reach between my folds and slide my fingers through my pussy. My fingers are wet and sticky, but I still wrap them around his cock.

"Fuck." His hand drops from his search in the nightstand drawer before his head falls back to the bed, and he covers his eyes with his arm.

"Deacon?"

"Yeah, baby?"

"I need to see your eyes." I grin, thrilled with the fact that I get to toss his sexy words back at him.

He huffs out a laugh but removes his arm, letting it fall to the bed. "That little move you just did is the hottest fucking thing I've ever seen in my life."

"Yeah?"

"Yeah." His hand slides behind my head, and he kisses me slow and deep. I reach between my legs again, grabbing more of my wetness and coating him with it. "Am I doing okay?" I ask, needing feedback. I'm way out of my element here.

"Perfect," he breathes.

The room is quiet except for our breathing and the sound of my wetness on my hand as I stroke him. I need to be closer. I want to watch as he spills over into my hand. Moving down his body, I rest my head on his belly as I stroke him.

Deacon runs his fingers through my hair, not once telling me to stop or commenting on my lack of experience. I stroke him and can feel his belly quiver. His hands tighten in my hair, his cock twitches beneath my palm, and suddenly, I want to taste him. Taste us together. This time I don't ask for permission. He said I could do anything I wanted, anytime I wanted, so for once in my life, I take what I want without the fear of repercussions.

Moving closer, I don't stop stroking as my tongue peeks out and tastes us together.

"Oh, fuck." His legs lift off the bed, and so does his back, but he settles and lets me do my thing.

I go in for another taste, this time pulling the head of his cock into my mouth. I can taste the salt of his early release on my tongue.

"Ramsey?"

"Hmm?" I say, my mouth still holding the tip of his cock.

"Fuck, baby, if you keep doing that, I'm going to lose it. I'm going to come."

I stop, letting his cock fall from my lips with an audible pop. I turn to look at him over my shoulder. "Isn't that the point?"

"Do you want me to come down your throat? I'm just warning you."

"Yes. That. Let's do that."

He huffs out a laugh before his face grows serious. "You're a gift, Ramsey. A precious gift and a light that makes my world brighter."

I blink back tears. "I'm already a sure thing," I tease. Something I could have never seen myself doing until Deacon came into my life.

"You're everything."

It's on the tip of my tongue to tell him that I'm falling in love with him, but I don't want it to be like that. Not when we're in the middle of being intimate. I want him to know it's coming from my heart and that it's not the orgasm talking. Instead, I turn back to the task at hand. I stroke him a few times before taking him into my mouth. I can't take him all, but I give it my best try.

His hand lands on the back of my head, but he doesn't apply pressure. He gathers my hair into what feels like his fist and lets me do whatever I want.

"Jesus, Ramsey. So hot."

His words fuel me to bob my head fast, stroke my hand faster. Another deep moan fills the room, and it's a heady feeling to know that I'm giving him this kind of pleasure.

"Babe, I'm close. You have to stop." His hand doesn't release my hair as the other taps on my shoulder. "Fuck, Ramsey, I'm going to come." He sounds pained, but I know that's not the case.

I don't stop.

I want this.

I want to give this to him. I want to taste him as he tasted me. I increase my efforts, my jaw starting to ache, but I keep going, craving his release just as much as I craved my own.

"Fuck!" he roars as he shoots his hot, salty release down my throat. I swallow, not loving the taste but also not hating it. When he relaxes, I let him fall from my mouth and move up to rest my head on his chest.

We both stay in each other's arms, not saying a word. For me, I'm still processing this night. Deacon coming to my work, bringing dinner, and then us ending up at his place, naked and tangled in his sheets.

I shiver, and he pulls me closer. "Come on. Let's take a quick shower, and we can go to bed."

"Together?"

"Unless you don't want that."

"No. I do. I've just never done that before." I lift my head to let him see my eyes.

"He was an asshole. If I ever run into him…" His voice trails off.

"If you ever run into him, nothing. He's not worth your breath or your fists."

"What makes you think my fists would get involved?"

"The look on your face. Besides, he can't hurt me anymore. My father and Robert, they no longer control me or my life. I'm doing just fine on my own."

"You're not alone."

My heart feels as if it could burst at his words. I don't reply, but I squeeze him tight, and he does the same thing in return.

"Come on. Let's shower." He climbs out of bed and offers me his hand. At the gesture, I realize that I would follow him anywhere.

Deacon sets out a couple of towels for us and starts the water. He waits until the temperature is right before climbing in and holding his hand out for me to join him. Placing my palm in his is an easy decision.

"As bad as I want to explore your soapy, sexy body, I'm going to stay over here." He points to the second showerhead. "While you do your thing over there. I know you're exhausted, and you need your rest."

"Is that a challenge?" I tease.

"No. Not with you, little minx." He flashes me a grin. "Get clean before I say fuck it and dirty you up again. We're both exhausted."

I do as he says and stay on my side of the walk-in shower, but my eyes still linger. He's toned in all the right places, and his cock, well, it's hard for me to process the fact that it was just in my mouth not long ago.

"You good?" he asks, his voice gruff.

"I'm good."

He nods and turns off the water. Stepping out, he grabs a towel and wraps it around me before doing the same for himself. He then hands me another. "For your hair," he says.

"You take good care of me," I tell him. My heart feels like a big warm puddle of goo, and it's not the orgasm. It's the care that he shows me each and every day.

"Always." My words were meant to be teasing, but his reply is not. He steps into me, holding me close. "I'll always take care of you." He dots a kiss to my nose before saying, "I don't have a hairdryer or anything. You should probably leave some things here for nights like this. Or tell me what you need, and I can make sure I have it for you."

"You'd be okay with that?"

"Yes." He takes our towels and tosses them in the hamper.

I comb my fingers through my hair and remember I have a hair tie in my purse. "I'm going to run downstairs and grab my hair tie out of my purse."

"Stay. I need to go lock up and turn out the lights. I'll bring it up for you."

While he's gone, I stare at my reflection in the mirror. I look like the same me, but I feel different. I don't feel like the meek girl who stood by and let those who were supposed to love her walk all over her. I feel strong and confident.

"So sexy," he purrs, handing me my purse. "Do you want something to sleep in?"

I bite my lip and shake my head. He gives me time like he always does to voice what I want from him. "Can we just sleep like this? Naked?"

"Yes." There is no hesitation in his reply. If I ask and he can give it to me, he will. He takes care of me.

Once I have my hair braided and tied off at the end, he places his hand on the small of my back and turns off the overhead light. He guides me to the bed, pulls back the covers, and motions for me to climb in. He then reaches over turns off the bedside lamp and slides under the covers next to me.

I waste no time curling up against him, and he wraps his arms around me. "I always wondered what this would feel like. Lying with someone skin-to-skin."

"Not someone. Me. You will only be lying like this with me."

"You can't foresee the future, Deacon." It's a gut reaction to his words. I've spent far too long not letting myself believe in happily ever after. However, I have no reason not to believe Deacon. He's been open and honest with me about wanting us to be together. I guess it's just hard for me to let myself hope for a future with him.

"No, I guess I can't. How about this? If I'm breathing, you're lying next to me."

"That's… okay." I started to tell him that's impossible to know, but I trust him. I know he's a man of his word.

"You make my heart race," I confess into the darkness.

"You make mine light up." I feel his lips press against my temple. "Good night, baby."

"Good night." I place my lips against his bare chest and close my eyes. It's not long before sleep takes me.

Chapter Eighteen

DEACON

I'M REACHING FOR THE DOOR OF THE WILLOW TAVERN WHEN MY cell phone rings. Stopping, I remove it from my suit jacket to see Orrin calling. "Hey, man."

"I just drove by your office, and you're not there."

"No. I'm getting ready to walk into the Tavern to grab some dinner."

"My cousin has you by the balls already." He laughs.

"Is there a point to this call or do you just want to give me shit?"

"It started out as wanting to give you shit, but it's been a long-ass day, and I'm starving. I'll meet you there."

"Sounds good. I'll be at the bar."

"Just grab us a table."

"I don't get to see her again unless she's behind this bar until Saturday morning. She works all the damn time. I'll be at the bar."

"Fine." He laughs. "I'll see you in ten." He ends the call, and I pull the door open, anxious to see my girl.

Walking into the Tavern, I see that it's dead, which I expected for a Thursday night. I head to what I like to call my corner of the bar, since

I spend so much time there. Ramsey spots me as soon as I walk in and pours me a glass of water. She's placing it in front of me as I lean over the bar and kiss her hello.

"Missed you today."

"I brought you lunch at work," she reminds me.

"That was what? Twenty minutes? Not long enough."

She smiles and shakes her head. "What are you having tonight?"

"Orrin is meeting me. He just called to give me shit about not being at the office. I told him I was here, and he said he'd come eat with me."

"Hi, Deacon." Tabitha, one of the bar staff, waves as she passes by.

"Hey." I nod in her direction before turning back to Ramsey. "What's that smile about?"

"I didn't tell you when I did it because I didn't want to get either of our hopes up. But…" she draws out the word. "I talked to Hank about changing my hours. I told him I'd like to have at least one weekend night a week off, if possible two."

"Seriously?" I lean my elbows on the bar to get closer to her. She does the same, and our faces are close. "When does this start?"

"Tomorrow night."

Leaning in a little further, I press my lips to hers. "What are we going to do?"

She shrugs. "We can just hang out. We don't have to make a big production over it."

"A big production over what?" Orrin says, interrupting us.

"I'm off tomorrow night."

"Really? Then we should all go out," he suggests.

"Where are we going?" I look over Orrin's shoulder and see Archer and Ryder, two of his younger brothers, standing behind him.

"Yeah, I picked up a few stragglers on the way. Well, they called and asked what I was doing, and well, here we are."

"And what are we doing?" Archer asks again.

"Nothing." Ramsey laughs. "I'm off tomorrow night for the first Friday night in forever, and I was just telling Deacon that we could just have a quiet night in."

"Rams, come on." Ryder grins. "You can't spend Friday night just sitting around with this guy." He points to me.

"Yes, I can," she counters, crossing her arms over her chest.

"Babe, you never get Friday nights off. We should go out."

"I never get quiet Friday nights at home either," she counters.

"What about Friday night?" another voice asks.

Glancing over, I see it's Rushton, another brother of Orrin's. "We're trying to talk my girl into going out tomorrow night."

"What's the deal?" Brooks asks Ramsey.

"No deal. I just thought it might be nice to stay in and have a quiet night with my boyfriend. However, if you want to go out with the guys, go right ahead."

"Baby, if you think for a second that I'm letting you spend your first Friday night off in months without me, you're wrong."

"Come on, Rams," Rushton encourages her. "The guy is practically begging for your time. Put him out of his misery," he says, smacking a hand down on my shoulder.

"I'm clearly outnumbered." She shakes her head, a smile playing on her lips.

"Why are you all hounding my best friend?" a voice that I know belongs to my baby sister asks.

"Palmer, help me out here." Ramsey waves her hands at our group. "Tell them it's fine for me to want to spend Friday night at home."

"You work on Friday nights," Palmer answers.

"Not tomorrow. I'm off."

"Then hell yes, we're going out. What are we doing, boys?" she asks, placing her arm around Archer's shoulders. They graduated together and have always been close.

"Fine." Ramsey holds her hands up in the air. "Tell me where to be and when," she says, moving down the bar to serve someone who just walked in.

"Seriously, what are you all doing here? Is this some kind of Kincaid family reunion?" Palmer teases.

"These jokers follow me around like lost puppies." Orrin points at his brothers.

"We're all bachelors, and we're starving," Archer counters.

"Fair enough. Let's grab a table. You coming, Deacon?" Palmer asks.

"I'm good here."

"Come on." Palmer grabs my hand and pulls me from my stool. "We need to make plans for tomorrow night. You can go sit with your girl after."

"I'll be there in a minute," I tell her, waving her off. She smiles and shakes her head. I know she loves that Ramsey and I are together. I have a feeling she's never going to let me live it down that she introduced us.

"You're not going to contribute to the planning?" Ramsey asks after serving her customer.

"If you really want to stay home, we can. I just thought you deserve a night out of fun."

"It's fine. I don't mind going out. I just hate that you always insist that you pay. You don't have to spend your money on me to make me want to be with you."

"That's not what I'm doing. Not at all. I'm paying because I want to take care of you, and before you say you don't need me to take care of you, I know that too. It's not because you need me to do it. It's because I want to do it. I like doing nice things for you."

"You're a good man, Deacon Setty."

"I'm your man," I say, leaning over the bar to press my lips to hers.

"All right, you crazy kids, break it up," Tabitha jokes.

I settle back on my stool. "I got you something last night."

"You did?"

I nod. Reaching into my pocket, I grab the item and slide it across the bar to her. "This is yours."

"A key?" She takes it in her hand and tilts her head to the side.

"To my place. If there are any nights you get off work and you want to come home to me instead of home alone, use that."

"Giving me a key to your place is a big deal."

Leaning over the bar once again, I kiss her. I can't seem to help myself. Thankfully, there are only a couple of small groups, minus the Kincaids and my sister. I hope they're not paying us a bit of attention. I don't want to get her into trouble, but I can't not kiss her either. "Don't you know we're a big deal, you and me?" I wink and stand from my stool. "I'm going to go see what they're planning for tomorrow night. Is there anything you absolutely don't want to do?"

"I just want to be with you. I don't care about the rest."

My chest does that tightening thing that happens when she's around, and it's on the tip of my tongue to tell her that I love her. In fact, I have to bite down on my cheek to keep the words from spilling out of my mouth. This isn't the place or time to confess something like that. I need to be where I can take her in my arms and hold her, make love to her when that happens. "Done." One more kiss and I turn to join her cousins and my sister at their rowdy table.

"There he is," Brooks calls out. "Did she finally let you off of your leash?" he teases.

"Unfortunately." I laugh. I can take their ribbing all day long. I'm very aware that I'm gone over this woman, and I have zero fucks to give about it. I'd rather be sitting on that stool close to her than here at this table with them.

"Stop." Palmer pushes on Brooks's arm, and he laughs but doesn't say anything else.

"So, what's the plan?"

"We're thinking of driving to Harris and doing some ax throwing at the new indoor go-kart place, Karting Express. They have the karts, ax throwing, a bar, and an arcade."

"Sounds good."

"Don't you need to ask your girl?" Orrin teases.

"He doesn't," Ramsey says from beside me. She places her hand on my shoulder. "I already told him if he was in, so was I."

I turn to look at her. "Are you taking your break?"

"Yeah. I ordered us food. I can change it if you want, but I just got you a burger and fries."

"That's fine, babe. Thank you." I scoot back and tap my thigh. "Sit." She does as I ask, and I wrap my arms around her. Damn, this turned out better than us getting a table together to eat during her breaks.

"This looks like it's going well," Orrin says, nodding in our direction.

"It is," Ramsey answers. She turns to look at me over her shoulder, and I place a kiss on the corner of her mouth. "What are we doing tomorrow?" she asks me.

"Oh, we're going to Karting Express," Palmer answers for me. "They have ax throwing, and I've been dying to try it."

"Sounds fun."

"Who's riding with who?" Palmer asks.

"We're going on our own," I speak up.

"You can ride with us," Archer tells her.

"Don't think you boys can let me tag along so I'll be your designated driver," Palmer says.

"It's my turn." Rushton raises his hand.

"You really take turns?" Palmer asks.

"Yep. That's the best way to ensure we're all home safe."

"What happens when you all go?"

"Well, the twins are still too young, so there's never more than seven of us."

"And all seven of you pile in your pickups?" she asks.

"Nah, if all of us go, we take two, and there are two DDs."

"Well, fine, if you need me to do it, I will."

"You give in to them too easily," Ramsey tells her.

"I'd rather volunteer to do it than have to depend on these goons to get me home safely."

"Hello? Older brother here." I point to my chest. "I'm not drinking since I'm driving."

"Then you should just let me ride with you."

"Can't. Date-night rules," I tell her. I expect ribbing for the comment, but surprisingly the guys all remain quiet.

"Since your date night is with my bestie, I'll let that slide." Palmer winks at Ramsey, who I'm sure is smiling at my sister's antics.

"Hey, Ramsey, order up!" Tabitha yells from behind the bar.

"I'll be right back."

"You need help?" I ask.

"Yes. You can carry the drinks."

Standing, I follow her and grab our drinks while she grabs our basket of food. I take my seat and pull her onto my lap.

"You need both hands to eat."

"I'm just fine where I am." She shakes her head but doesn't argue as she begins to eat her food.

Her thirty-minute break goes by way too fast, and all too soon, she's leaving my lap to go back to work. "I'll come to see you before I leave."

"Okay." She bends down and hesitates for a brief second before following through, placing a gentle kiss on my lips.

"Don't be paying my tab either," I call after her.

She ignores me like I knew that she would. She's paid for my tab a few times, so I've just shoved money into her tip jar. I like knowing that I can take care of her.

I sit while everyone else eats, and when they head home, I give my sister a hug, telling her to text me when she gets home, and make my way back to the bar.

"Hey, are you heading out?" Ramsey asks.

"I thought I'd sit with you for a few more minutes. They monopolized my time."

"Deacon, go home. You've worked all day. And you have to be up early tomorrow."

"You're worth losing a few hours of sleep."

"What am I going to do with you?"

"Keep me?" I suggest, making her laugh.

"Kiss me and go home and get some rest."

Not needing to be told twice, I lean over the counter and kiss her. "Use that key, Rams," I whisper against her lips.

"Are you sure?"

"If I had it my way, you'd come home to me every night. Yes, I'm sure."

Her eyes soften. "Drive safe."

"I always do. You got my bill?" I ask her.

"It's already taken care of."

Pulling two twenties out of my wallet, I reach over the counter and shove them into the tip jar with her name on it. She tries to stop me, but I'm not having it. "That's too much."

"You're my girlfriend. It's the same as me keeping it in my wallet." I toss her a wink and head out the door.

It's just after eleven, and I'm awake in bed. I can't sleep because I can't stop thinking about Ramsey and wishing she were here with me. I also don't want to miss her text, telling me that she got home safely. I hate her working late hours. Sure, Willow River is a safe town, but there are all kinds of people in this world who do bad things. I can't help but worry.

I'm holding my phone, waiting to hear from her, when my bedroom door creeps open. I don't know how in the dark of the room, but I know it's her. "Ramsey?"

"I'm sorry if I woke you."

"You didn't. I was waiting for you. Is everything okay?"

"You said I could use my key, well, the key you gave me, and I missed you."

"Come to bed, baby."

"I really need to shower."

"You know where everything is." I hear her moving around the room and then her arm patting mine.

"It's so dark in here," she whispers as she leans over and finds my lips in the dark.

"I can turn on the light," I say after getting my kiss.

"No, it's fine. Try to go to sleep. I'll be quick."

I listen as she walks back around the bed and disappears into the bathroom, with a soft click of the door closing. The light comes on, and a few moments later, I hear the water turn on as well. I'm tempted to join her, but I'm exhausted, and I don't want her to think that I gave her that key so I could use her as a booty call. Not that we've gone that far yet. The past week, anytime we're together, my hands are all over her, and vice versa, but I have yet to feel her pussy wrapped around my cock. We're taking it slow, and that's okay. This is a marathon, not a sprint.

I want this to last.

I want us to last.

As she promised, her shower is quick. Not five minutes later, the light under the door disappears, and the sound of the door opening filters through the room. The covers lift and she slides in next to me, her bare, freshly showered skin against mine.

"You sleep naked?" she asks as she settles in next to me.

"Yes."

"Always? Or did you do this because I was here?"

"Not always, but I took a shower when I got home and just bypassed underwear."

She's quiet for several minutes. Her breathing evens out, and I'm sure she's fallen asleep at least until she asks, "Are you sure it's okay that I'm here?"

I tighten my arms around her. "It's more than okay. There is nothing better than you sleeping in my arms."

More silence. I close my eyes and start to drift when I hear her voice. "Deacon?"

"Hmm?"

"I never want this to end."

"Me neither, baby. Me neither." I kiss the top of her head, and together we let sleep take us.

Chapter Nineteen

RAMSEY

"How are you so good at this?" I ask Palmer.

She shrugs. "It's a natural talent." She follows up with a teasing wink.

"I feel sorry for your future husband," Deacon says. He's standing next to me with his arm casually thrown over my shoulder.

Palmer wags her eyebrows at him. "Damn right."

"You need another beer?" Deacon asks.

"No, I'm trying to pace myself." What I don't tell him is that I want more than just heavy petting from him tonight, and I know if he thinks that I'm the least bit drunk, he's going to shut me down. "A water would be good."

"You got it." He kisses my temple. "Palmer?"

"I'm good. Thanks." She holds up her half-empty water bottle. She waits until he's out of earshot before turning to me. "How's that going?"

"Good." I don't bother to hide my smile.

"Just good?"

"He's... everything, Palmer."

Her grin matches mine. "I'm happy for you. For both of you. I just wish you two stubborn asses would have let me fix you up with each other sooner."

I laugh. "I don't know that I would have been ready sooner. He might not have been either."

"But you are now?"

"Yes." It's been two months since the photo shoot, and I can honestly say it's been the happiest time of my life. Deacon is sexy and bossy, but not in a controlling kind of way. He's thoughtful and considerate, and I've fallen head over heels in love with him. I'm not sure when it happened, but it did. I almost told him last night, but I chickened out. It's not that I don't want him to know, but I don't know if he feels the same, and not hearing it back would crush my soul.

"You're in love with him." It's not a question. Palmer knows me better than anyone, well, other than Deacon.

Tears well in my eyes. Not because I don't want her to know, but because she's right, and this will be the first time I've been able to admit it out loud. "I am."

"You know that he loves you too, right?" she asks.

"I'm not sure, but he's good to me."

Palmer's eyes soften. "That's how a man is supposed to treat a woman, Rams." Now it's not just me who has tears in my eyes.

"What's wrong?" Deacon asks, handing me a bottle of water.

"Nothing." I offer him a watery smile.

"Then why the shimmering eyes, baby?" he asks softly.

"Just telling Palmer how blessed I feel to have you be a part of my life."

He swallows hard before his lips find mine. The kiss is soft, but it's still potent enough to have me wishing we could call it a night and head back to his place or mine. I'm not picky. "I'm the lucky one," he says, pulling out of the kiss.

"Palmer? Deacon? Hey. It's so good to see you." A woman, who appears to be a few years older than me, leans in and hugs Palmer and then

Deacon while his arm is still wrapped around me. She gives him a one-armed hug. "How have y'all been?" she asks.

"Good. It's been forever. How are you?" Palmer asks her.

"Doing good. I actually just moved back to town."

"You were living in Indiana, right?" Palmer asks.

"Yes. I moved there for college and got a job at the local hospital right out of school as a radiology tech. When a spot opened up in Harris, I jumped at the chance to apply. I got the job, so I moved home. Sorry, I'm rambling. How's Piper?"

"She's good. Still working at the elementary school. She teaches fourth grade."

"That's great. How about you?" the newcomer asks Palmer.

"I started my own photography business. I have a small studio in Willow River. Captured Moments." Palmer's smile is one of pride, as it should be.

"That's awesome." She turns toward Deacon. "The last time I talked to Piper, she told me you were an attorney."

"I am," Deacon replies. "I work in Willow River too at Patrick and Gordman."

She nods before turning her attention to me. "Hi, I'm Jade." She thrusts her hand to me.

"It's nice to meet you. I'm Ramsey."

"My girlfriend," Deacon adds.

"You going to let me beat your ass on the track?" Orrin asks, stepping up to our little group. He stops when he sees Jade. He stares at her for a few minutes. Something flashes in his eyes, but he quickly masks it and turns to his best friend. "You in?"

"Yeah. Babe, you want to race?" Deacon asks me.

"I think I'll sit this one out."

"You sure?"

"Positive." He leans in and kisses me before walking away with Orrin.

"Damn," Palmer mutters. "That was hot."

"Stop." I laugh at her.

"Oh, yeah, I mean, we all know Deacon is in love with you, but I was talking about Orrin. Did you see the fuck-me eyes he was giving you?" she asks Jade.

"He was not." Jade waves her off. I don't miss the tint to her cheeks. "How long have you and Deacon been together?" she asks me, clearly changing the subject.

"A couple of months."

"He seems smitten." Jade smiles.

"He's not the only one," I reply.

"Come on. Let's go watch these men pretend to be boys." Palmer links an arm through mine and Jade's and leads us to the viewing room for the go-kart track.

"That was fun. I'm glad we did it," I tell Deacon.

"I'm glad we went too. It was nice to see everyone." He leads me into the house from the garage, through the mudroom into the kitchen. "You want something to drink? Are you hungry?"

"I'm good. It was nice to have a weekend night off."

"I'm glad you talked to Hank, and he was able to make it happen."

"Me too. I've actually been thinking about my job and my degree a lot the last few weeks. Well, since you asked me if I could choose what I would do," I tell him, following him into the living room. He takes a seat on the couch and pulls me down onto his lap.

"What did you decide on?" he asks.

"I didn't get to choose my degree, but I did enjoy it. I'd like to think that if the choice was my own, I would have wanted to follow in my dad's footsteps."

"And now?" he asks, moving my hair back over my shoulder.

"I never want to be anything like him."

"I'm an attorney," he reminds me. "I'm nothing like that piece of shit." He has no remorse for calling my sperm donor a piece of shit, as he shouldn't.

"You're the exception to every rule, Deacon." I kiss his jaw, the scruff of his beard tickling my face. I can't help but wiggle in his lap when the memories surface of what it feels like to have that beard between my thighs.

"You good?" He smirks.

I don't know how, but he knows exactly what I was thinking about. "Just fine," I reply with a smile. "Anyway, I've been thinking, I might start looking for a paralegal job or something. I'm qualified, and I think I would enjoy it. I never wanted anything to do with that field, fearing all lawyers were like my dad and Robert, but you've proven that theory wrong."

"We're not all like them, but there are plenty more assholes that I'm sure you will encounter like them no matter what field you work in."

"I agree." I relax into him. "Tonight helped me make my decision. For the last two years, all I've done is work and save and battle my past. I never want to go back there, and once I was settled in my jobs, I got comfortable and never tried for more." I pause, thinking about how far to take this, and decide to give him my words that he's always asking for. "Being with you makes me want that normal life. Having dinner with you after a long day. Being able to go out with our friends on Friday or Saturday nights. I'd love to be able to go to my aunt Carol's Sunday dinners. It's open, and whoever can make it that week shows up. I've never been. It's always at five that evening, and well, I'm at work by then."

"You do have a shitty schedule," Deacon agrees.

"Right?" I laugh. "You've never given me a hard time about it. Why?"

"Because as bad as I hate you working there, as much as I hate the hours, I refuse to be another man in your life that takes your choice away. Unless it's the choice of me paying for dinner." He winks.

"You hate me working at the Tavern?"

"Yes. I hate that you're there late at night, driving home late, coming home to an empty house late. Any drunk fool could follow you. I hate that men hit on you every fucking night that you're there."

"I wish you would have said something."

"It's your decision, Ramsey. I hate that too. I've had to bite my tongue many times, wanting to tell you to just ditch the job at the Tavern. You could move in with me, and I could take care of you." I open my mouth to argue, but he puts his hand over my mouth to stop me. "However, I know that's not what you want. I know you don't want to be dependent on someone else ever again. That's something else I'm working on. One of these days, you're going to trust that I will always stand beside you, behind you, and in front of you when you'll let me."

"All three, huh?" I ask, fighting back the tears. I don't know what I did to have this man come into my life, but I will forever be grateful.

"Beside you because I want to be your partner in life." He kisses my left cheek. "Behind you because you don't need me to speak for you. You need my support, and you will always have it." He kisses my right cheek. "In front of you because I want to protect you. I know you don't need it, but I want to do it all the same." He kisses my lips softly.

I move to straddle his hips so that we're facing each other. I place my hands on either side of his face and stare into his golden eyes. I've been fighting my tears, but I lose as one slides over my cheek. I open my mouth to speak but close my mouth just as fast.

"Never with me, Ramsey. Give me your words, baby."

It's time. No matter if he feels the same or not, my heart is screaming for me to tell him. "I love you." My voice is strong. "You are everything I ever dreamed of in a partner, in a man, and I-I love you so much, Deacon," I say. My heart is racing, and my hands are clammy as they rest against his cheeks.

One hand grips my hip while the other slides behind my neck. "Say it again," he demands huskily.

"I love you."

"Ramsey," he breathes. I watch as he swallows hard, and his eyes become glassy. "I love you too. I've wanted to tell you, but I didn't want to scare you away."

"We're a pair, huh?" I chuckle as relief washes over me. Deacon Setty loves me!

"I think we're the perfect pair," he says, kissing me deeply. My heart trips over in my chest from happiness. There are a million butterflies in my belly, and this moment is one I will never in my entire life ever forget. He pulls back and leans against the couch. "Before I get so far into your kisses that I can't think right, let's get back to your job. You know I work at a law firm, right?"

"Ha ha, funny man. Yes, I'm aware."

"The partners have been tossing around hiring a paralegal. They're slowing down and giving me more of the work. They're not ready to hire another attorney. In fact, I think they'll offer to sell to me before they do that, so the hiring will be my decision since I'm the one who will be dealing with the new hire."

"Thank you. I appreciate that. However, I don't want to get the job because I'm your girlfriend."

"What about as the woman I love?" He bats his eyelashes at me.

"That either." I laugh. "I want to know I can make it on my own. I know that sounds crazy, but that's one of the big things my father used to tell me. That I was nothing without him and that I would never make it in the world without his connections or his money."

Deacon's jaw twitches. "He's a piece of shit."

"I know, but I still need to do this. I want to do this. You've given me the courage and the motivation to take the risk. I've been living to work. Just saving every dime, but I have an education, and I think I would enjoy the work."

"If you don't, you can go back to college or find a new career. You can do anything you put your mind to."

"I always wanted more, but now that I have you, and you've been helping me express what I want, I know working at the Tavern forever is not my end game. I want a career. One day when I have children, I want to be home with them at night. I want family dinners where they tell me about their day. I don't want to miss a game or a practice or a school function. I want my kids to have the opposite of what I had. Don't get me wrong. I never wanted for anything, well, except for my parents' love and attention."

"Our kids will always know how much we love them. I promise you that."

"*Our* kids?" This is the second time he's said something like this.

"You did hear the part where we told each other that we were in love, right?"

"Yes, but kids, that's a big deal."

"We're a big deal, baby."

Those damn butterflies swarm, and I feel light-headed from how happy he makes me. The future kids he just mentioned, I can see them. I can see our life playing out like a movie reel in my head. "Yeah, I guess we are," I say, kissing him. "Thank you for the offer. I promise that if I need help or guidance, and I'm sure that I will, I will come to you."

"Or you could come for me right here," he says, sliding his hand under my shirt.

"That works too." I shiver as his thumb glides across my bra-covered nipple.

"This fucking bra is so thin. Let me see."

I raise my arms in the air and allow him to lift my shirt over my head. He licks his lips, and his grip on my hip tightens. "Like what you see?" I tease.

"Love, Ramsey. I love what I see." His head dips, and through my white lace bra, he sucks a hard nipple into his mouth, causing me to moan.

"Are you ready for bed?" he asks.

"I'm ready to go to bed. I'm not ready to go to sleep."

"No? You want to play?"

"Sure, but I also want you to make love to me."

He freezes, and I'm afraid I've pushed too far until a slow sexy smile tilts his lips.

"Anything my girl wants, she gets." He nips at my bottom lip. "I'm going to lock up down here. I'll meet you in my room."

"Okay." I move to climb off his lap, bending over to pick up my discarded shirt from the floor, and he smacks my ass. "Hey!" I pretend to be offended.

"It was right there in front of me." He shrugs.

"You're lucky I love you." I point my index finger at him.

He captures my hand and presses a kiss on my palm. "I know. Now, head upstairs before I strip you naked and fuck you here on my couch. You asked me to make love to you, and that's what I'm going to do."

I squeeze my thighs together at his words. "Your option works too."

He laughs, a deep throaty laugh. "I promise I will. Not tonight. Now go." He stands, bends, and kisses me. "Love you."

"I love you too." With my shirt in my hand, I take off for the stairs. I'm nervous and notice a slight tremble in my hands as I strip down for him, but I'm not scared. This is Deacon, and he'll take care of me. He always does.

Chapter Twenty

DEACON

Walking into the kitchen, I turn off the lights and make my way upstairs. Instead of taking the stairs two at a time like I want, I take slow, measured steps. Tonight is the night I make Ramsey mine in every way. When I push inside her, all bets are off. It doesn't matter who has an issue with us dating, whether it's family members or the world, because of our age difference. The reasons will no longer matter.

She's mine.

There is no turning back.

Ramsey's my future.

Now, I need to make sure she understands that before we take this any further. I've never told a woman I'm not related to that I love them, and if I have my way, Ramsey will be the first and the last. Pushing open my bedroom door, I halt when I see the low glow of the bedside lamp and my girl sitting on my bed.

Naked.

Waiting for me.

I'm just standing here, staring at her, taking in the fact that this beautiful woman loves me, and it hits me. This is not a one-time thing. I can have her like this for the rest of my life.

She reaches for the comforter to cover up, which spurs me into action. In a few long strides, I'm standing beside her. Reaching behind my neck, I grab my T-shirt and pull it over my head. Next I go for the button on my jeans, sliding them and my boxer briefs over my hips in one swift movement. My cock is hard and ready for her, but before we go there, I need to make sure she understands. We're both naked and on a level playing field, so to speak.

Dropping to my knees, I circle my arms around her hips. With our height difference, we're looking eye to eye, which is what I wanted. As much as I love her eyes on my cock, I need her eyes on mine for this conversation.

I pull her to the edge of the bed, feeling her soft skin against mine, where I'm nestled between her thighs. My hands lock behind the small of her back, holding her close. "You asked me to make love to you."

"It's okay if you've changed your mind." She pushes my hair back out of my eyes. Her past fears are not completely gone, but that's okay. We'll get there.

"That's… No, Ramsey. I haven't changed my mind. But I'm giving you the option to change yours."

She tilts her head to the side. "I don't understand."

"I've never told a woman that I love her. Aside from my family. That's a big fucking deal to me, and I mean it. You've burrowed your way into my heart, and I want you to stay there. Forever."

"I love you too." Her voice is soft, and her body relaxes at my confession.

"This is forever, Ramsey. I can't make love to you and then let you go. I know me. I know how I feel about you, and I know that I won't survive it. If there is any doubt in your mind, we can wait." She shakes her head, but I keep going. "I know there will be people who disapprove of our age difference, but all I see is the woman I love. I don't see age beyond who you are."

"That doesn't matter to me."

"I know this has been a fast-moving train, our relationship, and I wouldn't change a single thing. I think you were right when you said that we hadn't met before the photo shoot because maybe we weren't ready. I'm ready now. I'm all in. There is only Deacon and Ramsey as a unit from here on out. I want to make sure you know that I'm yours and that you're mine. I need to know that you feel confident in the love that we share and that you know you can always count on me. I want you to always speak your mind and use your words. I'll never silence you."

Tears shimmer in her eyes. "Thank you for loving me the way that you do."

"Never thank me for loving you, baby. It's as easy as breathing for me."

"You make me stronger. You're not afraid to call me out, and you won't let me hide behind my insecurities. I love you. The forever kind of love, Deacon."

That's all I need to hear. My lips find hers, and nerves bubble to life in my chest. I've had sex, I'm not a monk, but I've never made love. Yeah, I'm aware it's the same thing. At least, I used to think it was the same thing. Now I know better. I'm more nervous now than I was my first time. Losing my virginity was nothing compared to knowing that this woman is the last I'll ever be inside of. This is my last first time.

My Ramsey.

Her hands are buried in my hair, and her legs are wrapped around me. My hands are everywhere. Her hair, her breasts, sliding down her back. It's as if my hands are on a mission to touch every inch of her soft silky skin.

It takes effort to tear my lips from hers. We're both breathing heavily, and my heart is beating against my chest. I'm fearful I could break a rib. "Slide back, baby." She moves back and rests her head on my pillow. Standing to my full height, I grip my cock and stroke it lazily. Her eyes follow my every move.

"I need to get you ready," I tell her, reading her expression. "I don't want to hurt you." She nods, and that's my green light. Reaching into the nightstand, I grab the new box of condoms I bought a couple of weeks ago when our make-out sessions started to get hotter.

Tearing open the box, I pull out a strip and drop them next to her on the bed. I toss the box back in the drawer and then join her. On my knees, I settle beside her, just taking her in. She smiles up at me, and I notice the change in her. My girl is more confident, and I want to beat my fists against my chest. My love did that for her.

"What are you smiling at?" she asks, her voice soft.

"You're beautiful and all mine."

"Show me." Her legs fall open, and her pussy glistens for me.

Moving between her thighs, I lie on my belly and do as my girl asks, and I show her. I love her with my mouth, sucking her clit until she's writhing beneath me. I add one finger and then another, working her, getting her ready for me. She grips my hair, and it's as if that action is attached to my mouth. I tongue her clit, sucking harder, and she screams, calling out my name. Her pussy squeezes my fingers, and I don't stop until her body falls relaxed back to the bed.

Wiping my mouth with the back of my hand, I move over her. My hands are braced on both sides of her head. I'm holding my weight off her, giving her time to catch her breath, and I don't want to crush her.

Finally her eyes flutter open. "Hi," she whispers shyly.

"Hi." I grin. I love the fact that I can put her in this blissed-out state. "You good?"

"I'm great." She reaches between us and grips my cock. "Let me help you with this," she says, her voice dropping to a sexy rasp.

"No can do, baby. You asked me to make love to you, and that's going to be a struggle as it is. If you put your mouth on me now, this is all going to be over before it starts."

"I want more of you."

"You have all of me."

"Show me." Moving her hand from my cock, she reaches for the strip of condoms, tearing off a small foil pack and handing it to me. There's a slight tremble in her hands. Holding my weight with one arm, I take her hand and press a kiss on her palm.

"At any time you want to stop this, just tell me. I don't care when. If you want to stop, we stop."

"But won't that… hurt?"

"Not near as much as the thought of hurting you will."

"You won't hurt me." Her words are strong and confident, and I have one of those chest-beating moments again. My girl is using her voice. "I don't have to worry about that with you."

"Never with me," I confirm.

Sitting back on my knees, I tear open the wrapper and slide it over my aching cock. I'm hard as stone, and I'm a big guy, so I hope I've done enough to prep her. The thought of hurting her in any way causes my chest to ache. I never want to be the man who causes her fear, pain, or tears. I just want to love her. I never knew this sappy lovesick side of me existed. In fact, I'm certain it didn't until Ramsey walked into my life.

Ramsey bites down on her bottom lip as I grip my cock, and lean forward, sliding it over her wet pussy. Moving, I brace my hands on either side of her head while my cock weeps, begging to be inside her. I ignore him and his needs and focus on Ramsey. "All you have to do is tell me to stop."

"I won't."

"But tell me that you know that you can."

Her hands land on my cheeks. Her big blue eyes tell me she's speaking her truth. "I know that if I want to stop, you will stop. I know that you love me and that you would never hurt me. I know that this means that I'm yours, and you're mine. The forever kind of love. What I don't know is why we're still talking about it."

"So sassy." I bend my head and kiss her. "I love you."

"I love you too."

"Guide me inside, baby." I'm taking this slow. Not because I'm afraid of hurting her, but because every man in her life before me took from her. She was never allowed to choose before, and I want her to know she will always have a choice with me. Sure, I want to push inside and fuck her, chasing my release I've been craving since the moment I laid eyes on her, but I'm not going to do that. I'm a man who can show restraint when needed, and for the first time we have sex, it's needed.

There's a slight tremble in her hands as she grips me, reminding me again that this is more than just sex. This act is sealing our fate. It's as if she, too, is realizing this is her last first time as well.

Carefully, she guides me to her entrance, and I push in. She tenses, and that won't do. Lowering myself, careful of my weight not to crush her, I kiss her. Slowly, my tongue slides against hers until I feel her relax. I push in a little further and pause, giving her the time she needs. I kiss her and then give her a little more. Not just of my cock, but me.

"Almost there, baby," I mumble against her lips.

"I want all of you, Deac. Please," she pants. "Give me all of you."

With her words, I push all the way in, and she cries out. Only this cry, it's not of pleasure, it's of pain. I freeze and stare down at her. She's biting on her bottom lip, and a tear rolls down her cheek.

My tongue is thick. I can barely form words. I open my mouth to speak, but it's not happening. Slowly, I pull back and look between us. That's when I see her truth. The one she didn't use her words to tell me.

I take a deep breath, slowly exhale, and find my voice. "Baby, why is there blood on my cock?" She turns her head, not willing to look at me, but that's not going to work. Bracing my weight on one elbow, I move to cradle her face in my palm, and she flinches. "Hey," I say softly. "Ramsey, look at me." I wait until I have her full attention. "I'm going to need your words, sweetheart."

She nods.

"Tell me." It's still demanding but not as harsh as before. She shakes her head, and again I'm not taking no for an answer. Not with her words. "There is no wrong answer here, Ramsey. I just need to hear your words, baby. I need you to tell me."

"I-I wanted it to be you."

Fuck. Six words wrap themselves around my heart like a vise. I don't know what's happening to me. It's almost as if my heart physically leaves my chest and jumps into hers. The love I have for her is greater than anything I've ever felt in my life. Why is it that knowing she gave this to me, that she got to choose this, and it was me she chose, makes my eyes water? How did I not know she was a virgin?

What is it about her that has my heart dancing in my chest to a beat that can only be heard by her?

"Are you mad?"

I'm shaking my head before she's even finished asking. "No. I'm not mad. I'm honored. I'm humbled and ecstatic that he didn't take that from you. You chose me, and my heart feels like it's going to explode."

She smiles, wiping at her tears. "Can you maybe ask your heart to wait until we're done?" She lifts her hips, and I slide inside smoothly this time.

My lips find hers as I pull out and push back in. Leaning down on my elbows, I clasp my hands on top of her head as my hips slowly rock into hers. Just moments ago, I was racing to chase the high of my orgasm, and I still want that, but right now I want this moment more. This is her first time, and fuck me, I'm going to make it special for her. I'm going to be gentle with her and show her how much she means to me. We have the rest of our lives to have dirty, sweaty fucking. Right now, I'm doing exactly as she asked.

I'm making love to her.

Her request makes even more sense to me now. I don't know why we never had the conversation. She didn't bring it up, and neither did I. She said he never forced himself on her, and we left it at that. I didn't like thinking about the two of them together like this. Turns out, I didn't have to.

I'm the only man to ever be inside of her.

I roll my hips, and she moans. "Do that again," she instructs, and I give her what she wants. Her pussy begins to tighten around me, and I know she's close. I'm there, ready to fly over the edge, so I reach between us and circle her clit with my thumb. Her nails dig into my arms, where she's holding on. Her eyes close, and I want to demand that she opens them so I can see her, but I don't. I let her have this moment.

I memorize her every feature, and when her pussy grips me and she calls out my name, her eyes pop open. Liquid blue fire stares back at me as I still and release inside her.

She smiles softly. "I love you, Deacon."

"I love you too." I kiss her, sliding my tongue against hers once more, before slowly pulling out. "Don't move." I rush to the bathroom. Tossing the condom into the trash, I grab a towel from the shelf and clean up, then collect a washcloth for her. I run it under the warm water before rushing back to the bed. "Open for me," I instruct, sitting next to her.

"What are you doing?"

"Taking care of you. Open." I tap her knee.

"You don't have to do that. It's… messy. I can do it."

"I love every part of you, even the messy parts. Especially the messy parts I helped make. Let me take care of you, baby." My words work. She opens her leg just enough for me to clean her up. Satisfied that she's as good as can be without a shower, I toss the washcloth through the bathroom door. It hits the floor with a slap, but I don't care. I'll get it later. Right now, nothing is more important than holding her.

Sliding under the covers next to her, I pull her into my arms. She rests her head against my chest, and my heart calms, and our breathing evens out. This is the most content I've ever been.

"Is it always like that?" she asks.

"No. That's something that's only us. You were made for me."

"When can we do that again?" she asks, making me laugh.

"You're going to be sore. We have forever."

"Forever," she agrees.

Chapter Twenty-One

RAMSEY

"I REALLY NEED TO GO TO MY PLACE AND DO SOME LAUNDRY," I tell Deacon. We're sitting on his couch, curled up under a blanket to ward off the chill of the air conditioning. It's also a comfort thing for me. I like to be cuddled with my man and a soft fuzzy blanket. It's been a month since we had sex for the first time, and I never feel like I can be close enough to him. I don't understand it, but Deacon doesn't seem to mind me clinging to him when we're just hanging out, so I don't let it get to me either.

"We can go pick it up, and you can wash it here."

"But then I have to pack it back to my place."

"Just leave it here."

"So, I'll come over here and get dressed every day after my shower?" I laugh.

"No. If your things are here, then you will be too."

I sit up and turn to look at him. "What are you saying? Use your words," I tease, which earns me a playful poke in my side.

"I have no problem using my words. I want to be where you are. We have more space here, and I know you love the pool, but I can pack some things, and we can spend the week at your place."

"The week?"

"The week. The month. Forever." He shrugs.

"Deacon Setty, are you asking me to move in with you?" I wait for the panic to set in or the fear of not owning my own place, but it never comes.

"What would you say if I did?"

"I'd probably tell you that three months of dating isn't long enough." I pause. He starts to speak, but I talk over him. "Then I'd think about how I feel when I'm with you. I'd think about the love that we share, and I'd think about you telling me that there is no one that matters but us."

"And?"

"And I'd ask you what we're going to do with all of my furniture."

This time it's Deacon who moves to sit up. "Move in with me."

I open my mouth to agree. The decision is easy. I love him. He loves me. We've already promised to be each other's forever. I've spent more time here than at my place in the last month. I'm wasting money on rent. However, before I can give him an answer, he starts to plead his case.

"You're here all the time. I love sleeping next to you. I know we don't get to eat dinner together often, but when you change careers, that's going to change. You could save money on rent, and I have that extra hers closet in my room that has just a measly few hangers of things you leave here. It's being underused. That's a travesty. You moving in would fix that." He grins, proud of himself.

He opens his mouth to start again, but I place my fingers to his lips to stop him. "Okay."

"Okay?" There's a sparkle in his golden eyes that has butterflies taking flight in my belly. Will it always feel like this? Like I'm floating on a cloud of love. I'm happy. So happy, and for the first time in my life, I know true, honest love and happiness. All thanks to the man sitting next to me.

"You promised me forever, Deacon Setty. I plan to hold you to that."

"Done." He kisses me hard but quickly pulls away. "When? When can we make this happen?"

I shrug. "Whenever."

He leans forward and snags his phone off the table. He taps the screen before holding it out in front of him. It rings three times before a deep voice that I recognize answers.

"What's up?" Orrin asks.

"What are you doing today?"

"Nothing. I have adult shit to do like laundry, but I'm thinking about pushing that off until tomorrow."

"Good. I need your help. And your brothers'. As many of them that you can find that are free."

"What for?"

"Well, it's Ramsey who needs help, actually."

"What happened?" Orrin is instantly on alert, and my heart swells.

"She's fine. She's perfect." Deacon leans over and kisses me.

"Are you kissing her?" Orrin asks. "Can you not hold that shit until we hang up? Now, get your paws off my baby cousin and tell me what she needs."

"She's moving in with me, and we need manpower."

"Today?"

"Yes. Today. Before she changes her mind."

"I'm not going to change my mind," I speak up.

"Rams?" Orrin asks.

"I'm here. He has you on speaker," I explain.

"You sure you want to move in with this guy?" There's humor in his voice. "I could tell you some stories..." He lets his voice trail off.

"Nothing you could tell me would make me change my mind."

"Fair enough. When are we doing this?"

"We're heading to her apartment now."

"I haven't even packed anything yet."

"Bring boxes," Deacon adds.

Orrin laughs. "Congratulations, guys. I'll gather my brothers, and we'll head over to you in a couple of hours. Rams, will that give you time to start packing?"

"It really doesn't have to be done today. How about we play it by ear? I'm going to pack and purge some of my things and decide what to keep and what to donate. Then, when that's done, I would love it if you and some of the boys would help us."

"Can I tell them that you called them boys?" Orrin begs, the humor evident in his tone.

"Not until after they help me," I reply with a laugh of my own.

"All right. You do you, Rams, and let me know when you're ready."

"Thank you. In the meantime, I'll be staying here. So if you need me for any reason, if I'm not at work, I'll be… home. With Deacon."

"Damn right you will. We'll call you," Deacon says, ending the call and pushing me back on the couch. He kisses me like today is our last day together. His phone rings, and he groans. Pulling back, he glances at the screen and shows it to me before answering, again placing it on speaker. "What?"

"What are you two getting into tonight? You hanging out while Rams works?" Orrin asks.

"No. She's off tonight."

"Isn't there a band at the Tavern? I was thinking about rounding up a few of my brothers and going to check It out. You two should come."

"We'll discuss it and let you know. I'm sure Ramsey doesn't want to hang out at her place of employment on her only night off."

"Actually, I heard the band is supposed to be good. We should go."

"You sure?"

"Positive."

"Fine. We'll be there. Seven."

"Seven," Orrin agrees, and the call ends.

"Now, let's go to your place and grab what we can. Clothes, toiletries, and whatever else we can pack before you change your mind." Deacon stands and offers me his hand to help me off the couch.

"I'm not going to change my mind."

He nods. "I'm still not taking any chances with you. Come on. We'll take the truck."

"I need to get my phone and my purse, and I don't have shoes on."

"Hurry up, woman! It's not every day the love of my life agrees to move in with me."

"I need to call Palmer too."

"What? Why do you have to call my sister?"

"To give her the news. I don't want her hearing it from someone else, and I want to invite her to the Tavern tonight."

"We can call her on the way." He grabs my purse from the counter and points to my flip-flops that are by the door in the mudroom.

With a laugh, I follow him, only stopping to slide my feet into my flip-flops before following him out to the garage and to his truck.

"Good thing we have three bays, huh?" He smiles as he passes my car. He insisted that I park there. He cleaned out the space a couple of weeks ago, moving the lawnmower, and I don't know what else to a small shed he bought for that purpose out back.

I just smile at him and wait for him to open my door, knowing that he'll complain if I don't. Once the door is shut, I pull out my phone to call Palmer. I talk to her all the way to my apartment. She's thrilled that I'm moving in with Deacon, just like I knew that she would be.

"We're here," I tell her. "I'll see you tonight at seven. Do you need us to pick you up?"

"Nah, I'm all set. I have a shoot on Sunday, so I won't be drinking. Nothing like being hungover when you're shooting a third birthday party full of screaming kids."

"Yikes. Okay, well, I love you. I'll see you later."

"Tell my brother he makes me proud," she teases.

"Will do." I end the call and slide my phone into my purse. "Palmer is meeting us there, and she told me to tell you that you make her proud."

"She's going to remind us that she got us together until we're old and gray, isn't she?"

"Yes. Yes, she is."

"You really moving in with this guy?" Sterling points to where Deacon is sitting next to me.

"It's too late to back out now. We spent the day packing up the majority of my clothes and toiletries and moving them into his place."

"I admit, I didn't think I would see the day," Brooks confesses.

"You and me both. This one," Orrin points to Deacon, "worked so much I thought he was going to die a lonely old man."

"I was just waiting for the right one to come along."

"Ugh," Declan groans. "Now you've got him waxing all kinds of poetic shit. Ramsey, you broke him. You broke Deacon." The table erupts in laughter, including Deacon. His arm is slung over the back of my chair, and I can feel him shaking.

"Oh, there's Jade. Let's go say hi." Palmer stands and motions for me to follow after her.

"You want anything?" I ask Deacon.

"Nah, I'm good."

"You sure?"

"You already gave me what I wanted today." His eyes are soft, but my cousins can't see that. I know he's referring to me moving in with him, but to those not looking at him, the statement can sound suggestive.

"My ears." Archer places his hands over his ears, and again the table laughs at my man's expense.

"Oh, I gave him that too," I tell my cousins. "But what my boyfriend was referring to was me agreeing to move in with him."

"Isn't Palmer waiting on you?" Rushton asks.

"Fine, I can take the hint. Can I get any of you anything while I'm at the bar?" I offer.

"No. It's your night off. If they need something, they can get it themselves," Deacon speaks up.

"What he said." Orrin points at me. "Go, we're good here."

I make a production of standing and bending over to kiss Deacon.

My cousins grumble and groan about the kiss. When I pull back, we're both smiling. "I'll be back," I say softly, just for him.

When I reach the bar where Palmer is sitting, she waves her hand in front of her face. "Okay, so I know he's my brother, but damn, girl, way to put it on him." She chuckles.

"That was hot," Jade agrees.

"They were giving us a hard time, so I thought I would give them something to talk about." I shrug.

"Who are you and what have you done with my best friend?" Palmer asks.

"I'm still me. I just fell in love with an incredible man."

"Where do I get me one of those?" Jade asks.

"Right?" Palmer agrees.

"Ladies, I have a table full of single cousins for you to choose from. They're all great guys who welcomed me as if I were their sister. You'd be lucky to have any of them."

"They're all single?" Jade asks, glancing over her shoulder at the table.

"Yep."

"Which one are you looking at?" Palmer turns to look at our table.

"All of them." Jade grins.

"What about you?" I bump my shoulder into Palmer's. "Which one are you looking at?"

"All of them," she parrots Jade's earlier reply.

"Your sister's missing out. I called her to try and get her to come out tonight, but she already had a date."

Palmer sighs. "She's on this dating app and they're all losers."

"I need three drafts," Hannah, one of the servers, calls out from her spot next to me. "This is for your table," she tells me. "How do you handle being related to all of that hotness?"

"Um, did you not see her man? She's living with hotness," Jade replies. "Sorry, Ramsey, you know he's hot," she adds.

"He's very handsome." I smile at her. I'm not worried about her hitting on him. Sure, she might be closer to his age, but I know what we have, and I'm confident in that. It feels really damn good to know that what we have is solid and that others can look, but I'm the one snuggled up to him in bed each night.

"He's also ass over heels in love with you. Sorry, ladies, my brother is off the market," Palmer adds. She winks at me, and I smile. I appreciate her backing me up, but truly, I don't need it. Not with Deacon. It's taken me some time to get here, but I know without a shadow of a doubt he's one of the good ones.

"Here you go." Tabitha places three draft beers onto Hannah's tray, and she's off. "Ramsey, girl, what are you doing here on your night off?" she asks.

"Oh, you know, just hanging out," I reply. "We came to hear the band. It sucks that they had to cancel."

"Yeah, Hank was worried what it would do for the crowd, but everyone seems to be sticking around."

Before I can respond, I feel strong hands grip my hips. I know it's him without even looking. "I'm going to the restroom. Stay together or where the guys can see you." Deacon kisses my cheek. "Love you," he whispers, but not really judging by the awws coming from my friends.

"You two are serious, huh?" Tabitha asks as Deacon walks away.

"I'll say since she agreed to move in with him today."

"Wow. That's a big step," Tabitha comments.

"Do you blame her?" Jade asks.

"If any of the men at that table asked me to move in with them, I'd be all over it," Palmer states.

"Come on. You have to tell me which one you have your eye on. I can hook you up," I tell them.

"Oh, or let me do a photo shoot." Palmer claps her hands together. "Ask Ramsey… it works like a charm."

"That's how you met Deacon?" Jade asks.

"Yeah. This one," I point to Palmer, "convinced me she needed my help to boost her career. Little did I know she was setting me up the entire time."

"Hey, the photo shoot was gold. Pure gold. And I have gained some clients from it," she boasts. "Admit it. This will be a great story to tell your grandkids one day."

"And I'm sure you're going to be right there telling them that it was all your idea and that you're responsible for their existence." I laugh.

"Damn right."

"Six bottles," Hannah says, slapping her tray down. "My feet are already killing me."

"Coming up," Tabitha tells her. "Hey, Ramsey," she starts, but Deacon is back, sliding up behind me and wrapping his arms around my waist. "Never mind." She waves it off.

"What is it?" I ask her.

"Nothing. I was going to tell you how lucky you are. Go have fun. I'll catch up with you."

"Are you sure?"

"Yeah, we're on shift together next Sunday. You can tell me all about this new adventure with your man then."

"Okay. Then we can talk about finding you a man." Tabitha isn't someone I hang out with or even talk to outside of work, but she's a good coworker, and I blame myself for us not being close. I've had my walls up for far too long.

"You coming back to the table?" Deacon asks.

"Yes." I turn to look at him, and he presses his lips to mine. He releases me, laces our fingers together, and leads me back to the table. I hear Palmer and Jade talking about how sweet he is before we get out of earshot. I smile all the way to the table and for the rest of the night. Time with friends and Deacon is something I want more of. It's definitely time to focus on changing my career.

Chapter Twenty-Two

DEACON

It's Wednesday afternoon, and I'm buried deep into this deposition. My stomach growls, reminding me that I walked out of the house this morning and left my lunch on the counter. I can't even be mad at myself because the reason I forgot it was because I was kissing Ramsey one last time before leaving for the office.

It was worth it.

I need to take a break and go grab something, but then I can also work through and get home to her sooner, which sounds like a much better idea. I look up at the sound of a knock at my door. To my surprise, Ramsey is standing there holding my lunch.

"Hey. Come in." I stand and go to her. I bend to kiss her lips before taking the offered bag.

"I thought you might be getting hungry." She smiles.

"For you," I say, bending to kiss her again.

"Oh," comes a deep voice that I recognize as my boss Daniel Patrick. "I didn't mean to interrupt."

"Not at all. Daniel, this is my girlfriend, Ramsey. Ramsey, this is one of the partners, Daniel Patrick."

"It's nice to meet you." My girl offers him her hand politely, and he takes it, his eyes coming to mine.

"This is the Ramsey you've been talking about?"

"The one and only," I state proudly.

"That's actually what I was coming to talk to you about."

"Okay?"

"Spencer and I decided it's time to bring on more help. This is going to sound bad, but you were pulling so much of the weight around here, now that you've gone to somewhat normal hours, we're feeling the workload."

I start to apologize, but I keep my mouth closed. He's right. I've been working insane hours since the day they hired me, and I was okay with that until I met the love of my life. Now I need those hours for her. For us.

"With that said, we talked about what we needed. We tossed around another attorney, but we're both gearing for retirement, and hopefully, you'll be interested in taking this place off our hands at that point. We figured you could decide who that person is."

"Thank you, sir. I would be honored to take over the practice."

He nods and continues, "So, we decided a paralegal or legal assistant is what we're looking for. Someone who knows the field and can help with the research and screening clients. Those types of things." He turns to Ramsey. "Deacon tells me you have a poli-sci degree."

"Y-Yes, I do." She looks at me with wide eyes and back to Daniel.

"Whatever firm you're currently working for, we'll match it and hopefully do a little better."

"What?" she asks, confused.

"I want you to come work for Patrick and Gordman. This guy," he points at me, "sings your praises every day. I just figured he'd enjoy working with you, and we need the help. I assume you need to give your current firm two weeks?" he asks.

"Mr. Patrick, I'm not currently working at a firm. I work at the Willow Tavern full time, and I have two other part-time jobs just as I'm needed."

"Work here and only have one job. Do you think you can handle being with this one all day?" he asks, his belly shaking.

Ramsey turns to look at me. "Did you know about this?"

"No. You're hearing about it for the first time, just like I am."

"That's my mistake. I assumed you were using your degree. We really could use someone with your education. Willow River is a small town, and not many have your credentials, and want small-town living." He walks to my desk, grabs a Post-it and a pen, and writes something on it, handing it to Ramsey. "This is our initial offer. Forty hours per week. Take a few days to think it over, talk about it with Deacon, and get back to me." With that, he waves and walks back out the door.

"Did that just happen?" she asks.

"It did. What did he write on the paper?" I slide my arm around her waist and press my lips to her temple.

"I'm afraid to look."

"You don't have to. You can toss it in the trash and tell him thanks but no thanks. I won't be upset with you either way."

"Do you think we could work together?"

"Yes."

"Won't you get sick of me?"

"Never."

She nods. "I want to at least see what it says."

"That sounds like a solid plan. Weigh all your options." She bites down on her bottom lip, and the nervous energy rolls off her in waves. Releasing her, I walk to my office door and close it. I guide her to one of the two guest chairs and sit, pulling her onto my lap. "I'm right here, Ramsey."

She laughs softly. "I'm not scared. Well, I guess maybe I am."

"I know change is hard after the security that you've built for yourself. You've been wanting to do this. Just see what they're offering, and you can start your decision-making process from there."

Slowly she opens the folded Post-it note and instantly gasps. "That's more than double what I make now. At all three jobs."

"That's a good thing, right?"

"That's a very good thing. But can I do it? Can I do the job?"

"Yes. I know you can. Sure, there will be things that you have to learn, but that's any career. College doesn't prepare you for using what you've learned. Every job has a learning curve." She's quiet, and I don't push her. Instead, I wrap my arms around her and hold her close. Regardless of what she chooses, she has great things ahead of her. We both do. Together.

"Will you help me? I mean, I know that's a lot to ask with your current workload, but will you?" She turns to look at me.

"You know I will."

"And you had nothing to do with this?"

"I promise you I didn't know. You found out when I did. I am guilty of talking about the woman I love too much, but that's never going to change. I'm so proud to call you mine."

Her eyes soften. "I want to do it, Deacon. I want to take the job. I want a normal life with working hours like yours. I know there might be big cases and late nights for you, but not bar closing hours and every weekend. I want to be able to have Sunday dinners at my aunt and uncle's. I want to have dinner with you every night. I just… I want more than what I have. I've done well these past two years, but I'm not standing on my own anymore. I have someone to stand beside me, behind me, and in front of me. I have you, and I want this for us. I want it for me too, but I want it even more for us. I'd get to use my degree."

"Let's go tell him, and I'll take you to lunch to celebrate."

"Really?"

"Yes." I tap her thigh, and she stands. I lead her to my office door and pull it open. "His office is the last on the left. Do you want me to go with you?"

"No." She stands a little taller. "I can do this." She kisses my cheek and takes off down the hall.

"I'll get this put in for you," our waitress says as she walks away.

We settled on Dorothy's Diner for lunch. It's just around the corner from my office. "How are you feeling about your decision?" I ask Ramsey. Her beaming smile already tells me how she's feeling, but I still encourage her to tell me with her words.

"I feel excited and nervous and like it's my first adult job, even though I know that's not true. I love my jobs, all three of them, but none of them have ever excited me like this. I hope Hank isn't upset with me."

"I'm sure he's going to miss you. You've been working your ass off for him. But he's a good guy, and I don't know any employer who will ever give someone a hard time for bettering themselves or their lives as long as it's done with notice and respect."

"Definitely," she agrees. "I'm going to go see him after we eat. I want to tell him as soon as possible, and my shift doesn't start until five today."

"That's a good idea."

She does a little dance in her seat, and her smile is like a bolt of electricity to my system. I love seeing her happy and smiling. She slides her hand across the table and places hers on mine. "Meeting you has changed my life in so many ways. I can't wait to see what happens for us next."

I love how she says *us*, and I'm just about to tell her that when the sounds of sirens begin blaring outside. We're sitting in a booth next to the window, so we both turn, giving the loud noise our attention. Willow River is a small town, so when you see the town cop and the life squad and fire department rush by, you can't help but wonder if it's someone you know and love that they're rushing to assist.

"Here you go." Our waitress sets our plates in front of us. "I'll grab you some refills," she tells us and scurries off again.

"I wonder what's going on?" Ramsey says, picking at her fries.

"I don't know." I reach for the bottle of ketchup, and we start to eat. I tell her a little bit more about the firm and how we operate, and the kinds of tasks she will be assigned.

"I'm going to have to buy a new wardrobe."

"I'd like to do that for you," I tell her. "As a 'congratulations on your new job' gift."

"I can't let you do that."

"I want to. I like doing nice things for you."

"I can afford it. I've lived very frugally for the past two years, and I'm losing my rent and utilities soon. Which, by the way, we need to discuss me paying my way."

"I thought we talked about this months ago? When you're with me, you don't pay."

"Deacon." She laughs. "That was dinner. This is living expenses."

"You moving in costs me nothing more."

"More food, more water, more electricity."

"Hardly." I shake my head at her.

"I want to help."

"Fine. You can buy all the groceries."

"That's not enough."

"How about this? Whatever you think is enough, you put it away into a separate account and save it for our wedding."

She sputters and coughs. I slide her sweet tea toward her, and she takes a small sip. "Did you say our wedding?"

"Forever love, Rams. We've talked about this." My tone is teasing.

"Forever love," she agrees. She shoves one last fry in her mouth and pushes her plate away. "I'm stuffed."

"Me too." I smirk. My plate is empty, whereas hers still has about a quarter of her burger and about the same amount of fries remaining. "You ready?"

"Yes." Grabbing our ticket that our waitress dropped off when she brought our refills, I offer her my hand to help her out of the booth. I look at the total and toss some cash on the table for a tip. Together, we make our way to the register.

"You kids ready to check out?" Dorothy asks us. We're far from kids, but Dorothy is pushing eighty, so to her we are.

"Yes, ma'am. It was delicious," I tell her.

"You have a charmer with this one," Dorothy tells Ramsey.

"Don't I know it," Ramsey agrees.

I quickly pay, and she passes me my change. "You be safe out there. I hope they're getting that fire under control," Dorothy says.

"Is that what all the sirens were about? Do you know where the fire was?"

"Such a shame. Just a few blocks over. The Willow Tavern."

"What?" Ramsey breathes.

"Poor Hank," Dorothy replies. "You kids have a good day."

With my hand on the small of Ramsey's back, I lead her out of the diner. "I have to go see what's going on."

"I'll go with you. Let me call the office and let them know I'm taking a longer lunch."

"It's a couple of blocks, Deacon."

"I'm coming with you." I lace my fingers with hers, and we begin to walk. The scent of smoke fills the air. My other hand is at my ear. I call the office but there's no answer. Our machine picks up. Our receptionist must be at lunch too. "Hey, guys, it's Deacon. There's been a fire at the Willow Tavern. I'm walking Ramsey over. I'll be back to the office as soon as I can." Ending the call, I slide my phone into my pocket.

"I hope everyone is okay. This is terrible. How did a fire start at the Tavern?" Ramsey rambles on with questions through her worry.

We make it to the corner, but that's as far as we're allowed to go. The firefighters seem to have the blaze under control. I spot Hank a few feet away, and I point him out. "Let's go see what he needs."

"Hank!" Ramsey calls out once we're close.

He turns to look at her, his face showing a million different emotions. "Hey," he greets us.

"What happened?"

"It started in the bathrooms. I smelled smoke and came out of my office to see what was going on. Smoke was rolling out from under the door. I got everyone out as fast as I could before I called 9-1-1. The bathrooms are right next to the storage closet where we keep the extra bottles. Once the flames reached that room, it was out of control. Nothing my little fire extinguisher could handle."

"I'm so sorry." Ramsey gives him a quick hug and steps back into my embrace. I hold her close as we watch a staple of this small town being doused with water. "Where is everyone?"

"I sent them all home. There is nothing they can do here. After they were all checked by the EMTs, I told them to leave."

"Is there anything we can do?" I ask him.

"No. Just hang tight the next couple of days until we can see how bad the damage is. It's going to take some time to get this cleaned up and repaired. I'm hoping it's not a complete loss," he says solemnly.

"If there is anything at all that I can do, let me know. Ramsey can reach me."

"Thanks, Deacon." He offers me his hand.

"Me too."

"I'm sorry you're going to be out of work for a while."

"That's... fine."

"What? What's that face?" he asks her.

She sighs, glances at me, and I nod. "I was coming to put in my notice. I feel terrible even telling you, with all of this," she points behind us at the building, "going on."

"That's actually a relief. One less person I have to stress over. I know you live on your own and need the money."

"Well, I live with Deacon now, but I know what you mean. Once you get this place back up and running, I'm willing to help train new employees or paint or whatever."

"Me too," I chime in. "Whatever you need."

"Thanks, man. My brother, Heath, is on the fire department, so hopefully, we can get some answers."

Ramsey offers Hank another hug, and we turn and walk away. "I wish there was something we could do. I hate just leaving him there."

"I know, but they have it under control, and his brother is here with him. All we can do is be there for him for whatever he needs."

"I think I'll go to the store and grab a few things and make dinner. I can take it to the firehouse so the guys can eat later."

"That's a great idea. I'll help."

"Don't you have to get back to work?"

"Work will be there tomorrow. I don't want to leave you alone right now."

"You're a special man." She gives me a cheesy grin.

"And you're my special woman." I wink playfully. I kiss her on the temple, and hand in hand, we walk back to my office. I step inside and tell Daniel and Spencer what's going on, and they wave me off, telling me to let them know if they can help.

Willow River is a small town, but we're also like one big giant family. We're all going to be there for Hank, and the Willow Tavern will be back, better than ever before.

Chapter Twenty-Three

RAMSEY

"I HAVE SOMETHING TO ASK YOU." DEACON AND I ARE cuddled in bed. We've spent the entire weekend holed up in his house. Well, our house. That's going to take some time to get used to. We dropped two large foil pans of baked spaghetti off at the firehouse Friday night, and we haven't left the house since.

"What's up?" he asks. We're on our sides facing each other.

"First, I want you to know that you can tell me no. I won't be mad or upset or anything like that."

"You know I can't tell you no." He soothes my hair back out of my eyes. "What's going on in the pretty head of yours?" he asks.

"Today is Sunday."

"Is it?" He chuckles.

"My aunt does family dinners on Sundays. I never get to go."

"Then we go."

"You'll come with me?" I bite down on my bottom lip. I've made huge strides in dealing with my insecurities in the past several months, but I'm asking him to come to have dinner with my crazy family. That's another first for me.

"Ramsey, baby, you live with me. They know we're together. You and me, we're not a secret."

"I know, but I've never taken you there, and it feels…" I let my voice trail off. I don't know how to put this into words.

"How does it feel? Tell me." Ever so patient, he waits for me to find the words.

"It feels like a dream come true. I keep waiting to wake up and realize it was all just a dream and that you're not really mine."

"Are my eyes open?"

"Yes."

He takes my hand and places it over his heart. "Can you feel my skin? The beat of my heart?"

"Yes."

He takes my hand and moves it over his erection. "Can you feel what you do to me?" I grip his cock and stroke him gently. "Does this feel like a dream?"

"I guess it's because you're my dream come true. I've always wanted the kind of love that we share. I craved it. When I moved to Willow River, my aunt, uncle, and cousins, they showed me love. They showed me how a family should be, but what I have with you is something I've never felt before but always craved."

"Ramsey, you are the love of my life. We're going to go have dinner with your family, and then we're going to come back to our home. We are building a life together, and I want it. I want you, and I want everything our future holds for us."

"My heart feels happy."

"That's because it loves me," he says smugly. "Do you know what else feels happy?"

"What's that?"

"My cock."

"Yeah?" I ask as I lazily stroke him. "I think I can make him happier."

"You think so? I'm not sure." He pretends to think it over.

Pushing him onto his back, I straddle his thighs. Gripping his cock, I guide it inside me.

"Holy fuck." He tenses, and his hand on my thigh tightens. In one swift move, he sits up and helps me arrange my legs around his back. His hands settle against my cheeks, and he kisses me like we have all the time in the world. I rock my hips, and he breaks the kiss. His hands grip my hips. "Stop," he grits out. I freeze, not sure what to do next. "Baby, we forgot a condom."

Even with his grip on my hips, I manage to rock forward. "I'm on the pill."

His eyebrows raise, and I know what he's asking. When did this happen? "I've been on it since I was sixteen. I begged my mother, and she agreed. I think she assumed I was sleeping around, but I didn't trust Robert. I wasn't sure how far he would try to go or force me to go, and I just… wanted to be protected. That's probably the nicest thing my mother ever did for me."

"Let's not talk about that douche when I'm inside you. In fact, he no longer exists to us. He's insignificant." He kisses me hard. "Second, are you sure you're okay with this?"

"I've only ever been with you, Deacon. I never want to be with anyone else. Yeah, I'm sure."

"It's been a long time for me. Over a year before I met you."

I run my fingers through his hair. "I trust you." I kiss the corner of his mouth. He quickly takes control of the kiss as his hand slides behind my neck with the other arm and locks me tight to him.

"I've never felt anything like it," he confesses. "I've never been bare inside a woman, and now I never want to see a condom ever again." I lift up and then drop back down, and he moans. "There are risks. Not of diseases since we're both safe, but pregnancy. I know nothing is one-hundred percent."

"Is this the lawyer in you covering all your bases?" I tease.

"No. This is the man who loves you and wants to make sure this choice is yours. I'll wear them if you want me to."

"I don't want you to," I say, lifting on my knees again and slowly sliding back over him. We both moan at the move, and I have to fight to keep my eyes from rolling in the back of my head. Who knew that thin piece of latex made that big of a difference? Then again, maybe it's just because we know it's not there.

"And the risk of pregnancy?" he asks.

I stop moving and stare into his gorgeous honey-colored eyes. "You see, there's this man. He's kind, loving, and so damn handsome. He also loves me. He showed me what it truly means to be loved. He told me that his love for me was the forever kind of love."

"Sounds like a great guy."

"Oh, he is," I assure him with a small smile. "He's also the kind of man who you build a life with. The kind of man you want to start a family with." I pause, letting that sink in. "I love you, Deacon. I don't think we're ready for kids just yet, but if it were to happen, I know I won't be doing it alone."

"Never with me," he says, his voice gruff. "You will never be alone again. Never." His arms wrap around me, hugging me so tight I can barely breathe, but I don't tell him that. Instead, I hold him just as tightly. When I feel his arms start to relax, I begin to lift my hips.

He lets me set the pace. I find a steady rhythm as his hands roam over every inch of my skin. When he reaches between us and thumbs my clit, I call out his name. His hips thrust upward, and he stills. I feel him release inside me, and it's hot as hell knowing he's doing so with nothing between us.

He holds me to him. We're both breathing heavily. He somehow manages to move to the side of the bed, with his cock still buried inside me. "What are we doing?" I sputter with laughter when he stands, gripping my ass cheeks.

"We need a shower. I made a mess of you, and it's got nowhere to go."

Realization dawns on me. "Good point." He carries me to the bathroom and manages to turn the water on. He kisses me while he waits for it to warm and then steps under the spray with me still in his arms. My body slides over his, and I can feel the result of our lovemaking on my inner thighs.

Deacon manages to wash us both, dirty me up again, and then wash us both again before we leave the shower. Maybe we should skip Sunday dinner and stay here.

"What time do we have to be there?" Deacon asks, handing me a towel.

"Five. But we can stay here."

"Nope. We're going. You've worked every Sunday for the entire time you've worked at the Tavern. It's time to get to spend some quality time with the people who love you."

I don't dispute that. I miss my aunt and uncle, and it's been a really long time since I've seen the twins too. They're not old enough to hang out at the Tavern. It will be nice to get to see everyone. "I hope they can all make it. That would be nice to have everyone together."

"I'm sure they'll be there." He kisses me and strides out of the bathroom.

A few minutes later, I'm dried off, and walking out to find my clothes. Deacon tosses his phone on the bed. "Everything okay?"

"Let's see, I made love to you twice today, and it's not even noon. I'd say everything is perfect." He slips a pair of jeans over his hips. "I'm going to go make us some lunch."

I nod and watch as he slides a T-shirt over his head and grabs his phone and a pair of socks off the bed. Suddenly he's right in front of me.

"Rams, if you keep looking at me like that, we're going to have to take another shower."

"Okay."

He chuckles. "Love you." He kisses me quickly and strolls out the door.

Stopping at the front door of my aunt and uncle's, I raise my hand to knock. The door swings open, and Aunt Carol is standing there. She glances at my raised hand and places her hands on her hips. "Girly, I know you weren't just about to knock on this door. How many times have I told you? You are family, and this will always be your home. You don't knock here. You come and go as you please." She pulls me into a tight hug. "I've missed you so much." She steps back and turns toward Deacon. "Deacon Setty, it's been too long. How have you been?" She steps up to him and wraps her arms around him in a hug as well.

She's nothing like my mother. It's hard to believe they are sisters. Not only that, but as soon as we pulled into the driveway, I could feel the love of this place. It's a home where love and hugs are shared daily, and I owe my aunt and uncle a lifetime of gratitude for showing me what that feels like.

"I'm doing well. Met a nice woman, fell in love, moved her in. You know, living the dream," he tosses it all out there like it's no big deal.

"You be good to my girl." She points at him.

"It's the only way I know."

"Come on in, you two. I made Ramsey's favorite."

"How did you know we'd be here?" I ask her.

"It seems that man of yours sent out a text to his best friend. It said something like my girl is coming home for dinner, and she wants you all there." Aunt Carol winks and disappears into the kitchen.

"You did that?"

"You wanted them all here. I told you there's nothing I won't give you if it's within my power."

Tears well in my eyes. It's stupid really to get so emotional over something like him sending out a notice to my rowdy brood of cousins, but it's more than that. It's the effort and the way he loves me. There are so many emotions bouncing around inside me. I love this man with my entire being, and I wish I knew how to tell him. I wish I could find the words he's always asking me for, to explain to him what he means to me. Then it hits me. Something that I can say that will tell him not only how I feel but what he means to me. I'm nervous to even put them out into the universe, but I'm going to do it anyway.

Taking a deep breath, I let my hand rest against his cheek. He's smiling down at me. His eyes are soft and so full of love for me. All my nerves melt away, and it's just the man I love and me. I open my mouth, and the words escape freely. "I'm going to marry you someday, Deacon Setty." My voice is strong, my heart is full, and the confidence I feel in my statement fills me with contentment.

He swallows hard before his lips press to mine. "Ramsey Setty, it has a nice ring to it." He hugs me, but before we can say anything else, my cousins appear.

"Come on, man, not in my parents' house," Sterling jokes.

"Let the girl come up for air." This is from Brooks.

"Are you making babies in the hallway?" Declan asks loudly.

"Ma! We need popcorn." This is from Orrin.

"All right, funny guys." I turn to face them. "Just you wait. You're all going to fall, and I'm taking notes." I point my finger at them.

"Hey, we're innocent," the twins, Maverick and Merrick, state at the same time. It's that freaky twin thing.

"Yes, the two of you are off the hook. For now," I add, giving them a pointed look. "Bring it in." They both come to me and wrap me in a huge Kincaid sandwich.

"Can't breathe." I pretend to be choking on air, making them laugh.

"Give them some room," my uncle calls out to his sons. My cousins fall away, disappearing into the kitchen and living room, leaving us with Uncle Raymond. "Ramsey." He opens his arms for me, and I walk into them. He's hugged me several times since I called Aunt Carol that fateful night, but this time it feels different. Almost as if I've accepted Deacon's love, and now, I realize I've had theirs all along as well. I knew that, but this... it just feels different. It feels free.

"Uncle Raymond, you know Deacon." I step out of his embrace and look behind me. Deacon steps forward and shakes my uncle's hand.

"You're taking care of her?" Uncle Raymond asks.

Deacon looks at me and smirks. "I'm going to marry her someday."

Uncle Raymond tosses his head back in laughter. "Well, alrighty then. Welcome to the family, son." With that, he turns and walks away.

I swat at Deacon's arm. "You did not just say that."

"I did. You're not the only one who gets to make declarations, darlin.'" He winks, and with his hand on the small of my back, he leads me to the kitchen.

It's a flurry of activity as we all make our plates and take them to the huge dining room. Just as we sit down to eat, the house phone rings. I think my aunt Carol and uncle Raymond might be the only people left with a landline.

"Excuse me." Aunt Carol steps out of the dining room to the kitchen to answer the call.

Merrick reaches for a spoon, and Uncle Raymond smacks at his hand. "Wait on your mother. She worked all afternoon cooking for you. She's not going to eat last." He gives his youngest, well, one of the two youngest sons, a stern look that has Merrick nodding and placing his hands in his lap.

A few minutes later, my aunt comes back into the room and takes her seat. I can tell by the look on her face that something is wrong. "What is it, dear?" Uncle Raymond asks.

She looks at her husband, and then her eyes find mine. "It's Angela."

My heart squeezes in my chest at the sound of my mother's name. "What about her?" I ask. My voice is calm, even though I know that whatever it is that she's about to say isn't going to be good.

"She's sick. That was your father. That was Donald," she quickly amends. "She's not got much longer, and she's been asking for you. For both of us."

Deacon slides his arm around my shoulders and pulls me close to his chest. I feel his lips press to the top of my head. "Sick?" I clarify.

"Yes. He didn't say much else. Just that it wouldn't be long and that she would like to see both of us."

"You're not going, right?" Maverick asks. He's one of the twins. "They weren't good to you. Dad, we can't let her go. And Mom? No. They stay here." He crosses his arms over his chest as if his word is final. He's sitting around a table with his seven older brothers, his father, Deacon, and his twin, and he doesn't seem to have a single care about being the one tossing out orders. My heart melts.

"You're right, Mav. They weren't good to me. However, you and your family taught me what family is supposed to be." I turn to look at Deacon. "And you," I say softly, but I know my family can hear me. "You erased him and showed me what it's like to have the unconditional love of a man."

Deacon swallows hard. "Tell me what you want to do, Rams. Whatever you decide, it's your choice. There will be no judgment. You have every right to deny her request."

He's right. I do. "I know. However, I can't help but think that if she's asking for me, maybe she's changed. Maybe she's realized that turning a blind eye to my father's abuse all those years wasn't the right choice. Maybe she wants to apologize."

"And if she doesn't?" Archer asks.

Tears well in my eyes. "If she doesn't—" I clear my throat. "Then I have all of you. I have my family, and I have the love of a good, honest man who would rather die than ever hurt me. It might hurt, but it won't break me. I have too many people who love me now. Too many people who are in my corner for that to happen."

Murmurs of agreement greet me, and I smile through my mist-filled eyes. "As Deacon said, we stand behind you," Aunt Carol tells me.

"What about you? Are you going to go?"

She takes the time to think about her answer while the table full of rowdy boys, well men, are as quiet as mice waiting for her reply. "No. I'm not going. Things with my sister have been strained for years. I will never forgive her for the hurtful things she's said to me, and there is no way I can see either of them without starting a war after learning how they treated you. My relationship with Angela ended long ago. And before you boys say anything," she glances around the table at each of her sons, "I know I talk about forgiveness. I know that it's important, but in this particular case, I just can't do it. Too much has been said. Too much has been done, and in Ramsey's case, too much was left alone." She pauses when her eyes land on me. "Ramsey, you make the choice for you. This might be the closure that you need. You simply walked away. Maybe you need for them to see how strong you are. Maybe you need for them to see that you didn't need their money or their name to be happy or make a life for yourself. The choice is yours and yours alone to make."

I give her a weak smile. "Thank you. I'll consider it. I'm not going to make a decision right now."

"You let us know if we can help," Uncle Raymond tells me. "Now, let's eat."

For the next two hours, we eat and laugh and enjoy one another's company. I've never been this relaxed, even with the recent news, and I owe it all to the man sitting next to me with his hand on my thigh. Every once in a while, he leans in and presses his lips to my temple, but he never misses a beat in the conversations he's having with my cousins.

No matter what I decide, and no matter what the outcome if I do go to visit my mother, none of it will affect the life I've built in Willow River.

This is my life.

This is our future.

I can't wait to live every minute of it.

Chapter Twenty-Four

DEACON

"Y<small>OU KNOW YOU DON'T HAVE TO GO THROUGH WITH THIS</small>," I tell Ramsey. We're lying on the bed in our hotel room. Our flight landed two hours ago. There was no way I was letting her come back to her hometown and the men who tore her down and abused her on her own. No. Fucking. Way.

"I know. I think Aunt Carol was right. I need to know that I was here, even if she never loved me. She's my mom." She shrugs.

I understand her reasoning, but I hate that she's going to have to see them. The people who should have loved her beyond anything else in their worlds and they failed. I'm on edge, and my nerves are frayed, because the thought of them hurting her or even looking at her crossways, sets my blood on fire.

Her cell phone rings and Carol's name flashes on the screen. "Hello," she greets. Ramsey's quiet as she listens, and her eyes fly to mine. "Really?" she asks, with tears in her eyes. I'm immediately concerned, but then a small smile tugs at the corner of her mouth, and I feel myself relax. I feel uneasy. I won't let them hurt her, but I don't know. Something just feels off. I guess it's just the feeling of loving someone more than life and being worried about them. This is a new concept for me, and I can't say that I'm a fan. "Okay. I'm glad you're here." She ends the call and turns to me once again.

"Aunt Carol and Uncle Raymond are here." A single tear slides over her cheek. "She changed her mind. She said she wanted to be here for me. She's not doing it for my mom and her request. She's here for me."

"She loves you."

My girl nods. "It's hard for me to reconcile that they're really sisters. They couldn't be more different."

"Money changes people."

"Some," she agrees. "I would never let it change me. Sure, I could work less and not constantly worry about the balance in my bank account, but I would never be cruel or greedy or just plain mean. Especially not to my daughter." She wipes at another tear and gives me a sad smile. "If we ever hit the lottery, promise me you won't change. Promise me I don't have to worry about losing you to money and greed."

"Never with me," I say softly. "I couldn't care less as long as you're by my side. Some might say that money is their definition of rich or poor, but I tend to disagree. Yes, I went into law to be financially stable. Not to get rich. However, I am rich. I just didn't get that way until you came into my life. Love, friendships, and a happy heart. That's what makes me rich. Loving you and receiving your love makes me the richest man in the world."

"Smooth, Setty, real smooth," she teases.

I wink at her, making her laugh. "So, are they here?" I ask.

"They are. Their flight just landed. They're staying in the same hotel."

I nod. "This doesn't change the fact that I'm going with you. You know that, right? I'm not letting you go there without me."

"So protective." She places her palm against my cheek.

"I don't know a man on this planet who wouldn't walk through fire to protect his heart."

"You're on fire today." She smiles.

"Just making sure you know how much you're loved. Whatever

happens, when you go to see your mother, I want you to remember that. *You* are loved." My voice is strong. Fierce. "Don't let them get into your head. You've built a life for yourself in Willow River, and you and me, we're building our future. They're insignificant in that."

"I know. I agree with you. However, there is still a part of me, the little girl who just wished to be loved and hugged by her parents, that hopes they've had a change of heart. I know the chances of that are slim to none, but the wish is there all the same."

"Come here." She moves to cuddle next to me, and I wrap her in my arms. "I love you, Ramsey. That love is unconditional. Whatever happens, we go back to Willow River and live our life." The uneasy feeling washes over me once more. I want to take all of her pain. I want to shake her parents and knock some fucking sense into them. Sick or not, if they're cold and callous to her, we're leaving. I won't stand around and let them treat her that way.

They won't stomp all over my heart.

I won't let them.

"This is it," Ramsey says as we pull into the driveway of her childhood home. "Pretentious, I know. My father is all about the show." There's a pain in her voice I've never heard from her before. Not even when she was telling me about her past. It's this place; it brings all the pain back in color, and I'm moments away from turning this fucking rental around and driving us straight to the airport.

"Ladies, are we ready to get this over with?" Raymond asks from the back seat. A glance in the rearview mirror tells me he's not looking forward to this either.

"Ramsey?" Carol asks.

"I'm as ready as I'll ever be." She reaches for her handle, and the rest of us follow suit. I meet her at the front of the car and lace my fingers through hers. I don't look behind me, but I'm confident Raymond is giving Carol a similar show of support.

We reach the door and Ramsey knocks. Knocks. At her parents' place. In the home she grew up in, she has to knock like a fucking stranger. The door swings open, and a man I recognize as Donald Smithfield stands before us. Ramsey pulled up his picture on his firm's website while we were waiting to catch our flight. He's aged since that photo was taken, but his stance and cold eyes tell me he's still a dick.

"How is she?" Ramsey asks.

"Come in." His eyes flash to mine and then to our joined hands. They then flash behind me. "Carol. Raymond. I wasn't expecting you."

"You called me," Carol says, her dislike for him evident in her tone. "Tell me, Donald, how did you know Ramsey was with us?"

He smirks. "She ditched her phone, but you were her last call. It's not rocket science."

"You've known where I was all this time?" Ramsey asks.

He scoffs. "Of course, I knew where you were. It's a man's job to keep track of all of his assets."

My shoulders stiffen, and I squeeze her hand tighter than I should. I count backward from ten and then do it one more time to calm myself down. "She's your daughter." My voice is hard, my anger unmistakable.

He ignores me. "Your mother is upstairs. She's been asking for you."

"I want to see her."

He nods. "She's in her room."

This prick doesn't even share a room with his wife. Not that I blame her. I wouldn't want to lie next to the bastard either, but then again, she's not much better letting her daughter suffer at the hands of her father.

"Ramsey, you know the way. Your friend and your uncle can follow me to the den."

"I'm going with you," I tell Ramsey.

"It's okay, Deacon. We'll go see my mother, and then we can go." Ramsey's eyes tell me a different story. She doesn't want to be here any more than I do. She's here to see her mother and get the fuck out.

I don't like letting her go anywhere in this fucking house without me, but this is her show. I'm here. That's what I keep reminding myself. He won't hurt her while I'm here with her. I lean in and press my lips to hers. "Love you." I whisper the words. Not because I don't want him to know, but because my words are for her.

"Love you too."

"Gentlemen." Donald nods and turns, expecting us to follow.

I don't move until Ramsey does. She links arms with her aunt, and they head up the spiral staircase. It takes everything in me not to chase after her.

"We're here, Deacon. He's not going to touch her," Raymond says, clapping a hand on my shoulder.

I nod, and together we follow after Donald. "Can I offer you a drink?" he asks once we're in the den.

"No," Raymond and I say at the same time. I have to bite back my smirk. This fucker isn't going to schmooze us.

"Suit yourself," he says, pouring himself a generous glass of bourbon. He sits in a black leather wing-back chair, while Raymond and I both choose to remain standing behind the matching black leather couch. "You seem fond of my daughter."

"If you weren't such a prick, you'd already know that." His eyes flare, and it's obvious he doesn't like to be called out.

"Such hostility. Should I be worried about my daughter's safety?" He raises a bushy brow in question.

"Cut the shit, Donald," Raymond speaks up. "We all know you're not in the running for any father of the year awards."

Donald laughs. "Don't pretend to know what it's like to be me," he sneers. He opens his mouth to say more but yelling from what sounds like upstairs stops him.

I take off running, with Raymond hot on my heels. When I make it to the top of the stairs, I see Ramsey with her back against the wall, a guy in a suit caging her in. My eyes scan the area, and I don't see Carol. The blood is whooshing in my ears. I take a deep breath, and that's when I hear it. It sounds like fists beating against the door and Carol's voice calling for help.

"Son of a bitch." Raymond sprints to the door and tells her to back up as he busts it open.

At the same time, I rush toward the bastard who has my girl pinned to the wall. Gripping the back of his suit, I tear him away from her, tossing him to the floor. I pull Ramsey into my arms as the schmuck climbs to his feet.

"What the fuck?" he seethes.

"Back up," I snarl. My voice is commanding.

"Who the hell are you to tell me what to do?" the fucker asks.

"I'm hers." I point to Ramsey. I pull her a little closer. "We're leaving."

"Oh, this is classic." The young douche laughs. "You're pathetic," he spits. "Running to the first man who will have you and spreading your legs for him."

"Ramsey, you've tarnished our family name," Donald says. "You're wretched." I didn't even realize he followed us up here. He sure as hell didn't care that this fucker was restraining his daughter.

I glance over to see Raymond with Carol in his arms. He nods, letting me know that she's okay.

Rage unlike anything I've ever known courses through me. He had his hands on her. I want to step in front of her to shield her from their vile words. I want to protect her from them, but I know that I can't do that. I know that she needs this. She needs to realize how strong she is. Walking away from the toxic life she was living and moving to Willow River shows that. Now she needs to show them for the second time who she is.

So, instead of standing in front of her, glaring at them, I settle for my arm around her waist, holding her next to me. I want her to know she has my full support and that she always will. I'm her partner, not just for this moment, but if I'm lucky, for life. Age differences and family acquaintances are dammed.

She's mine.

"You finally come to your senses and come home, yet you bring him with you," the douche, who I assume is her ex, sneers.

She glances up at me, and I wink, which makes her mouth kick up in a grin before the scowl returns as she faces off with her ex and her piece-of-shit father. "I'm not home. My father made it very clear to me that I was no longer someone he wanted in his life. I believe your exact words were: you're dead to me. Does that ring a bell, Father?" she asks, her voice void of emotion.

Robert, the douche, takes a step toward her, but the growl that escapes my chest stops his movement. He glares at me before turning back to Ramsey. "It's good to see you had to find a man to take care of you—another lawyer at that. Do you think of me when he's inside you?" He gives her an evil grin.

She stiffens next to me, and I want to rip his fucking head from his shoulders. "You and I both know you were never inside me." Her fist grips my shirt. "I see you've done your homework, though. Yes, Deacon is an attorney. A damn good one. Do you know what else he is? He's the love of my life." Her voice is strong, and I want to kiss the hell out of her.

"I knew you couldn't do it on your own, you little slut." Spittle flies from his mouth, and I've had enough. I'm a man, and I can only take so much of another man yelling and insulting the woman I love. She might be pissed at me for stepping in, but I'll handle that later. Nothing a few orgasms can't fix. Then I can explain my standpoint. No one gets to talk to her that way.

"Ramsey doesn't need me to take care of her. She's doing just fine all on her own." I feel her relax into my hold, inching her body a little closer at my confession. "What she does need is for me to be her pillar of support. She needs me to be there on the good days and the bad. She needs me to tell her how incredible she is." I glance over to find her eyes on mine. "How beautiful she is." Her eyes soften, and it takes every ounce of willpower I have not to lean in and press my lips to hers. "She needs to know that she's cherished and that her smile lights up a room." I swallow back my emotions and keep going. "She needs me to hold her as she falls asleep at night and kiss her good morning. She needs to know that if she has a good day, I want to hear about it. She needs to know if she has a bad day. It's my shoulder I want her crying on."

"Deacon," she whispers.

I turn now, facing her, cupping her face in my hands. "She needs to know she's loved. She needs to know that no man has ever loved a woman this much." Her eyes well with tears, but there's a smile pulling at the corner of her mouth.

I turn my head to face the douchebag. "She needs to know that my love isn't conditional. I'll love her no matter what she wears, the career she has, or what she orders to eat at a restaurant. I'll love her if she wants to stay home on a Friday night instead of going out. I'll love her if she wants to lounge all day on Sunday in her pajamas. I'll love her even after I leave this earth. Unconditionally. Irrevocably."

Ramsey crushes her body to mine, wrapping her arms around my waist, and buries her face in my neck. I don't hesitate for even a single second to return her embrace. I place my lips on the top of her head and breathe her in.

A slow clap fills the quiet room, reminding me where we are and that I just let these two assholes witness an intimate moment between us. Not my finest moment, but my anger at her ex and her father and her mother's blatant disregard for their actions, mixed with the love that I have for her, pushed me to the edge.

"Nice show. It's over. We're getting married. I'll overlook your indiscretions. This time." Robert, the douche, reaches for Ramsey, and if I thought I felt rage before my speech, I was dead wrong. Seeing him reach for her, the thought of him touching her after all the times he hurt her, I see red.

I start to release Ramsey, but even with trembling hands, she's able to hold onto me. "No," she whispers softly. "He's not worth it."

"Aw, look at that. She has you trained. That pussy must be good," Robert says, licking his lips.

"Motherfucker." I step forward, but Ramsey wraps herself around me, jumping in my arms. I stop moving, my hands landing on her thighs.

"Let's go home, Deacon. Take me home."

"You're already home," her father says, his voice booming. He's losing his aloof appearance, and that gives me some satisfaction. He's pissed he can't control her.

Not anymore.

"Raymond?"

"We're good," he assures me.

"Let's go." I don't put Ramsey on her feet. I turn and make my way to the stairs with my girl still in my arms.

"Donald!" Robert screams. "Do something. You said she would stay and all of our problems would go away. You started this mess. You better fucking fix it." Robert's voice sounds panicked.

"You ready, baby?" I ask Ramsey. Fuck these assholes. We don't owe them a damn thing. They can work this shit out on their own. I don't give a flying fuck what they need to fix.

"Take me home, Deacon."

Chapter Twenty-Five

RAMSEY

"You can't just let them leave!" Robert shouts as Deacon starts to move toward the stairs.

"Donald. Fucking stop her!" Robert yells.

I don't know why, but I say, "Stop." Deacon freezes.

"Rams?"

I release my legs from around his waist and slide to the floor. I turn to face my father, which places Deacon at my back. He wraps his arms around my waist, holding me to his chest. My aunt and uncle are standing next to us, and Uncle Raymond moves into the same pose as Deacon, wrapping his arms around Aunt Carol. We're a united front.

"What's going on?" I ask my father.

"All you need to know is that you're moving home, and you will marry Robert."

Deacon growls from his spot behind me, and that sound gives me courage. This man loves without boundaries. I open my mouth to tell my father to go fuck himself, but it's my mother's voice that stops me.

"Donald, it's over." She stands in the doorway of the room where Aunt

Carol was locked. She's the one that held her while Robert pulled me into the hallway, leaving Aunt Carol and my mother locked in the bedroom.

"Shut the fuck up!" my father yells at her.

My mother rolls her eyes, which is more emotion than I've seen her show in years. "You got yourself into this mess. It's not Ramsey's job to fix it."

"Angela," my father sneers.

"He's in debt. The firm's in debt," my mother speaks up.

"I told you to shut the fuck up!" my father screams, causing the vein in his forehead to pop out.

"I've remained quiet long enough." My mother's eyes flash to mine. "I never wanted to be a mom." Her eyes flash to her sister. "You suffered because of that," she says, finding my eyes again. "However, this has gone on long enough."

"Angela." My father's voice holds a warning that my mother doesn't heed.

"Your father and his firm invested money that wasn't theirs."

"Shut. The. Fuck. Up." My father moves toward her, but I'm surprised when Robert steps in front of her.

"You did this," Robert seethes.

"Your hands are all over it too," my father reminds him.

"You think so?" Robert smirks. "You need not be so trusting, old man."

"Fuck you," my father spits, but there is less venom and more worry in his tone.

"Your father gambled with some money belonging to his clients. Made some bad investments," Robert explains.

"What does that have to do with me?"

"Your grandparents, your father's mother really, left you an inheritance," my mother informs me.

"What? Grandma Edna?"

"Yes."

"How did I not know about this?" I ask her.

"Your father is a control freak."

"That's enough," my father demands, but he's losing his ire.

"Legally, you weren't to have access until you were twenty-one."

"I don't understand. Why keep it from me? Why insist that I marry Robert?" I shudder even at the words, and Deacon pulls me closer. I feel his lips press to the back of my head.

"Your grandmother stated in the guidelines of the inheritance that any man that you marry would also have access. She was a sucker for love, as you know, and she insisted that any man you found worthy enough of changing your last name was also worthy enough to have access to your money."

"Is that even legal?"

"It's written in the will that the man you marry is set to receive fifty percent of the funds."

"How much money are we talking about?"

"One hundred million."

"W-What?" I sputter.

"She left you everything!" my father yells. "All of it. My family's fortune goes to you."

"Why? I mean, why on earth would she leave me that kind of money?"

"She left you a letter."

"Jesus, Angela. Shut the hell up." My father runs his fingers through his hair. He's losing his cool.

"Where is the letter?"

"With the family attorney."

"So your father," I say, glancing over at Robert.

He nods. "The plan was for us to get married. I'd get fifty million, and I could clean up the mess the firm was in."

"Why? You could wash your hands of it all and leave."

"My father."

That's all he needs to say. I know that his father has always been his idol, and he's always strived for his attention to make him proud. He thought this would have done it, but we both know that Robert Barrington wouldn't have given a single fuck as long as his ass was covered.

"You're not sick?" I ask my mother.

"No. Not physically. Mentally." She shrugs.

I stand here at the top of the stairs in the home I grew up in and see my parents for what they are. Money-hungry fools. And Robert, and his father, they're no better. My eyes swing to my aunt Carol and uncle Raymond. They've been quiet through all of this, as has Deacon, but they're here. All three of them. My pillars of strength reminding me that this is my life, and I can do with it as I wish.

"Thank you for telling me. Robert, please tell your father that Deacon Setty, my attorney, will be in touch." I turn in Deacon's arms. "Take me home."

Deacon nods, slipping his arm around my waist. He motions for my aunt and uncle to precede us down the stairs.

"Ramsey!" my father yells. "Get back here. You can't just leave. You can't take what's mine."

I ignore him, taking each step in time with Deacon. We make it to the door, and my father calls out for me again. I don't bother looking back. I have no desire to be a member of this family any longer.

Deacon opens the passenger door of the rental for me, while Uncle Raymond does the same for Aunt Carol. No one says a word as he pulls out onto the road, leaving the two people who gave me life behind.

My mind is racing with all that I've learned. My mother isn't sick. It was just some ploy for my father to get me here and try to force my hand to marry Robert. My grandma Edna left me more money than I can spend in a lifetime. She passed when I was nine, and I have nothing but fond memories of her.

I can't help but think about my life two years ago and the fear I felt when I left. Fear mixed with freedom. Today, all I feel is… happy. I made a choice, the hard choice two years ago, to walk away. Today that choice was easy as I walked away for the second time, and I have no regrets. Removing my seat belt, I turn to look at my aunt and uncle.

"Rams, put your belt back on," Deacon says softly.

I ignore him, which causes him to signal and pull over to the side of the road. "Not risking your safety, baby. Say what you need to say. We're listening," he assures me.

"I love you both," I tell my aunt and uncle. "Thank you for saving me. You gave me a safe place to land when I needed it. You helped me get on my feet, and every day since the first, you've treated me as if I were your daughter. I can't tell you what your love and generosity mean to me."

"You are our daughter," Uncle Raymond speaks up. "And you know, sweetheart, us Kincaids, we work hard, but we love even harder." He winks.

"If I didn't plan on letting Deacon change my last name, I'd beg you to let me change it to Kincaid."

"Setty sounds better," Deacon chimes in.

I turn to look at him. "Yeah, I agree." I settle back into my seat but keep my eyes on him. "Deacon, you are everything I never knew that I needed. You brought me back to life and showed me the true meaning of a man loving a woman. I love you with every part of my soul."

He blinks hard a few times before leaning over the console of the rental and kissing me soundly.

"I'm starving," Uncle Raymond announces once Deacon finally releases me.

"You hungry, Rams?" Deacon asks.

"Yes. Let's grab something at the hotel and then see if we can all catch earlier flights. I'm ready to go home."

"So, it's legit?" I ask Deacon. We're sitting in his office two days later.

"It's legit. You get access to all one hundred million now, and once you're married, your spouse is entitled to fifty percent of what's left."

"You're welcome," I say, smiling.

"What?"

"I'm going to make you a millionaire." I grin.

"Baby, you already gave me your heart. I'm already a millionaire."

"You looking to get lucky tonight?"

"I'm lucky every day that I spend with you," he counters cheekily.

"You're impossible."

"Only when it comes to you."

"So, what's next?" I ask him.

"You've signed the papers. Once you're married." He smirks. We both know he's the one I'll be marrying. "Your spouse needs to sign as well once you submit a copy of your marriage license."

"How is that going to work when it's you?" I ask him.

His smile can't be rivaled. "I've asked my partners to take over. I took care of the paperwork, but it's their names on them. Not mine."

"Always thinking ahead. I like it." I stand and walk around his desk, placing a kiss on his lips. "I'm heading home. Palmer is meeting me."

"You girls have fun."

"We will. You better enjoy today. It's your last day working without me hovering over you."

"I look forward to it." He smiles. "I'll see you at home later. Love you." He pulls me into another quick kiss before I force myself to leave his office. As I'm pushing open the door, Palmer and Piper are entering. "Hey, I was just on my way to meet you."

She grins. "I had to drop something off to Deacon first." She motions toward the package in her hands. Piper is carrying one as well.

"What are those?" I ask her.

"Come." She motions for me to follow them.

"Piper?" I ask Deacon and Palmer's middle sister.

"All I'm going to say is that I love the love that the two of you share. It was evident from day one."

What in the world are they talking about? Following them down the hall, I step into Deacon's office behind them.

"Hey, you just missed Rams," he greets his sisters.

"Oh, we found her." Palmer steps aside so that he can see me.

His eyes soften. He holds his hand out for me, and I go to him. How could I not? He pulls me onto his lap and kisses my cheek. "Missed you."

"It's been like two minutes." I laugh.

"Two minutes too long."

"Aww," Piper and Palmer say at the same time.

"You got them?" Deacon asks.

"I do." Palmer sets the brown paper-wrapped package on his desk and slowly unwraps it.

I gasp when I see what it is. "Oh, my word." I'm looking at a canvas print of one of our photo shoot images. It's the one where Deacon has me sitting on the wall, his hands holding my face, his lips pressed to mine. It's sexy and intimate, and Piper's right. You can see the love. Sure, we weren't in love then, but the way that Palmer captured the shot, anyone looking at this image would argue that there was love between us that day.

"That one's going in our bedroom," Deacon tells me.

"Is that another one?" I point at the similar package that Piper is holding.

"It is." She grins and goes through the same unwrapping process that Palmer just did for her unveiling.

"That one, it was your smile," Deacon tells me. In the image, he's standing behind me. His face is buried in my neck. My head is tilted back, giving him access like the hussy I am for him, and he's right. The smile on my face is wide and carefree. It's everything Deacon makes me feel captured for us to remember for always.

"Palmer," my voice cracks.

"Stop." Palmer shakes her head, swallowing hard. "I'm just glad you two stubborn asses finally let me do this." She points at us.

"What? You're not claiming naming rights to their first baby?" Piper teases.

"Don't encourage her." I laugh. "She's already mentioned that."

"I'll tell you what. You find me the love of my life as I did you, and I'll gladly give you naming rights of my firstborn." Palmer laughs.

"Be careful, Palmer," I tease her. "I just might do that."

She shrugs. "I don't need a man to be happy. I have my family, you, who will soon be family once my brother makes it official, and my studio. Captured Moments is doing great, and this shoot brought me so much business. So, it's me that should be thanking you."

"Are we still hanging out?" I ask her.

"Yes. Since we're all here, we should head to the diner for lunch and then back to your place."

"I'll finish up early, and we can throw something on the grill for dinner."

"Wow," Piper breathes. "You really are a changed man," she teases.

"That's what the love of a good woman will do to you." Deacon winks and all three of us burst with laughter. I kiss him goodbye, promising to get the canvas prints home safe and leave him to finish his day while I spend the day with his sisters.

I'm technically a millionaire and don't have to work, but I'm looking forward to starting on Monday and getting to spend my days with Deacon. I don't know if it's my forever, but it's my right now. The only forever I need to be certain of is Deacon and that Willow River is home.

Epilogue

RAMSEY

It's been six months today since the Willow Tavern caught fire. Hank has been working tirelessly to finish the rebuild on the Tavern.

Today, is finally the day. Hank is reopening his doors to the Tavern. Well, kind of. It's what he's calling a soft opening. Where people he's close with come and check the place out. He has his staff run through procedures with a small, forgiving crowd of patrons. His real opening night is next weekend. Turns out most of the patrons are my family, or Deacon's. That's small-town living for you. Deacon and I have helped with painting and a few other odd jobs to help Hank get ready for the opening. I assume they're all here to support us, and by default, support Hank.

"Everything looks so different," I say to Deacon as we take in the new look.

"Yeah," he agrees. "Hank said there was so much smoke and water damage, the insurance called it a complete loss."

"I'm glad he was able to rebuild. Willow River isn't Willow River without the Willow Tavern," I say.

Deacon laughs. "Say that three times fast."

"Hi, brother," Palmer says, taking me by the hand. "Bye, brother," she calls, pulling me toward a table in the back. Jade and Piper are already there waiting for us.

"Hey." I wave as I slide into the booth.

"How did you get her away from Deacon?" Piper asks.

"I just grabbed her hand and ran." Palmer grins, proud of herself.

"Damn," Jade mutters, her focus somewhere over my shoulder.

We all turn to follow her gaze, and it's hard to tell who she's talking about. But I can see the appeal. All nine of my cousins, even the twins, are here with my aunt and uncle. Deacon's parents are here as well as a few other people like Hank's brother, Heath.

"I'm calling dibs on that one." Piper points to the group of guys.

"You're going to have to be more specific," Jade tells her.

"Heath." Her face goes red.

"Heath, huh?" Palmer asks.

"We kind of went out on a date last weekend."

"What?" the three of us ask. "And you didn't tell us?" Jade comments.

The four of us have become really close. Palmer will always be my number one, but the other two are great girls, and it's nice to have friends who are friends with me because they choose to be, not because of the size of my parents' bank account.

"Which one for you?" Palmer asks Jade.

"They're all gorgeous."

"Come on now. Fess up," Piper encourages her. "I told."

Piper and Jade reconnected, and they are now besties like Palmer and me.

"Fine. Orrin," Jade whispers quietly.

"Yeah?" I ask, nodding. "He's a sweetie."

"It's just a thing. As I said, they're all easy on the eyes."

I glance over at Palmer, and I can already see her wheels turning. "What about you?" I lean my shoulder into my best friend. "You can only pick one," I tell her.

"Hmmm, Brooks," she confesses. "Have you seen that fine man in his scrubs?" she asks, making us all laugh.

"You're lucky," Jade speaks up.

"How so?" I ask her.

"I'd give anything to have a man look at me the way that Deacon looks at you."

"I am lucky." I'm quick to agree with her.

"Speaking of my brother." Piper nods, and when I turn my head, my man is standing next to our booth.

Epilogue

DEACON

I've been packing this ring around with me for weeks. It wasn't until Hank invited us to this soft opening that I knew tonight was going to be the night. I called him and told him my plan, scoring invites for her family and mine to be here. I basically highjacked his soft opening for my own purposes and I don't feel a damn bit guilty for it. I paid for an open bar and food for everyone. After all, it's a night worth celebrating.

I've been calm all week, knowing today's the day that I ask the love of my life to marry me. I thought maybe once the day arrived, I'd be nervous, but still nothing. I made love to Ramsey this morning, and all I could think about was that the next time, she's going to be my fiancée.

I'm not worried that she's not going to say yes. We're solid, and we're forever. I am, however, excited. I can't wait to marry her and change her last name. I want her stripped of that name and the family it represents. She's more of a Kincaid than a Smithfield, and soon she's going to be a Setty.

I can't fucking wait.

Everyone knows what's going to happen today. Her family, my family, even my sister who just stole her away from me. Everyone is in on it, except for her. It's time to change that. Tossing my empty water bottle in the trash, I catch my best friend's eye and nod. He grins and starts letting everyone know it's time.

Making my way to their booth, I can feel all four of them staring at me, especially my sisters, but I only have eyes for Ramsey. "Can I have my girl back now?" I ask, still keeping my eyes locked on the love of my life.

"Brother, why must you always steal my bestie?" Palmer asks. She's not letting even a hint of what's about to happen show in her actions or her words.

"Because I love her. Because it's easier to breathe when she's next to me. Because she's my best friend. Need me to keep going?" I ask.

"Uh, no. No, that'll do." Palmer moves to stand and motions for Ramsey to do the same. "Sorry, bestie, he wins. That was some deep shit."

Ramsey grins, slides out of the booth, and takes my hand. Without a word, I lead her to the stage, and I don't have to worry about all eyes being on us. I know that Orrin spread the word that the main event is starting.

With both of her hands in mine, I stare into her deep blue eyes. "I wish there was a way for you to see inside my heart. If you could, you'd see that your name is written all over it. You would be able to see that it beats for you."

"Deacon." Her eyes shimmer with tears.

This is it. It's time.

I drop to one knee and watch as her mouth falls open. "If you could see into my heart, you would know that there will never be anyone for me but you. You would see that my love for you runs deep in my veins. Ramsey, baby, will you do me the incredible honor of spending the rest of your life with me? Will you marry me?"

"Yes." Tears slide over her cheeks and her hand trembles as I slide the one carat princess-cut diamond onto her finger. I stand and pull her into my arms, kissing the hell out of her.

Our friends and family cheer all around us, but I block it all out.

All I see is the woman in my arms. Breaking the kiss, I rest my forehead against hers.

"I told you I was going to marry you someday," she teases.

"That you did." I chuckle.

"Were you nervous?" she asks.

"Nah, I know we're forever. What about you?"

"Nah, I know I never have to be nervous with you."

"Never with me, baby."

Thank you for taking the time to read *Never with Me*.

Want to read Palmer's story, and the rest of the Kincaid family? Pre-order your copy of Stay Over now.

Looking for your next read while waiting for Stay Over to release. Download Play by Play, a Riggins Brothers prequal novella for free.

Never miss a new release:
http://bit.ly/2UW5Xzm

More about Kaylee's books:
http://bit.ly/2S6clWe

Contact Kaylee Ryan:
Facebook: http://bit.ly/2C5DgdF
Instagram: http://bit.ly/2reBkrV
Reader Group: http://bit.ly/2o0yWDx
Goodreads: http://bit.ly/2HodJvx
BookBub: http://bit.ly/2KulVvH
Website: www.kayleeryan.com

More from
KAYLEE RYAN

With You Series:
Anywhere with You | More with You
Everything with You

Soul Serenade Series:
Emphatic | Assured
Definite | Insistent

Southern Heart Series:
Southern Pleasure | Southern Desire
Southern Attraction | Southern Devotion

Unexpected Arrivals Series
Unexpected Reality | Unexpected Fight
Unexpected Fall | Unexpected Bond
Unexpected Odds

Riggins Brothers Series:
Play by Play / Layer by Layer
Piece by Piece / Kiss by Kiss
Touch by Touch | Beat by Beat

Standalone Titles:
Tempting Tatum | Unwrapping Tatum | Levitate
Just Say When | I Just Want You
Reminding Avery
Hey, Whiskey
Pull You Through
Remedy | The Difference
Trust the Push | Forever After All
Misconception | Never with Me

Entangled Hearts Duet:
Agony | Bliss

Cocky Hero Club:
Lucky Bastard

Mason Creek Series:
Perfect Embrace

Out of Reach Series:
Beyond the Bases / Beyond the Game
Beyond the Play / Beyond the Team

Co-written with Lacey Black:

Fair Lakes Series:
It's Not Over | Just Getting Started
Can't Fight It

Standalone Titles:
Boy Trouble
Home to You
Beneath the Fallen Stars

Co-writing as Rebel Shaw with Lacey Black:
Royal

Acknowledgments

To my readers:

Thank you for your continued support. If you've made it this far, you've devoured another one of my books, and I can't tell you what it means to me that you picked my words for your escape. Thank you for choosing Never with Me.

To my family:

This story consumed me in the best of ways, and you let me do my thing. Thank you for always standing by my side and supporting my dream. I love you.

Champagne Book Design:

Thank you for making the paperbacks beautiful. You're amazing, and I cannot thank you enough for all that you do. I owe you one.

Wander Aguiar:

Thank you for an image that brings Deacon to life. It was a pleasure working with you and your team.

Sommer Stein:

I love the traditional cover, but this one, this special edition, is probably one of my favorites of mine if not my favorite. Thank you for being so patient with me during the design process. I appreciate you more than you know.

Lacey Black:

I don't really know what I can say that I haven't already said, except I love you, my friend. Thank you for being my constant pillar of support and sounding board. Even when it's not one of our co-writes, you're there to bounce ideas and read scenes, and your friendship is invaluable. Thank you for being amazing.

My beta team:

Jamie, Stacy, Lauren, Erica, and Franci, I would be lost without you. You read my words as much as I do, and I can't tell you what your input and all the time you give means to me. Countless messages and bouncing ideas, you ladies keep me sane with the characters being anything but. Thank you from the bottom of my heart for taking this wild ride with me.

Give Me Books:

With every release, your team works diligently to get my book in the hands of bloggers. I cannot tell you how thankful I am for your services.

Julie Deaton:

Thank you for giving this book a set of fresh final eyes.

Jenny Sims:

Thank you for helping polish this book to be the best that it can be.

Jo Thompson:

Thank you for helping make this book the best that it can be.

Becky Johnson:

I could not do this without you. Thank you for pushing me and making me work for it.

Brittany Holland:

Thank you for your assistance with the blurb. You saved me!

Chasidy Renee:

Thank you for everything you do. How did I survive without you before now? No matter what the task, you're always there with your never-ending support. Thank you so very much for all that you do.

Stacy Garcia:
Thank you for the amazing promotional graphics. You're the best.

Bloggers:
Thank you, it doesn't seem like enough. You don't get paid to do what you do. It's the kindness of your heart and your love of reading that fuels you. Without you, without your pages, your voice, your reviews, and spreading the word, it would be so much harder, if not impossible, to get my words in the reader's hands. I can't tell you how much your never-ending support means to me. Thank you for being you. Thank you for all that you do.

To my reader group, Kaylee's Crew:
You are my people. I love all of the messages and emails you send me. I love the little book community we've created. You are my family. Thank you for all of your love and support, not just with books but with life. No matter what I decide to write, you are there, ready to consume every word. Thank you for being the amazing group of people that you are.

Much love,
Kaylee

Made in United States
Orlando, FL
27 July 2022